HYPOTHESIS

HYPOTHESIS

A Story of Mineral Rights and Wrongs

JIM MAY

Tate Publishing & *Enterprises*

Hypothesis
Copyright © 2010 by Jim May. All rights reserved.

No part of this publication may be reproduced, stored in a retrieval system or transmitted in any way by any means, electronic, mechanical, photocopy, recording or otherwise without the prior permission of the author except as provided by USA copyright law.

The opinions expressed by the author are not necessarily those of Tate Publishing, LLC.

Published by Tate Publishing & Enterprises, LLC
127 E. Trade Center Terrace | Mustang, Oklahoma 73064 USA
1.888.361.9473 | www.tatepublishing.com

Tate Publishing is committed to excellence in the publishing industry. The company reflects the philosophy established by the founders, based on Psalm 68:11,
"The Lord gave the word and great was the company of those who published it."

Book design copyright © 2010 by Tate Publishing, LLC. All rights reserved.
Cover design by Amber Gulilat
Interior design by Jeff Fisher

Published in the United States of America

ISBN: 978-1-61566-741-3
1. Fiction, Mystery & Detective, General
2. Fiction, Suspense
10.01.15

[Jim] caught the magic of the lake moments so well. I also think his handling of the dialogue was exceptionally natural, which is difficult... Being able to hear the voices as distinct, and getting the colloquial flow... to sound natural was well done. I also personally liked unraveling the intricate details of the conspiracy toward the end as it got complex. Mostly, it's just damned good. This can't be his first. He must be returning to writing he's done more of before his business career. We'll take more.

—Marian S. Miskell
Editor, The Community Foundation magazine

DEDICATION

For Ann, my patient editor and inspiration throughout the writing of this book.

PREFACE

For truth is always stranger, stranger than fiction.

- Lord Byron, 1788–1824

Truth is stranger than fiction because fiction, after all, has to make sense.

-Mark Twain, 1835–1910

Truth is more of a stranger than fiction.

-Silver Lake Police Chief, Jim Mitchell, 2008

Truth and fiction are not necessarily polar opposites, as the facts in this account attest. However, while the quaint background of Susquehanna County, Pennsylvania, and its people are characterized in this story as interesting and specific to some individuals and locations, they are composites of various traits I have observed, rather than specific biographical accounts of any single person or place. Still, they can easily be interpreted as a particular individual or location since the personalities and attributes about which I have written are widespread and common in this part of the state. Nonetheless, the characters and situations are fictitious except for one: Susquehanna County itself and its current encounter with the Marcellus Shale natural gas drilling phenomena.

The natural gas drilling rush by energy exploration companies, primarily with Texas roots, is a real event occurring in northeast Pennsylvania and northern New York state, consuming conversations, hopes, and dreams of much of the population hoping to benefit somehow. It is the single largest worldwide discovery of natural gas and promises to greatly influence the region, for better or for worse.

Truth and fiction are credibly entwined, and it is most often difficult to determine which is which. My proofreaders familiar with the situation firsthand have expressed interests to become involved with the manifestation of *Hypothesis's* concepts. My hope is that all readers will have the same feeling and take to heart and hand some of these ideas.

Mankind will be better for it.

1

Lottie Carpenter's visitor appeared at the end of her driveway, trailing a cloud of dust as his car headed toward the house. Her long-extinct farmland looked like a museum of agricultural life. Littered with relics of rusting tractors, wagons, and haying equipment lining the horizon, it was an eerie effect at dusk, resembling foreboding monsters on the prowl. Other than hay harvesting three times a year by a neighboring dairy farmer, it had been eighteen years since any productive farm work had occurred there. A few raindrops, accompanied by muffled rumbles of thunder coming from a distance to the northwest, greeted him as he hurried from the car and up the steps. His suit-and-tie manner was friendly but strictly businesslike, briefcase in one hand, the other extended in greeting. It was a cordial meeting, and both of them were anxious to finalize the details of the document they had been discussing for weeks now.

Once inside, after some small talk and catching up on the state of everything rural, it was time to discuss the important matters contained in the briefcase. While seated at the kitchen table, they each read from the same document, he viewing it upside down while highlighting things of interest from time to time, using his pen as a pointer extended from his cupped hand, and she with a trusting smile indicating satisfaction that an agreement was close at hand. In order to emphasize the significance of a chosen item on one of the pages, he stood, purposely eyeing it on the page, and came around to stand behind her, leaning over her left shoulder.

Without a warning, he suddenly clasped her across the mouth with an open hand, stretching her head unnaturally upward and back, and filled her mouth with an open bottle of Smirnoff vodka. He squeezed her into submission from behind against his chest, tipping the bottle into her mouth, and forced her down into her chair. Pouring the contents, intermittently allowing a gasp of air but then violently again and again without chance hardly to breathe unless she swallowed in concert, he persisted as her resistance weakened. She kicked and flailed about, her slight-framed body rising from the chair, falling back, writhing with fear, rising and falling again and again. He held on, clenching even tighter. The cycle repeated in a synchronized rhythm—back and forth, back and forth—until the bottle was almost empty. She sank in a slump; he fell to the floor behind her, saying nothing, doing nothing. She was motionless but groaning in a low tone, stunned by what had just happened. It was swift, violent, obviously rehearsed in his mind many times.

The two figures remained in position, exhausted from the exchange as the room dimmed with the darkness of the approaching storm. Perspiration bled through his clothes, and he stood to see the results of his efforts, looking down upon her from behind still. Her delirium was obvious. Her hand movements were strained and slow, ineffectual.

He watched for any slight movement as he methodically went about wiping his fingerprints from the bottle with his handkerchief, forcing it into her hands multiple times to imprint hers. He took out a fresh bottle of vodka and did the same, then carried it within his handkerchief and placed it in a highboy in the dining room. Looking ever constantly at her, he fit his hands into a pair of rubber gloves and then packed up all the paperwork into his briefcase and placed it by the door with the empty vodka bottle and cap, removing his shoes afterward. He kicked open the door and carried her body, cradled in his arms, through the misty rain to the garage. He dared to look at her eyes. They were closed, straining to open but unable.

He steadied himself against the side of the garage and stood her up while opening the door. Straining to pick her up in his arms again, he struggled to bring her around the car to the driver's door, opened it, and shoved her in. He arranged her clothing and moved her into a proper driving position behind the wheel, all the while looking around for any intruders.

Fired with adrenalin now, his small stature managed the task, but only barely. Wiping perspiration from his eyes, he trembled almost to the point of weakness. The empty vodka bottle was stuffed in his suit coat pocket, and he used the end of his ballpoint pen, inserted in the mouth, to place it on her lap. He positioned it again in her hands, wiped down the car door handle, and pulled her left hand out to impress some fingerprints on it as though it was opened by her. He propped her upright and took the car keys from the dash, where he knew they would be from previous visits and conversations, and started the car. He dropped the cap of the vodka bottle on the seat after pressing it into her fingers.

He closed the car door and left with the garage doors closed and went back to the house, first wiping his feet in the grass and removing his socks this time. He located the vacuum cleaner and ran it over the carpet and then scuffed the nap slightly with his feet to remove any traces of his footprints. With the vacuum returned, cord neatly wound into position as befitting the way he found it, he shuffled lightly to the door, carried his socks, shoes, and briefcase to the car, drove to the end of the driveway, and got out. The rain was steady now.

He put on his shoes and walked the fifty yards back to the house carrying a hemlock branch he had stowed in the back seat. Starting at the porch, he retraced his footprints into the garage and then followed his tire marks exactly away from the house, brushing away all signs of a visitor's tracks. When he had driven in earlier, he drove up the left side of the driveway, leaving any of Lottie's car tire tracks on the right intact. When leaving, he just drove out over his old tracks. But now both of his traverses were removed with the hemlock broom and the rivulets of rainwater running on the driveway. The booms of the evening thunderstorm sounded louder now, and heavier raindrops fell as he got into his car, just as expected when he made his appointment with Lottie earlier in the day. Within a few minutes the driveway would be washed with a fresh summer bath, the product of a warm day and quick evening cooling of the atmosphere in summertime Pennsylvania.

Not far away, in another part of town, Pete Woodard had just arrived at his summer lake house after a tedious trip from Michigan. Prompted by the approaching storm, he hurried to bring down the last piece of luggage from the car and placed it at the door with the others. The phone could be heard ringing inside as Pete's cold hands fumbled with his keys to open the door. He rushed across the room to the desk. "Hello, this is Pete."

"Pete, it's Mitch; welcome back."

"How are you?"

"Fine. Listen; I'd like to come over to see you if you have some time. It's important."

"Mitch, I just walked in the door. I haven't even unpacked yet."

"There's lots of time for that. I've got an urgent favor to ask of you, and it's gotta be face-to-face. I'm sorry to do this to you, but I think you'll understand."

"Your choice; come on over. I'll be lighting the pilot to get some heat in here, so just come on in."

Pete Woodard's R-and-R was already interrupted. He was planning a quiet respite away from it all, fishing and sunning on the dock by the lake, getting back to nature, all the good things he enjoyed here at Silver Lake over the years. Only, this year he would be alone. Each of the previous months were supposed to get easier and easier, and instead things seemed to spin around him aimlessly without his being engaged. His wife of forty years had the audacity to pass before he did, a prediction she often jokingly made.

She was the healthy one, jogging eight or more miles a day, rain or shine, and never ate meat, only fish and vegetables. The best cook in the world, but she only quietly and humbly enjoyed everyone's praise for the myriad of meals and baked goods she abundantly created. She remained ingrained with her Russian heritage and memories of helping her nana bake wonderful meals, soups, breads, and desserts for the local railroaders and miners who flocked to their quaint hotel restaurant and bar when she was a little girl. They were mostly Russian and Irish immigrants saving their meager wages to bring families over from Europe to enjoy the blessings of America.

Her grandfather had run the small hotel and restaurant operation since the early 1900s, while also providing banking security for all the patrons. They were not trusting of bankers and were only comfortable placing their savings with a fellow immigrant like him, and to this day there are hundreds of descendants who will never know the extent of what they owe to the dedication of the simple Russian couple with a mission to help anyone without expectation of personal gain.

The furnace gas pilot just would not hold a flame after repeated tries. This was an annual trial of patience. A standby replacement thermocouple hung from a nail on the wall, but that was the last thing he wanted to tackle on this cold evening after a long trip. Laying almost prone, with flashlight in one hand and propane lighter in the other, Pete just held the flame on the thermocouple for two long minutes until it was red hot. He released the gas pilot valve, and the flame finally stayed lit—so much for leaving all utilities off for the winter and expecting everything to work just right when returning in the summer. The thermostat read 45 degrees, even though it was May 24 in Pennsylvania.

He was glad to have a central-boiler heating system; many homes on the lake depended on fireplaces and a good supply of dry logs to ward off the chill, even on summer evenings at this cold, breezy altitude. He plugged in four electric heaters reserved for emergencies and placed them around the living room. It was a still, damp cold, probably more so inside the house than outside, and darkness was soon approaching, which would make it even much colder at Silver Lake this evening. The heat should come up to a comfortable level from this dead start in about three hours. In the meantime, he sought out a comfortable woolen sweater from the closet and tried to keep himself moving to counter the cold. He checked to see that the water was working as previously arranged with his plumber and then stored some basic groceries in the refrigerator.

Pete took some time to look around for any winter damage or anything unusual. Some large tree branches and one small tree had fallen down outside the kitchen window during the winter, probably the result of heavy snow accumulation and wind during the usually bitter winter season. He walked from room to room, mostly to appreciate the fine work he had done over the years in expanding the small fieldstone house built in 1948 to four times its original size.

HYPOTHESIS

All the rooms had high-vaulted ceilings and oak-stained pine walls with an amber patina that matched the red oak flooring. The living room featured a double-opening see-through fieldstone fireplace that reached twenty-two feet to the ceiling and separated the dining room on the other side. There was the warm embrace of a lodge feeling throughout. The sitting room adjoined a full glass conservatory overlooking the lake through a framework of eighty-feet-tall hemlock trees between the lake and the house. He saw in it quite a bit of his life's work and hours of enjoyment in getting the home to where it was today. Now, however, there would be little joy to share without someone else.

Loud rapid knocks on the door announced the arrival of Police Chief Jim Mitchell. A tall bear of a man, his Irish good looks and ready smile were always welcomed by anyone who met him. His best years were behind him, but you would not know it by his attitude. He simply exuded energy, and plenty of it. The small town of Brackney could only support a part-time salary, and the residents knew they got a good deal in Mitch. He was a retired technical manager from a large architectural and engineering company. His early retirement promised many good years ahead in the comfortable little town of Brackney, Pennsylvania, with almost just a public relations function to manage as police chief.

Crime in Brackney was nonexistent. The close-knit family community almost policed itself; everyone knew everyone. No one was going to do wrong, and if anything did happen, Mitch knew about it instantly. He was the authority figure they needed when a community issue arose—the two or three automobile accidents a year, a domestic altercation once in a while, and the regular violations by the recreational snowmobile and off-road quad drivers year round. Actually, he secretly enjoyed the unauthorized freedom these drivers took in crossing rural roads and fields in public and privately owned areas; their worst fate was a stern warning, if he even cared to pursue them at all.

Chief Mitchell was mainly on call at home. On weekends he did a little cruising throughout the sparsely inhabited community in the Jeep Cherokee police vehicle, but for the most part he was not out looking for trouble. He was enjoying life, his farmhouse and home with his wife, Helen, and the few farm animals they both loved to care for. He was a country boy through and through.

"Pete, it's sure nice to see you," Mitch greeted with an extended handshake after brushing the rain from his sleeves and drying his hand on his shirt. His dark blue jacket with a Silver Lake Police emblem sewn on the left sleeve was the only indication of his higher authority.

"Yeah, you literally caught me with the key in the door and luggage in my hands. How've you been?"

"Just fine, couldn't be better. Let me say again, I'm so sorry about Janice. She was a fine, fine lady."

"Thanks. I miss her a lot. I know I appreciated her all those years, but now I really do."

"Pete, I'm sorry to barge in like this. First, here's a little something from Helen." He handed over a freshly baked apple pie covered with a tea towel, still warm and filling the air with an unforgettable aroma.

"You know, this was worth the trip. Please tell Helen thanks."

"Now let me at least help bring in some of those bags outside. It looks like more rain. We're having a cool, rainy spring as you can see; typical Silver Lake." They carried in the various pieces of luggage and bags of groceries that Pete had lined up outside the door when he arrived. "At least you didn't have to worry about the frozen items thawing out."

"Yeah, what's up with the weather? I've been watching it all month long, and it was really warm earlier in the month."

"Oh really, what day was that?" answered Mitch.

"Funny man; just what I need after a long day. Maybe I should come back in the summer. What week is that again?" Pete laughed.

"You know, if that weren't so true, it would be funny."

The two acquaintances were, by all accounts, friends, and enjoyed the back-and-forth banter, but Pete was a loner, now even more so. It was more of a professional admiration on each part; in fact, it was an intellectual admiration. They found bits of news to catch up on; however, there was a tension in the air, and both of them were anticipating what it was Mitch wanted to discuss on such an urgent basis.

As far as Chief Mitchell knew, Pete Woodard was a very special person in many ways that were obvious to anyone who met him, and in some ways he could never account for them. Pete was quiet and unassuming. Confident, even cavalier, he emanated an unintentional air of command in any situation, social or otherwise. His tall, handsome figure filled a room when he entered, and all who met him knew someone of capability was in their presence. He was the last person to speak or voice an opinion, almost unless requested. Yet his clear thinking and balanced views were particularly free of emotion and prejudice, all traits of a varied and successful career, both in business and something else in his background, which seemed better left alone.

Pete had mentioned many times in the past that his career was "problem solving." Even as a young engineer, he took on projects that were abandoned by teams of others, completing them successfully with no apparent difficulty. Accordingly, he rose rapidly at a young age to positions of responsibility in the corporate world. Mostly, though, they were turnaround situations, and he knew turnarounds were ideal matches for his cavalier attitude; he could do no wrong. Where others had failed previously, he could just pull out all the stops to prevail; coupled with an unrelenting work ethic, some of his project successes seemed godlike to his peers.

There was, however, a void of some sort in Pete's background, which Jim Mitchell could not unearth; that is, not without being obvious. Ashamedly, he had done a background check on Pete a few years ago. Pete's past two decades as a business consultant were quite stellar, according to comments by the clients in his portfolio regarding his expertise and accomplishments on their behalf. Before that, his career in the corporate world was highly regarded by those who remembered him. An early stint in the military after college seemed normal, with no outstanding events mentioned. Otherwise, it was almost boring. Still, there was something else to be known. He was sure of it.

"When's it going to warm up in here?"

"In an hour or two. I just lit the furnace and plugged in some electric heaters. It'll take a while, especially with these high ceilings. Sit down, Mitch. What's on your mind?"

They made themselves as comfortable as could be, sitting in direct line with two of the electric heaters, but it was still bone-chilling and left them feeling uneasy under the circumstances.

Mitch strained forward in his chair, searching in his mind for a way to begin. He pulled off his baseball cap and ran his fingers through his bushy, curly hair, a particular habit he had when in deep thought. "Pete, you've been a help before on that Saunders family thing a few years ago, and I still say it would be a mystery today if it weren't for your thinking. 'Outside the box,' they say."

Pete said nothing.

"I suffered quite a bit personally on that, although the outcome was accepted hands down by everyone. But even to this day I still don't think I have 100 percent local support or acceptance of that situation."

Pete cautioned, "Well, the Saunders family was highly regarded, and finding their own son guilty of murder was as much an offense to the community as to the family itself. Time will heal, but I guess it must be something like killing the messenger, if you know what I mean. And you're the messenger."

"Well, it's been a factor. I can see it in people's eyes when they're talking to me. I don't know; maybe it's my imagination."

HYPOTHESIS

The murder of Cassie Saunders by her brother two years ago had taken its toll on the entire community. Everyone was under suspicion for months before the truth was discovered. State police and FBI teams questioned everyone even remotely related to the comings and goings of the town. Whether he wanted it or not, Chief Jim Mitchell was in a storm of activities, suspicions of neighbor on neighbor, accusations, and mistrust. It was all necessary to eliminate as many suspects as possible so that there was left a clearer picture of what really happened. Her nude body was found in the woods by hunters a month after she went missing; strangulation was the apparent cause of death.

As fortune would have it, Mitch discussed the case with Pete one afternoon while sharing a quiet fishing tour of Silver Lake. Pete listened casually, with his attention more on the movement of his fishing line than on the storyline. His job that day was to get the chief's mind off his problems for a while. Instead, the problems were all that were discussed. Mitch just could not let up in his quest. He had a murderer in his town, and not only was it an assault on the community, but he felt it was a personal assault. The storybook town of Brackney in Silver Lake Township would now always have a black chapter. Pete felt that day to be a failed effort and pledged to do a better job of psychological mending next time.

Later that week, Pete sat straight up in bed one night with a thought about what he had heard in the boat that day with Mitch. Cassie and her brother, Josh, were very close, ages seventeen and fifteen respectively. They kept to themselves with just occasioned friendships at school. A household search was standard operating procedure with nothing unusual except, Pete thought, one thing. Josh's entire world of possessions consisted of a common .22-caliber rifle with a box of bullets, some foreign coins, a video game machine connected to a TV in his room, and a wallet with the obligatory pack of condoms every schoolboy seems to think will come in handy some day. Pete thought, *Was he using them, and with whom?* His mind raced to the unthinkable. He got up and found Chief Jim Mitchell's phone number in his address book and dialed it immediately. "Mitch, I have a thought about the Saunders thing. Can we get together?"

The chief's reply was as expected. "When? Now?"

"Mitch, it's important. You're gonna want to hear this."

Within fifteen minutes the two sat together over cups of tea in the wee hours of the morning while Pete offered his theory about the brother and sister having sexual relations with one another, and who knows what transpired to cause Josh to act as he did. Mitch sat, dazed, saying nothing. It was the longest silence, but somehow fit for the occasion. When he spoke it was thunderous.

"Pete, I know that family. They're all good churchgoin' people! This is not even a consideration! The FBI and state police already covered that as far as suspecting anyone in the immediate family."

Pete was prepared for the reaction. "Mitch, you've got to admit that it does add up. The kids are home alone for long periods of time. They don't socialize. They spend all their time together. And it is a somewhat remote location. It certainly is worth exploring. You have to admit that. And you did mention that she wasn't a virgin."

"Maybe, but how do we go about confronting this, especially with the family in the state they are now and, of all things, involving their own son?"

They both sat quietly for a moment while Pete prepared for the suggestion that was to be the crack in the case from the most unlikely source. Pete's calm, deliberate suggestion left no room for interpretation. "Mitch, you need to open their septic system. Those things float, you know. And unless the parents fess up to using them, there's only one other possibility in that house."

Chief Jim Mitchell's political capital was pretty much used up by the time the court order process allowed the opening of the septic tank. A team of FBI agents, state police officers, and a truck from Country Septic Systems assembled with Mitch in the field behind the Saunders home. It was an old-fashioned system with a gravity feed from the house, and no pump or filter system to deteriorate the latex rubber condoms. When the concrete lid was removed, the truck driver shined his flashlight down into the opening. Right on the surface of the water floated at least a hundred of them, a murky mess attesting to the unspeakable.

Within three days everything was confirmed, and Cassie's fifteen year-old brother confessed right in front of his court-appointed lawyer and a room full of people, almost just as Pete theorized. The psychological rationale of the strangulation was left to the experts' interviews of Josh. Pete was sickened. There was no gratification. He and Mitch never spoke about it or even referred to the case until Mitch's mention of it earlier tonight.

"Anyway, why am I here? I value your input, as you know by now. You're here to relax, and I respect that, except I really would like your opinion on a particular situation. And you always said that when I want your opinion I should give it to you."

"You mean I should ask for it, don't you?" Pete chuckled.

"Whatever. You know what I mean."

"Sure. What is it?" Pete really enjoyed talking with Mitch, but his tiredness was quickly creeping in and he had all he could do to keep his eyes open.

Mitch settled back in his chair. "I've got a situation, and I'm definitely alone on this."

2

Brackney Police Chief Jim Mitchell filled out the large upholstered chair from arm to arm. It embraced him snugly as he spoke. Sipping tea and telling a tale, normally a pleasant experience, these two Irish traits were not to be enjoyed this evening. Pete reached to switch on a lamp and handed over a plate with a piece of Helen's pie as the chief began.

"About a month ago we had a suicide, or it could have been an accident, here in Silver Lake Township. It was Dr. Danields, Lois and Bill Danields' son, Bill, Jr. He was found on a Monday morning in his Montrose office. Been there all weekend. Both parents have been dead now for a few years. No one even missed him. The joke was, people don't especially care about or miss dentists if they're not around. I believe there is some truth in that."

"Was he despondent? Any known problems?"

"No, in fact he had a very good practice. He did quite well from what I understand."

"My dentist does quite well too. He charged me ninety dollars for a filling the other day. I told him that was a lot of money for ten minutes' work, and he said he could drill more slowly if I want next time."

They both laughed.

"Anyway, I thought you said the incident was in Silver Lake. Montrose is nine miles away, a different township and all."

"No, you're right. He lived here in Silver Lake just up from the south end of the lake on Crowley Road; had a nice little place there too, about two hundred acres or so. But the suicide happened right there in his office in town." Pete listened as Mitch began to lay out all the details. The facts were pretty straightforward. "Apparently he was dead since Friday evening. Took an overdose of ether, diethyl ether, or something like that."

"Ether? I thought dentists didn't use that stuff any more. Kinda primitive, isn't it?" Pete asked.

"You're right. The doc had a whole supply of it. He was a collector of antique dental equipment. It was on display in cases and shelves in his office and waiting room. I've seen it myself. You know, tongs and drills, the way they used to do things. There was an old carton of ether made by a company that no longer exists. More than half the bottles were empty, but the caps were screwed back on."

Pete again questioned, "Even the bottle he was using?"

"No; there were two empty bottles, one on his desk and one on the floor, along with some gauze, two ounces each. It looked like a cut-and-dried case. If the other empty bottles were an indicator, he seemed to have been a regular recreational user, but this time on a binge. You know, relax and forget your worries. I got all this information from County Coroner Jim Davis and Montrose Police Chief Al Dorrance. They're pretty good guys. I believe they reviewed it well. Didn't find anything. And that's that."

"So what's all the urgency about? That was a month ago you said." Pete was tired from his trip, and he was edgy, to say the least.

"Well, I'll get back to that. But there's more. We now have another suicide here just up the road. Pete, my biggest concern around here is generally that someone's cows got out and onto the road. Now I've got multiple suicides, to say nothing of the Saunders thing two years ago."

"Mitch, what's the big deal? I mean, suicides, especially among dentists, are not all that rare. So who is it this time?"

"A computer manager named Jane Morson, a very nice lady, quiet, kept to herself. Widowed a few years back when her husband had a heart attack right in their yard splitting firewood. She blew her brains out with a shotgun."

"Geez, what a way to go! How'd they find her? And don't tell me everywhere, if you know what I mean."

"She was home. Her car was in the driveway. Mail was accumulating in her box. I got a call from her employer and went over. I could smell it outside. She was there four days, slightly longer."

"What was the scene like?"

"Pretty gruesome, as you can imagine. I called the coroner and state police. I like to keep the state police in the loop for a number of reasons, mostly that they get to see the countywide picture of what's happening. Things sometimes add up to where they appreciate the inputs for some of their other work like robberies and things like that throughout the region." Mitch also knew that the state police could be a big asset, especially when he needed to project authority. Sometimes a small-town law officer doesn't get all the respect and cooperation he should.

"It looked like she had the gun between her legs with the barrel in her mouth when it went off. We figure her dog ate everything that landed on the floor."

"Geez." Pete wondered what Mitch's concern was. "So are you saying there's a connection to the dentist?"

Mitch gestured with both hands extended over his lap, palms down and waving. "I'm sure not saying that. Not to anyone, believe me. Not with my rep as the town prince of darkness. That's why I wanted to talk to you. Think about Doc Danields—forty-five years old, pretty well off, nice business, the only dentist for miles around, friendly personality, mildly involved in community functions, a great guy all in all. In fact, he was sitting on some recent large income from a natural gas drilling lease he put together with a Houston well driller last year. He shouldn't have had a care in the world. Yet one thing sticks out: the ether."

"What do you mean?"

"I mean the absolute amount of it. There were two bottles opened. Davis's blood test came back, and it was off the charts! It was believed that he may have been in a stupor over a period of ten hours or so while using it off and on as he awoke. Doc Davis said that it is pretty easy to overdose. That's why dentists use nitrous oxide, laughing gas, and that's only for extreme cases. They have a lot more latitude with the dosage before anything serious happens. Any more, with the high-speed drills used today, they just use a shot of general anesthesia in the nerves."

Pete commented, "I see what you're saying. But someone in an induced state like that could not be in control of dispensing exacting amounts."

"That's true." Mitch added, "There was also a lot of alcohol in his system. Under the conditions, it was hard to be sure after two and a half days how much he took, but that combination was also a major part of it. He kept a bottle of Jack in the office, and it was almost empty."

Pete wondered, "Who was last to see him?"

"You took the words right out of my mouth! His dental assistant, Claire Woods, left about four thirty Friday. He had no more patients scheduled. No notes were on his calendar or in his personal schedule book. It looked like he was just going through the mail and kicking back after a full day. She's the one who found him on Monday."

"Doesn't he normally have office hours on Saturday?"

"He does, but nothing was scheduled that Saturday. Claire said that happens once in while, mostly because they try to encourage people to come in during the week."

"Well, I'll say he had a full day and a full evening planned too. So we have two suicides, or possibly a suicide and an accident, in what, almost six months since the beginning of this year? That can't be abnormal," Pete observed.

"I don't think we had any suicides last year in the entire county, and maybe only one or two the year before," said Mitch authoritatively. "I'm going to check that with the coroner. But see, this is where I don't want any notoriety, at least not yet. So that's why I'm talking to you, crossing the i's and dotting the t's, you know."

Pete chuckled. "You mean the other way around; t's and i's, that is. How about homicides? Anything out of the ordinary?"

"Maybe there's one a year in the entire two- or three-county area, and then not every year. There was a murder-suicide a few months ago down toward Tunkhannock. A father blew up his whole family, a handgun deal, sad—little kids and all. Speaking of Tunkhannock, there was an, I guess you could call it, an accident, at least that's how it was ruled. A graphic artist fell off the roof of the Dietrich Theater. It seems he was shooting photos by the amount of equipment lying around."

"How do they think it happened?"

"It was at sunset. You know how these artsy types are, trying to get some colorful shots of the Susquehanna River. At least that's what was recorded in the camera. The rumor mill said it was a lover's quarrel. He was light in the loafers, if you know what I mean. But nothing was ever proven. It's possible that he could have tripped and fell. Anyway, a kid on his bike found him at the back of the building in the afternoon the next day. He might have lived a bit longer after the fall. He had crawled, it seemed, some distance along the building, but still too far in from the street to attract any assistance. So as you can see, we haven't been lacking for excitement around here."

"Mitch, I'm still trying to figure out what we're looking for. All you have is the suicide of a lonely widow. Other than that, the doc in Montrose and the shootings and accidents in Tunkhannock are so far removed and months ago. What are you trying to come up with?"

"I just want to bounce things off you as I look at a couple of facts. This shotgun thing doesn't add up. First, there's no record of them owning a shotgun, and of all things, this one was a fairly new Mossberg with the serial number freshly filed off. Another thing: her fingerprints were the only ones on it. You would think maybe her husband's might still be on it from a few years ago."

"It wouldn't be the first gun with the serial number taken off. That's what people do. And people do clean their guns after using them."

"Yeah, I guess, but I knew Jane, and she was rock solid, even after her husband's death. I also know things can wear away on people, but she was strong, a churchgoing type. And she was well off, no financial worries, from what few details people knew about her personal situation. She was highly regarded in her career connections. My God, she was only forty-eight years old!"

"Any relatives?"

"No, there were no close relatives. Maybe that's part of the problem; loneliness, more than likely. There'll be a service on Friday. And as far as the doc and his ether party, that doesn't make sense either. I just wanted you to hear these things. Maybe something will pop into that head of yours. Do you mind?"

"I never mind, if you think I can be a help."

Mitch knew Pete to be a problem solver extraordinaire. It was obvious when talking to him about even the simplest of things. He always had the right approach. He didn't hesitate or vacillate when something had to be decided. He was accustomed to dealing with large risks and rewards in business, and it resonated in his personal life in even the simplest issues. He seemed to always have a handle on situations when others continued to be perplexed. The reason was simple as far as he was concerned. As Pete often quoted, "Everyone wants to go to heaven, but no one wants to die." What he meant was that you can be pretty sure that when someone can't make a decision, it usually means he isn't willing to pay the price. "Almost everyone, and I mean 999 out of 1000 people, wants the cheap way out," he would say. Pete didn't work that way. He made his decisions without regard for cost or time involved, and then he would figure out how to offset the cost factor afterward.

Pete's attention was wavering. It was a long flight, and the hassles at the airport, rental car booth, and supermarket on the way to Silver Lake had taken the best of him. His eyes were closing uncontrollably. He was in no condition for deep thoughts. "You made your point. I'll be glad to help. Call or come over any time."

"Thanks. I will."

"I really do want to help. Let me give it some thought."

"Okay, my friend. I just might need it."

"I'm afraid right now, though, I've got an appointment with some clean sheets and pillows. I am planning on some quality hook-and-worm time tomorrow, first thing in the morning. You know where to find me."

"Ah, the beauty of full retirement! It must be nice."

"Say hello to Helen for me. And don't forget to thank her for the pie. It was great."

"Thanks, Pete. This is kind of a one-man band effort around here. I appreciate the contact with you. Sleep tight. Hey, it's still cold in here. You sure you're okay?"

Pete's farewell wave and smile was all he could muster. He was badly in need of rest, and there was a lot to think about. He actually enjoyed this.

Pete didn't even unpack. He went to his dresser for a pair of pajamas and changed into them. The thermostat read 57 degrees inside. He put on a pair of socks and crawled into bed under the sheets and hoped that the heat would come up soon.

Evenings at Silver Lake were stark. There were no lights except for a few faint glows from the small cottages across the lake. It was catacomb-like. A person had the feeling of a guarantee of not being disturbed, and it was a very restful state of mind. You were away from the world when you wanted to be. No one knew or cared if you were here, and that's a very different sense, which is rarely experienced. It was why Pete looked forward to being here, a withdrawal from the world into oneself. Rest and peace of mind are very much assured.

3

Susquehanna County is a northeastern county of Pennsylvania, 860 square miles shaped in a rectangle, measuring about twenty-five by thirty-five miles. Other than cleared farm fields, some beautiful lakes and streams, and a few small towns, the absolute entire land area is populated with trees, most commonly maple and oak leaf-bearing trees and hemlock and white pine trees. The population of 42,000 rural residents consider themselves some of the luckiest people on earth. Time and prosperity surely has passed them by. There have been no driving economic forces to speak of other than dairy farms and blue stone quarries, large and small, mostly small. The official working population is seventeen thousand, half of whom leave the county each day to pursue a living in adjacent, more prosperous—but not by much—counties.

The largest town is Montrose, somewhat centered geographically and home to 1,843 residents at last count. Its name is a conjoining of two words, the French *mont* for mountain and *rose* for Doctor L. R. Rose, whose family settled the area as emissaries of

HYPOTHESIS

Benjamin Franklin after helping with the surveying of the undocumented lands in the area. It is the county seat, with a courthouse and a lawyers' row of converted Victorian-era homes and buildings that house the legal profession within walking distance to the courthouse across from the Currier and Ives town green. Not much deep legal expertise is required for the constant flow of property deeds and realty transactions, wills and estate reconciliations, divorces, and only minor criminal offenses. Many legal issues are still handled the old-fashioned way, with one lawyer handling the legalities for both parties in a matter. It speaks loudly to the spirit of trust and good fellowship found throughout the area.

Personal income and family assets fall well below the state and national averages. Yet what is missing in dollar-measured wealth is far more than made up for in value—community, family, religion, absolute scenic beauty, all bound together with something of a peaceful human spirit found almost nowhere else on earth. It is truly a marvelous thing to observe. It may not be spoken, but it is a matter of pride in everyone's mind, at least it seems, every day—a quiet, unassuming self-esteem that simply shows.

Life spans are longer than average. The local obituaries pretty much average eighty-five years of age for each death, with frequent mentions over age ninety. The only medical facilities are two small hospitals about twenty-five miles from one another. While a larger community hospital is planned, major medical services are now found only in neighboring counties to the north and south: Broome County, New York, and Wyoming County and Lackawanna County, Pennsylvania, respectively. It is seriously thought that the health and longevity of the population probably would not support a new hospital anyway. It would merely be a local convenience. The joke is that the only one who died recently was the funeral director; he starved to death.

The county's many lakes and hills are weekend tourist and summer resident attractions. You can go back in time with just a short drive through the Endless Mountains region, as it has been called for centuries, with regard to the many scallops of long, rolling mountains defining this and the adjoining three county topographies. From most roadside vistas, as many as seven mountains layered behind one another can be seen dissolving into the distance. Bob Johnson, a member of the Montrose Chamber of Commerce, jokingly coined the phrase, "We are a half hour from nowhere," and while there is no such official town motto, however, there is a barely-functioning Chamber of Commerce that tries to promote business and whatever scarce development opportunities come their way.

The few local businesses are comprised sparsely of a paint store, flower shop, antique shop, art studio and gallery, bookstore, gift store, candy store, sporting goods, hardware, two car dealers, and a few grocery stores, restaurants, pharmacies, banks, a dentist, a veterinarian, two doctors, realtors, and of course, accountants and attorneys. The businesses have a captive audience by virtue of their "half hour from nowhere" location, and better yet, the residents have the attention of the businesses to keep them shopping locally with the best services and products to be found. Symbiotic at least, quixotic at best, there is always the hope of economic improvement.

The drive from Montrose to Silver Lake Township is as picturesque as can be along a gentle upward mountain slope of nine miles lined with pastures, trees, and quaint farms. There are a few lakes and streams; the crown jewel is Silver Lake itself, one hundred acres of the purest spring-fed waters sitting at one of the highest elevations in the state, at 1,790 feet above sea level. Two-thirds of the shoreline is dotted with cottages and some year-round homes. A nature conservancy with abundant hemlock trees occupies the other third of the land along the water, offering a stunning atmosphere to relax in and enjoy during any season. It was settled in the early 1800s by Dr. Robert Hutchinson Rose, who built a mansion on the lake and started many industries in the area, including tanneries, logging and lumber mills, quarries, gristmills, and home building. He deeded property to anyone who would stay and work in his empire, predominantly Scottish and Irish immigrants who were coming through upper New York state nearby, laying railroad tracks at the time. The local cemeteries are a testament to the Celtic bloodlines that are still dominant to this day. Development has not found its way to these shores, nor would it be welcomed by the entrenched attitude of its longtime inhabitants. Things are just right here, and everyone wants to leave the rest of the world behind and keep it that way.

The relaxing qualities of the lake itself are enhanced by a predominant northwest breeze flowing over its mountaintop location on most days. Viewed from one of the surrounding hills, the lake sits in a bowl with most of the land on its circumference angling upward except for an inlet on the north end and a dam outlet on the south end. It gives a comfortable feeling, sort of like being fortified by the surrounding forests. The main road from Montrose passes unnoticeably by the east shore of the lake and meanders for another ten miles through breathtaking countryside to the border of upstate New York.

Silver Lake Township is one of twenty-seven separate townships in Susquehanna County. Each has its own governance of elected township supervisors, and many have a volunteer fire company and a township maintenance building for road repairs. There are no towns as such within the township, just a post office in Brackney that is across the road from the volunteer fire station. There are a few hard-to-find businesses located on back roads, such as furniture makers, machine shops, craft and gift shops, and one notable military surplus depot. Kublo's Government Surplus carries an abundant supply of olive drab Jeeps and two-and-a-half-ton trucks and other army vehicles in the outside lot and everything from ammo boxes, tents, and boots to personnel clothing items inside. When you consider that there are two skeet shooting, pistol, and rifle ranges in town with more than seventy members, it has been said that Brackney is constantly at one of the highest states of militarily preparedness in the nation in case of a Ruskie invasion, or anyone else who would be silly enough to try. Other than a bar and restaurant called the Colonel J.W. Brackney Inn, named after a civil war colonel who operated a tannery in the area, and Tucker's grocery store and gas station, which is now out of business, there is nothing else.

Silver Lake is probably second only to Ireland as the largest per capita consumer of tea in the world, and perhaps beer too. They take both seriously, especially the tea. You will find it on nearly every breakfast table and throughout the day for an afternoon break of a *cupan tae,* Gaelic for cup of tea. Most people think of high tea as a formal afternoon affair for the privileged, but it was originally a working man's afternoon break with scones or biscuits that served as a small meal before arriving home for dinner very much later in the day. It can still be expected in many homes today after a customary Irish wake when a family member passes away or during any family occasion. These traditions followed from the arrival of Irish immigrants, who were mostly poor trades people and farmers locating here. Tea once served as a common currency among these early residents. The small grocers originally took butter and eggs from local farmers as a barter payment for tea, sugar, and salt sold at their stores, and then the farmers made payments of tea to one another for services such as purchases of wood products, blacksmithing, candles, honey, soap, and the like. Irish tea is a strong blend of exotic tealeaves from various regions in Kenya, India, and Sri Lanka, marketed by such familiar Irish companies as Barry's, Lyons, and Bewley's. It is brewed to be very strong, and to this day in Silver Lake, it is made to be combined in a cup filled one-third with rich milk before pouring in the tea and adding sugar.

HYPOTHESIS

There are 1,320 registered vehicles in the township, 1,081 of which are pickup trucks. The 1,700 residents traverse forty-two miles of township roads, only two miles of which are paved. This discounts the four stretches of two-lane state highways that lace through the area as the main travel fares. The other forty miles are dirt, known locally as hardpan, artfully manicured roadways with smooth surfaces crowned in the center for water runoff into perfectly engineered drainage ditches, country style. Country style is a sincere compliment. Whether it's a road, a barn, or just a fence, it's built with fortified structuring, no skimping—deep foundations, extra-thick substructures, wider and thicker beams, double welds, longer nails, and anything else one could do to assure longevity against the elements. Things are done right the first time so that they don't have to be revisited again and again. This culture prevails in the small-town government run by three elected residents as town supervisors, any one of whom is handy enough to get on a snowplow or road grader and do the job well. Accordingly, town budgets are tightly scrutinized and managed.

Much of the township's business is conducted by volunteers and part-time employees. A dollar travels quite a bit farther under the watchful eyes of these proud and prudent people. Their priorities are sensibly decided, and the financing of projects always begins with an analysis of whether secondhand equipment can suffice or a weekend volunteer crew can get the job done. The newest piece of fire equipment is a tanker truck entirely built from a truck frame and engine with a buttressed frame and water tank added by the volunteer fire company members over the course of one winter. Taxpayers get their money's worth in Silver Lake Township.

Pete Woodard loved it here. His annual summer visits since retiring sometimes stretched through much of the early fall. Snow has arrived at this high elevation as early as October 11; however, colorful leaves and the scents of the autumn forests can be enjoyed throughout much of November in most years. Pete's plans were open-ended this year. Without Janice, his focus had been nonexistent, unable to make plans or caring to make decisions. He was surviving.

4

"Mitch, this is Nora. How've you been?" The cell phone crackled as Chief Jim Mitchell strained to hear.

"Nora? Oh, fine; long time no see. I hope you can hear me. We're still waiting for that infamous cell tower to arrive over here," spoke Mitch very loudly.

"Yes, a little broken up, but all right."

"What's up? No problems, I hope," he returned. He pulled over to the side of the road to continue his conversation.

She explained, "No, but my sister and I have some questions, and you're the only one we'd like to discuss something with. You remember Carol, don't you?"

"Sure."

"She's visiting for a few days while we settle some family business. It's about the gas lease thing."

"Well, I'm probably the last person to ... can you hear me?" he said.

"Just barely; can I call you at home?" she answered loudly.

"Sure. Anytime after six I'll be there," he squawked back.

He thought, *I've gotta get some action on that cell tower. It's a safety issue for sure and undoubtedly a missing comfort factor for people traveling these roads, especially in the winter. The squeaky wheel gets the grease, but now I think the wheel fell off on that tower deal.* He made a mental note and drove over to the township office to see what was going on.

The Silver Lake Township building housed the road grader with some plow equipment and a pickup truck. There was a meeting room with a capacity of about one hundred chairs for town meetings and other gatherings. It was run part-time by the single most effective government official in the history of man, Ella Pierson. She also recently was elected to the position of township supervisor, and served as secretary/treasurer, one of three governing positions for the township. The entire community placed its unwavering faith in her guidance, deservedly so. Mitch picked up his duty roster, and as usual, there was nothing on it. Ella did mention that two residents at the last supervisors meeting wondered if he could drive by Laurel Lake Road to check whether he thought a twenty-five-mile-an-hour speed limit sign there would be effective. He said he would, and then left for the day.

Nora Connely lived in a farmhouse on over five hundred acres just southwest of Silver Lake along Nasar Road. Her husband of twenty-six years had passed away unexpectedly last year. Mitch and Helen helped out with the funeral proceedings, and they kept in contact with her for a few months until they felt she was on her feet emotionally. Helen stopped by with baked goods once in a while on the pretense that Mitch was watching his weight and she didn't want the calories tempting him, which was true, but only conveniently so. Nora's only living relative was a sister, Carol, whose home was an hour or so away in Waverly, New York. Both sisters taught school and were nearing early retirement age but were not yet financially comfortable enough to end their careers. They vaguely discussed moving in together on the family farm, which Nora now occupied, but only cryptic mentions of it came up when they spoke. Now, with the advent of the number of gas well leases being offered to residents including Nora, serious life-changing decisions must be made, and quickly.

As decided, Nora called after dinner, and she and Mitch planned to meet the next day at noon. Mitch and Helen tended to their animal kingdom after that. They relished this time every evening. Their property sat on fifteen acres and could not be called a farm by any measure, but it looked like one. To the west side of the house was a horse barn with two horses and a few chickens. There were also two cats and two dogs. The cats stayed in the barn, and the dogs were afforded prime bedding in the house. All the animals were jostled by their fur in a communicative manner then fed and watered. It was a nightly parade as each of them followed behind, expectantly anticipating their evening treat. It was what kept Mitch and Helen alive, they said; a responsibility, a daily set of tasks, an elixir.

Mitch's mind never wavered from his discussion with Pete. That was the first time he was able to compile all his thoughts into one cohesive set of impressions. His plight as the single law enforcement entity in his district of responsibility put an unusual demand on him. Normally it was all about a tree fallen on the road or some other rurally inspired happening. But this suicide matter needed consultation, and under the circumstances, there was no one else available at this time to discuss things with. Pete's arrival was perfect timing, and he would use him as much as possible. He knew Pete enjoyed it, so he didn't feel as though he were taking advantage, but rather adding to the interest of Pete's visit.

Nora Connely's homestead was a marvelous sight once the turn from the main road was made. A long, curving dirt road led right to the front of the turn-of-the-century home. A white-painted barn stood to its left with a wide courtyard between. On the southwest corner sat an old itinerant farmhouse where the temporary field workers stayed during the harvests. An old circular stone wall housed a roofed well along the barn. The view of the descending topography to the south was well worth the visit in and of itself. It was at least a thirty-mile vista, sloping south, comprised of rolling hills extending far beyond Montrose.

The once-farmed fields were overgrown now. It seemed a waste, but on the other hand, it was inevitable. The number of active farms in the region had been decreasing year by year. Landowners in Susquehanna County can afford such vast properties, however, since they aren't taxed if they are registered as "clean and green." This is a quasi-environmental/anti-development state law that allows landowners to discount all land tax liabilities, even if they are not farming the land, as long as no development is permitted on the property itself forever. It entirely stifles developers from subdividing and putting up half-acre cookie cutter home sites. But on the other hand, it freezes the tax base because there are no continuing developments to offset increasing government costs. That's the way of these country folks, and that's the way they want to keep it. No development is a good thing. So goes the fate of Susquehanna County.

Nora was probably a beauty as a young woman, and she still was quite attractive. Her welcoming smile was always aglow. When she walked, her carriage was magnificent—shapely, but not overly so. The passing of her husband, and life alone for the past year, had begun to leave their mark. She wore her hair up in a bun, and it was now graying away from the blond mantle it once was.

Her trademark smile was accompanied by some wrinkles now, which recorded pain in her countenance. The lively attitude was still there, but one felt she was putting on a good outward appearance. It just didn't seem the same. She was well regarded as a classic high school teacher, the one people remember most at their class reunions—tough but fair, and responsible to her students and the community in giving them the best education possible, traits only appreciated years and years after graduation.

"My gosh, you never change!" Nora commented as she welcomed Mitch.

"Is that good or bad?"

"Only you know that answer, Mitch. Mitch, meet Carol. I know you met last year."

"Yes, how do you do? How are things in Waverly?"

"Oh, fine. But if it weren't for the Guthrie Hospital over in Sayre, we wouldn't even exist. You know how it is these days. There's just no economy there," Carol said.

"It's getting to be the same everywhere around here. I swear it's better to never have had an economy than to have had one and lost it," Mitch said. He often thought of the marked difference in attitude between the Susquehanna County residents who had virtually nothing by way of infrastructure and economic status and the formerly prosperous cities of the adjoining southern-tier counties of northern New York state, including Waverly, which once had many large high-tech companies and now had very few left. There was, however, a double-negative situation just south of Montrose, where a large electronics plant was located from the 1960s through the 1980s. It was shut down as a federal super fund toxic cleanup site and had yet to be put back on the market for lack of reconciliation of all the chemicals remaining in the ground. No one would touch it. You couldn't give it away. What was once a boon of prosperity for the area was gone, and had left behind a deficit that had not been overcome.

"Well, that's part of what we would like to get your opinion on. First, let's get that sandwich in front of you as I promised. Iced tea?" Nora asked. Mitch nodded.

As they ate the extra-thick chicken salad and cheese on toasted rye, quartered and accompanied with a pickle, they enjoyed the vastness of the southerly view and breeze of the early afternoon from the wraparound porch, which extended the view to the rear of the property. "I think I can make a career out of this kind of living," Mitch said.

"Glad you're enjoying it. It's somewhat why we want to talk to you," Nora said. Mitch nodded silently and continued with his lunch. "Carol and I are discussing plans to retire and continue living here together. She may even decide to move before her retirement and put in the sixty-mile drive each day to and from Waverly. But that's beside the point. I've been approached by two gas well drillers to enter into a mineral rights lease and drilling contract, and I wonder what you think." Carol had all of the physical traits of her sister and even mirrored her expressions and mannerisms as they both sat facing him. They seemed so innocent and needing of help. He quickly realized he was the only male figure in their lives and that's why he was there. It gave him a sense of ponderous responsibility for which he was definitely not prepared.

"Well, I am no expert on natural gas well drilling, much less an informed legal contact." Mitch laughed.

"I know. That's why I asked you over. You see, everyone is in a frenzy over this thing, and we just want to do the right thing at the right time. Two years ago people signed on leases for fifty dollars and one hundred dollars an acre for a five-year period. Now the going rate is $2,400 an acre and rising. In Houston, Texas, word is that they ended up paying $24,000 an acre for some leases years ago." Nora's nervousness was obvious.

"Nora, I definitely can't tell you what or when to do anything with these companies. But I do know it's the talk of the town no matter where you go, from Tunkhannock forty miles to the south to forty miles north into New York State," Mitch said. "It will surely change things around here, and I'm afraid for the worse. You're talking environmental problems probably worse than quarries or farm runoffs ever were. To say nothing of the truck traffic, water pollution, scarring of the land, reduced property values, and who knows what."

"I'm well aware of all that. It's just that I think I can get an offer of a $2,500-an-acre sign-up bonus right now, plus 15 percent of the natural gas revenues extracted for the next five years. You know we have 517 acres. That's a lot of money even if they don't ever drill here," Nora said. "There's gas, plenty of it, I'm sure. Our old well over there feeds into the old itinerant labor house, and methane gas comes right up through the water. Grandpa used to tell people not to smoke over there in the old days for fear of blowing up the place. The same gas comes up through the spring over at Salt Springs State Park. Even the old shallow drillings there used to get plenty of gas out of those wells in the early days. Used to light the lanterns and fire the stove and fireplaces as history tells. It was a panacea. No timber harvesting or wood chopping to heat the homes or cook. It was an unbelievably fortunate geological find. People thought an entire city would evolve around those well sites. They tried to make a commercial go of it, but eventually it lacked the consistent pressure and flow to be profitable. The technology just wasn't there at the time."

"So what's the problem? If you're asking if it were me, what would I do, I think … well, I really don't know what I'd do. A bird in the hand, if you know what I mean." Mitch was purposely being evasive. He was in a no-win situation.

If Nora entered into a contract now, the rates were sure to go up farther and she would regret it. If she waited for higher rates, it could be years before there was further interest in her particular property. The gas drilling companies knew this torment that the landowners went through, and they played on their fears as long as they could before increasing the offer. Then there were rumors of over-commitment on the part of some of these energy exploration companies. So should a person enter a contract now, while the gettin' is good, so to speak? It was not an easy position to be in. No matter whom you spoke with regarding the timing of entering into a contract, they were not satisfied. The early participants regretted not holding out for more money and actually entered into lawsuits to rescind their lease agreements. The later participants felt they should have held out for more. The current participants just getting involved felt they may have missed the drilling cycles, at least for the five-year period that their lease is applicable, since there are major restrictions at the government level holding up progress as well as water and wastewater processing availability problems. Those who have not yet signed up and are holding out for the best deal are becoming fewer and fewer. And by holding out, a landowner may just end up being bypassed in his or her lifetime even though the property may have very great production possibilities. Nora knew her property had great production potential.

Nora just stared off into the distance. Carol was busying herself cleaning up and freshening drinks, not caring to be an active part of this high-finance discussion. "Nora, I do know this. When you think about the assets of this property, you do have a lot of clear land, and it's completely cleared along Silver Creek, which just about divides the land equally east from west. These drillers need water for the drilling process, and lots of it. That creek is perfectly located, and it never runs dry. The pipeline is only about a half or three-quarters of a mile away to the east. They'll want to tap into it from the wells drilled here. That's probably a lot better situation than most people who have already signed."

"Thanks. I've thought about that. I just wanted to see if you would come up with that same opinion independently. I guess it's like a poker game of who is going to bluff the best or flinch first,"

Nora said. "When you think about the short history of these gas leases around here, everyone without exception who signed a lease early in the game resents it. There's even a lawsuit being prepared now against the first gas company to rescind the low-paying leases they set up with over twenty land owners." Nora's confidence was building as she related the happenings.

"Yeah, I've heard all about it," Mitch said. "I don't have to worry about it with our few acres. Fifteen acres in the country with a pond and some animals is a dream for most people, but these guys are looking for two hundred or three hundred acres at a clip. They want big deals first, and then let the little guy come begging."

"Mitch, how about some apple pie? The apples are store bought but good; no local produce for another seven or eight weeks," offered Carol from the kitchen.

"Don't mind if I do." Mitch breathed deeply while pressing his hands down in behind his belt as if to make room.

"Nora, you know Pete Woodard is back. Just talked to him day before yesterday. He just arrived."

"He's a great guy. How's he doing on his own now?"

"Seems fine. I'll see him this week again to do a little fishing together. He looked a bit tired, and I know he's anxious to just kick back. But I think everything is copacetic."

Mitch enjoyed what had to be one of the best apple pies he had ever tasted, including Helen's. Carol would have made a good catch for some lucky man. She had the same carriage and mannerisms of her sister and was easily mistaken for her, but she remained single for all these years and, apparently, happily so.

"Mitch, I know what I'm going to do. I think I'll just wait it out, this gas thing. I know in my heart that a better deal is in the offing. Look what happened to that Morson woman. It didn't seem to make her life any better."

"What do you mean? She had a gas lease too?" Mitch asked.

"Oh my, yes, and a sizeable deal it was, around $650,000. It's almost like there's a curse with these deals," Nora said quickly. "Doc Danields and all."

"How do you know about her arrangement with the gas drillers?" Mitch asked.

"The gas companies. They must want you to feel you're in good company, making the same decisions as your neighbors, I guess." Nora turned to her sister for reassurance. You could tell they had discussed this at length and didn't resolve their thinking. Mitch didn't respond. His mind was filing the new information among the details already there.

"My duty calls, ladies," Mitch said as he slapped both knees with his palms and quickly rocked himself forward, rising from the chair. "I hope you come to the decision that's right for you."

"You've been a great help," the sisters said together. "Come again soon."

"Hey, Nora, give Pete a call. He might like to hear from you. He might have a better opinion as to what to do than I can offer. He's quite a businessman, you know."

"Thanks, maybe I will. See you. Say hello to Helen."

"I will." Chief Mitchell swung into police mode as he drove away. He would spend the afternoon on his computer, researching. Ether, suicides, and shotguns seemed to be good places to start. He went into his former engineering mindset: *Start scratching around to get started, and some direction will take shape.* It always worked for him before. The important thing was to just get started.

5

Marcellus Shale is a sedimentary rock formation running under the southern tier of upstate New York, through Pennsylvania, and into Maryland. It is named after its discovery in an outcropping of rock in Marcellus, New York, just northeast of Skaneateles Lake in the Finger Lakes region. It's about a mile below the surface, and until 2005, it was thought to be only a minor source of natural gas held within the fractures between the layers of shale. Drilling in the 1980s was at best uncertain, producing moderately low volumes, and as a result, all but a few efforts were abandoned as financially risky. Only a few wells in northern New York and western Pennsylvania continued to operate this way for the past few years.

However, new horizontal drilling technology allows the wells to be drilled down to five thousand or more feet where the shale layer lies and then angle somewhat horizontally to intersect a multitude of vertical seams in just one pass. Voila! A major change in events! The announcement of a compatible shale structure by two Penn State professors was immediately verified by more than twenty oil and gas drilling companies, and their focus turned to northeast Pennsylvania, where the thickest and therefore richest concentrations of shale containing natural gas ever discovered lies. In particular, Susquehanna and Wyoming counties in Pennsylvania were the first to be approached by gas company land men offering sign up bonuses for five-year leases and a 12–15 percent payout of the gas production revenues for the exclusive use of the property owners' mineral rights. The industry estimates this to be the single largest find of natural gas ever. If technology proves to be able to prevail, the lives and fortunes of these country folk will definitely change forever, and some already have.

    Susquehanna County is a godsend to the gas drilling companies. There are two major gas pipelines already running north-south through the very sparsely populated region. They serve the colder northeast and mid-Atlantic states, which consume the majority of natural gas production for heating and cooking. A spider web of connections from the drill rigs will feed into these nearby lines for a most convenient delivery of gas production. In order to fracture the layers of shale once the borehole is drilled, sand and chemicals mixed with thousands of gallons of water per day are forced down the hole and horizontally to induce more fractures to release the stored gas from between the layers.

    The Susquehanna River runs southward from Otsego Lake in Cooperstown, New York. It begins as a small stream gathering millions of gallons of water per day that drain down from 27,500 square miles of the New York and Pennsylvania mountains and flow into the Chesapeake Bay at Havre de Grace, Maryland, over four hundred twisting and turning miles away. Only a few miles of it flow through Susquehanna County, but more of it curves around to benefit Wyoming County to the south, cutting diagonally through the entire area. Susquehanna is an Iroquoian and Lenape Indian word meaning "curvy river." Although the shale formations are thinner in Wyoming County, that is where the gas companies' initial wells were placed, water resources from the voluminous river flow there being the priority. This established the infrastructure for water transport by tanker truck without which drilling would be impossible. Local water sources are more practical than trucking water to the drill sites, but the approvals and system implementations take much more time, and it was imperative to get established quickly and then fine-tune the infrastructure.

Further, coalescence of economic forces regarding the quickly rising costs of energy since the turn of the century have made the search for new reserves of natural gas plausible, where it may have just been marginal before.

Pennsylvania state mineral rights regulations do exist and have been adequate for the relatively few wells in the state, particularly the western counties around Erie and Pittsburgh. However, the escalated events in the northeast around Susquehanna and Wyoming Counties have been unprecedented, much akin to a gold rush, and the state resources for permits and inspections are straining to just keep pace. In order to be responsive and ensure public safety at the same time, the price of drilling permits has increased from $100 to $2,500 to offset the government costs involved with the service demand requests of the exploration markets. More state government employees have been added along with expanded offices, equipment, vehicles, and field inspections.

It seems like everything is happening at once, and actually, it is. No fewer than twelve major energy exploration companies have set up operations locally. Equipment can be seen rolling in on trailers twenty-four hours a day. Motels and restaurants are filled with new faces. Meetings and presentations for landowners are being held. Bankers and financial firms are contending for the nest eggs being paid to landowners by the gas companies. Environmentalists and newspapers are warning of dire consequences. In a short period of time, about eighteen months, two billion dollars has bent spent by the exploration industry on the Marcellus Shale potential, and there is much more to come.

Right now it is a land grab, frenetic on one hand and a gamble on the other. The typical rural landowner would never think of defacing his land with drilling rigs and roads cut through his pristine forests, not even for a minute. Now, however, after the right amount of dollars is dangled in front of him, values have changed. He will allow trucks, drill rigs, and crews to develop the mineral rights, regardless of what it looks like from his kitchen window. One landowner said, "When I look out the window, I see my children's college education out there, and that's all I care about." It's a greed experiment at its best. Everyone, and you can say without a doubt or exception, everyone has a price.

Once these forces all start to take hold, the face of Susquehanna County, Pennsylvania will never be the same, for better or for worse.

6

"Pete buddy, how're ya doin'," bellowed Chief Jim Mitchell, interrupting the otherwise silent day Pete was having. His cup of tea and view through the hemlocks of the placid lake waters and the tree-filled shoreline mirrored reflection were undisturbed, except by an occasional fish bite on the surface, and now this phone call.

"Okay I guess, until now. What's up?" He stood there in his pajamas with a cup of tea in one hand as he spoke.

"I want to talk to you about something. I have some more information about that thing I discussed the other day," Mitch said hurriedly. "It's kind of urgent."

"You want to come over and catch some fish for tonight's dinner?"

"You know, I think I will. How's ten o'clock?"

"Okay, look for me down at the lake. I'll get the boat and rods ready."

Pete thought, *I've been waiting all year for this. Glad to have Mitch with me for my first trip onto the lake.*

Later, the two floated silently, watching bobbers dip, ready to start reeling in, anxious for the first catch of the season.

"When I was leaving, Helen asked why I call it fishing when I never come home with any fish."

Pete laughed. "Just tell her it's like shopping when she spends all day and never comes back with anything."

"I'll have to remember that." Mitch laughed. "I tell her it's like in the Bible. You know the guy who loafs and fishes. He eventually feeds the whole village."

Pete couldn't help but split a gut laughing. "You mean *loaves* and fishes."

"Whatever. Last time, all I caught was a cold out here. I'll have to do a lot better than that."

Helen had a great trout recipe—herbs rubbed on the flesh and slow grilled in butter on the barbeque. It was what summer was about. They both thought of that and what an incentive it was. Now they had to deliver. "But just in case," she had told Mitch," I'm making sure there is some macaroni and cheese and some ground beef as a backup meal for the evening."

They bobbed along as fishermen do, each with an eye on his line, looking for the slightest irregular movement. Mitch was anxious to discuss his recent research and his low-key discussions with his police buddies in other towns in the area, and he was first to break the silence. "Pete, tell me what you think of this."

"Okay."

"There are about 1,460 suicides in Pennsylvania per year. These are records from two years ago, latest figures they have. That's 11.6 for every 100,000 people."

"I never thought about it before. It sounds like a lot."

"There are 32,000 per year in the whole United States. Eighty percent are males, mostly white, two-thirds over fifty. The reasons are depression and those sorts of things. You know, widowers, sick people, and retirees. People without a life, I guess. Most all of

HYPOTHESIS

them have attempted to take the pipe many times before they pull it off in the final curtain call. A good ten to twenty times more people attempt suicide than actually die from it! That's a lot of hurting people."

"Mitch, you just described me! Is that why you're here? You think you can solve your mystery by following me around?"

"Hey, Pete, don't you go gettin' me nervous now."

"I'm sure there's a world of hurt out there we will never know about. At least I hope not."

"Listen; if you do the math, a little area like Silver Lake shouldn't have hardly any, and the whole county maybe three at the most per year," Mitch calculated. "And it's only early June, and we're batting two right here in one town."

"Averages are just that: averages. Everything will even out over time. Probably you won't have another for a couple of years from now," Pete guessed. "But what are you getting at?"

"Well, it's something Nora Connely said the other day. By the way, did she call you yet?"

"No, why would she?" Pete couldn't imagine a reason.

"I just mentioned you were back at the lake and that it might be nice to say hello. Plus, I was hoping she would dump off onto you her concerns about whether she should sign one of those gas leases for her property or not. You'd be a better help than I would with your business background and such, you know." Mitch also thought that maybe they could be good for one another. Actually, it was Helen who was the budding matchmaker, but he didn't want to be obvious. Pete quickly surmised that and said nothing.

"Anyway, she mentioned that the Morson woman had recently signed a gas lease and gotten a decent chunk of change, a cool $650 K!"

"As in $650,000?" Pete whispered, knowing how voices traveled over water and that people were taking in the beautiful morning along the east shore he was facing.

"Yep, I didn't know the property was that large, but there are two parcels shown on the Platt map, and I never realized it. The back section is 180 acres, almost right up against the pipeline."

"She shoulda had life made! What would make her do it?"

"I don't know, Pete, but that's what I'm thinkin' about. Her and the dentist. Same deal." The two floated silently. A northwest breeze pushed them along slowly, neither man saying a word, just the thing of fishermen on a perfect day. "First real nice day this year. That little storm last night pushed on through and left us a beautiful weekend comin' up."

Mitch's cell phone vibrated. "Damn! I shoulda left that thing in the car. Hello, Chief Mitchell." Mitch listened to the caller. "What! How long is she dead? Call back and tell him I'll be right over. Did you send an ambulance? Get someone there from the state police too." Mitch clicked off the call. "Let's get to shore, Pete. We've got another one."

"What? You don't mean a suicide?" Pete said as he turned toward shore.

"Durn right. Lottie Carpenter lives right over there about two miles. Lived, I should say." Mitch was perplexed. "Wanna come?" He beckoned Pete. "Your take on this stuff is appreciated."

"Yeah, okay. But I've never been to a crime scene before. Bad choice of words; a suicide, I guess. How do you know it's a suicide?"

"The kid who mows her lawn found her in the garage, dead in her car with the motor running. That's all I know. He's waiting for me there right now." Mitch readied for his quick departure as Pete piloted the electric boat to shore about one hundred yards from where they were. Neither spoke as they moved over the water and contemplated the day's rapid change of complexion.

The two-mile drive over to Lottie Carpenter's house was quick. "Damn, what's goin' on around here, Pete? Is it a full moon or what?" Mitch lamented. He could feel his prowess diminishing

HYPOTHESIS

somewhat. His command of Silver Lake Township was something less than what it was just this morning, whatever amount that was to begin with anyway.

Pete said nothing. He was now engaging on this thing that Mitch had already begun. He thought, *Could there be something to this? But let's wait and see.*

The chief's Jeep Cherokee drove up the long driveway to Lottie Carpenter's house, where they were met by Jake O'Neil, the kid who was there to cut the grass. His truck was parked at the garage door. They got out of Mitch's Cherokee and walked over. The ambulance's siren could be heard nearing them from behind as Jake rushed over to meet them. "In there," he yelled, pointing to the garage. The side door was open and so was the overhead car door. The threesome walked purposely together.

"Were the doors open?" Chief Mitchell asked.

"No, I opened them and shut off the engine." Jake's voice quavered, hoping they would agree he did the right thing. Young country men like him are very self-sufficient, decision makers in their own way.

"Everybody wait here!" commanded Chief Mitchell. Exhaust fumes still hung in the air as he entered the garage. His head turned from side to side repeatedly, taking in everything in sight on the interior walls, floor, and ceiling. Nothing out of the ordinary. He peered through the windshield at the lifeless body. He walked around to the driver's door, opened it with the two forefingers of his left hand while his hand was still in his pants pocket, and felt the slumped body at the neck for a pulse. There was none.

The ambulance siren blared as it stopped in front of the garage. "Fellows, check her out. Looks like asphyxiation," the chief advised. The volunteer EMTs quickly agreed, setting down their oxygen tank rig and stepping back.

"What do you want us to do, Chief?" one of them asked.

"Let me think for a minute," the chief responded. "I don't want to move her." Another siren sounded in the distance. The state policeman was on the way.

Corporal Carl Grady arrived in the state police car. He and Chief Jim Mitchell went back a long way. Mitch met him at his car and waited for him to get off the radio and get out. They spoke quietly for a while. Mitch walked Grady over to the garage to view the scene. They continued their discussion at the open driver's door and then returned to the state police vehicle for more conversation.

Pete observed the obvious respect and courtesies being afforded Mitch by Grady. Grady got back in the car and got on his radio while writing continuously. Mitch waved for Pete to come over and join them. Pete was instantly recognized by Grady with a wave. Grady was involved with the Saunders murder two years ago throughout the five months of investigation and particularly regarded Pete as extraordinary. Pete was acknowledged by those close to that case as insightful and clear thinking, an example repeatedly used in local police work since. Much to his dislike, Pete developed a celebrity status, which was definitely not sought out nor acknowledged by him.

"I asked Corporal Grady to get a crime lab team out here," Mitch confided. "I don't want to leave anything to chance on this one. The gloves are off, and I want it thoroughly documented. Don't anyone go near the house either!" he yelled. "Everyone, over here!" Chief Mitchell was definitely in command. On his phone, he loudly instructed the comm center, "I'm going to need coroner Davis out here ASAP. Yes, right now I'm treating it as a crime scene until I decide otherwise. That's right, Davis, and no one else... I don't care. You're gonna have to find him."

Coroner Jim Davis was in his car heading south down Route 81, en route to the Delaware shore with his family when the comm center located him. He had just passed Scranton, sixty miles south of Montrose, when he returned the call to Chief Mitchell. "Chief

Jimmy, if it was anyone else but you, I'd be long gone. Your word that this is important, am I right?"

"Yeah, Jim, you're the one I want on this. Can you do it?"

"Okay, give me about two hours to get there." He turned off the Montage exit just south of Scranton and headed back north. His family understood, disappointed as they were.

Chief Mitchell dismissed the ambulance crew but asked them to have someone stand by for transport when the time came. He and Pete looked at each other. "What were we saying about the law of averages? We now have a year's worth of suicides for the entire county right here in one percent of the county! Durn! Somethin's not right. Not by a long shot." Mitch said with a scowl.

He walked on the grass, looking down at the dirt driveway for a hint of any comings or goings, but it was too late for that. Four vehicles had arrived and one left in the last hour. Everything was obliterated. Footsteps were everywhere in the dirt around the house and garage. *So much for protecting the ... uh, "crime scene,"* he thought. But the garage and house in particular were preserved. He asked Jake to stay until the lab team arrived. They might have some questions.

Odd as it may seem, after the two-man state police crime team arrived, they started with a tour of the house. Just one of them, Sergeant Mann, entered and took photos while the other stood at the front door and took notes from the verbal communications from Mann inside. Nothing out of the ordinary was noted, downstairs or up. Everything was so perfectly in place that they commented whether anyone was actually living there. No dishes or clothes left about. All floors and carpets cleaned, furniture recently dusted. They did examine the refrigerator contents, and it was fairly well stocked, as though a food order was recently purchased.

Pete observed the proceedings. To him it was interesting, even exciting, as sad as the events of the day were. He watched as the team was shown to the garage by Chief Mitchell. Mitch waited outside and made his way over to Pete as the lab team repeated the same procedure, one man inside and the other remaining outside. After a few minutes they were both moving around the vehicle together, observing its interior and in particular, the body of Lottie Carpenter. "It looks like eighteen to twenty hours that the body's been dead. We'll be able to tell more at the lab. When's Doc Davis getting here?" one of them asked.

"Anytime now; won't be but another half hour," Mitch answered. "Anything look outta sorts?"

"Nothing yet," came the voice from the garage. "We did find another vodka bottle in the dining room. So I have to say that ties in to what we're seeing here."

"As in ... what do you mean?" answered the chief.

"As in, if you ask our opinion, we would have to guess depression, drunk, walks out, and starts the car for sleepy time. Pretty much plain and simple."

The two officers continued to take notes, make sketches, and take photos and samples for their plastic evidence bags. They spoke for a few minutes with Jake O'Neil and verified that he made his phone call from the phone in the kitchen of the house; otherwise, he was nowhere else inside. They worked for another half hour without speaking to anyone.

"Here comes your Doc Davis," Sergeant Mann announced as a car arrived.

Doctor Jim Davis was engaging under the circumstance of his interrupted vacation. He did a thorough review of the scene with the crime team and, after taking some photographs, turned to Chief Mitchell. "Mitch, I'll give it my best. I'm having the Endless Mountains Hospital pick her up. I'll look her over thoroughly tonight and give you a call."

"Thanks, Doc. That's all I can ask. Let me have something as soon as you can, will ya?"

HYPOTHESIS

Corporal Grady had already run yellow police tape around the entire house and garage, changing the character of the farmhouse from quaint to morbid in one pass. "Keep us in the loop, will you, Chief? The lab team will copy you on everything. Give them a day or two to file a report. There's not much that meets the eye, but you never know," Grady advised.

The Silver Lake ambulance crew arrived back at the scene and wheeled Lottie Carpenter's body out to the ambulance on a gurney and placed her in a zippered body bag, as instructed by coroner Davis. They left immediately for the hospital, where Davis would begin his examination.

Pete Woodard and Chief Jim Mitchell had quite a day, and in each of their minds, it was not over. They rode back together, both of them with the gnawing feeling that there was more to know than what was seen today. "Pete, I've got to make some calls. I have to try to locate some of Lottie's family and friends."

"How do you do that? She lived all alone, and didn't you say she had no local family?"

"I did, but we have our ways. I'll connect with the local grapevine. It'd put the CIA to shame. Everyone knows everything, or at least something, around here. The way of the country, you know. I'll just start with Helen. She's got a network the CIA would be proud of."

"So that's how you know what's going on."

"It's never failed me yet."

Mitch arrived back at Pete's home, and the two parted company in body only, but not in spirit.

"Thanks, my friend. Back to your fishing. Sorry to take up so much of your day," consoled the chief.

"Mitch, you got my interest. Let me know what transpires in the next day or two. I'll see if I can be of any help."

Mitch knew he had him. Pete was a born problem solver. The gears of his mind would be turning. Pete now had all the same information as he did; only Mitch knew Pete would process it differently.

When Mitch arrived home, Helen had already heard the news. She knew of Lottie's personal situation to some degree, but most important was that Nora Connely would definitely be the one to contact regarding any burial arrangements and such. It was Nora who was her next-door neighbor, albeit by a distance of a quarter mile, their farm properties sharing a common border. Although Lottie did keep to herself, Nora was her closest friend. However, they usually only met at the monthly Silver Lake Ladies Club meeting, and the extent of their socializing would be that they would try to be on the same committee when something special had to get done. Otherwise, Lottie was humble and unobtrusive, but in a friendly, neighborly way. She did go out of her way to not attract attention as a widow living alone on a large farm property, where it could be expected that things needed to be taken care of from time to time. When matters arose, she was always able to rely on local handymen for repairs and services. Otherwise, she had been self-sufficient and more than able to care for herself these past few years.

When Mitch called Nora, there was no answer, and he left a message. Later that evening, Nora returned the call and informed Mitch that she had been down to Montrose with some other neighbors, making the burial arrangements. He thought, *It is like a revolving door around here this year, one sad event after another. When will things settle down?*

7

Pete Woodard was hooked. His innate makeup welcomed questions and problems without obvious answers. His DNA had a gene that needed this challenge. He would think of nothing else.

He was a very organized thinker. *What is known so far?* he thought. *I'll make a chart, a spreadsheet of everything. It will be a concrete model of events, sort of like sitting on a cloud and seeing everything that happened down below and maybe some obvious, or not so obvious, relationships.*

He dragged out his copies of Mitch's reports and research into one stack of papers and started logging facts. There were no ties one to the other, no similarities, no social connections as far as he could tell. He poured through all the facts back and forth and came to the conclusion that if there was something to this thing, it was yet to be discovered.

His working method was derived from his past business career, where it seemed arcane to others who first encountered it as they worked with him. But after the ease of use and clarity of most situations emerged from the format, its appreciation was quickly realized by them. Simply, he stretched an eight-foot length of wrapping paper over the surface of the dining room table and began making headings as things came to him. They were in no certain order or priority, just parking lots for any thought that needed a category. It evoked a creative freedom, an orderly thought process when there was no order, and most important, a way to simply get started thinking things through. He had done it many times before, and it never failed him, ever. Something good or creative always came of it as a result.

He made a few notes, but nothing was coming together. This time he had a problem getting farther along. *At least it is a start,* he thought, *and that is something.* He decided that another creative problem-solving technique was needed; that is, put it all aside and give it a fresh look tomorrow. *This wasn't the most original idea, but sometimes it works,* he thought.

Mitch and Helen were coming by anyway to attend the afternoon funeral service of Jane Morson. Pete wanted to attend also, and thought it would be best to accompany Mitch and Helen in accordance with their invitation. When they arrived, Helen looked her usual pleasingly plump-but-beautiful self, and Mitch looked very uncomfortable stuffed into his suit, which had to be at least one, maybe two sizes too small.

As the three of them drove to Saint Augustine's Church just two miles north, all thoughts were of Lottie Carpenter. "Her family was nonexistent, and local friends and neighbors are helping to handle the final affairs," Mitch mentioned. "It looks like yet another funeral." He sighed. "What a start to the summer."

The small group sat quietly while Monsignor Frank Quinn conducted the Catholic mass in Jane Morson's memory. No mention of the horror of her passing was made during the service or by the small group in attendance. One member of the audience stood out, but he was unknown to Pete, quickly squinting his eyes and tilting his head toward the stranger in a questioning manner to Mitch.

Mitch whispered, "State Senator Bob Wellman. I think she helped him with a fundraiser a while back."

Senator Wellman sat with a woman and another man; presumably the woman was his wife. The group emerged from the church and walked across the road to the cemetery burial plot for the finality of it all. After a brief outdoor ceremony, Senator Wellman and his group offered their respects to the only two apparent family members present, a young lady and an elderly man who seemed bewildered by the activities. She was accompanying him as a caregiver of some sort, who tended to his needs in standing and walking with assistance. The senator smiled graciously as he passed by the dozen people in attendance and left quietly.

"Senator Wellman is pretty popular around here, Pete. He's been a good help to our region over the years. He certainly knows about the voting potential among rural folk, and he sure has been making his presence known lately. You know, the money's coming here now with all this gas well drilling, and I'll bet he's not going to be shy about asking for funds for his reelection campaign. His picture's been in the paper regularly the past few years. I don't even remember who his predecessor was. No one was ever interested in us before up here in this corner of the state."

"That's typical. You said the Morson woman held a fundraiser for him?"

"Yeah, I would say late last year. Didn't even know she was politically active. Maybe she was just trying to help in her own way. It didn't seem to be that big of a deal at the time, as I remember. There was a notice in the 'Grapevine' village newsletter, and I think a few people got written invitations. I know we did," Mitch remembered.

"Did you attend?"

"No. We're not into that sort of thing. Even as police chief, I sort of avoid getting involved."

"Will you stop for lunch, Pete?" Helen asked.

"Thanks, Helen, but I think I'll just head over to the house, if you don't mind. I'm working on something, and I want to get back to it." His thoughts were on his empty worksheet.

When he arrived back home, almost without hesitation, he sat in front of his notes and started writing. His work carried into the early evening, leaving him with very little to show for his efforts. He rocked back onto the two rear legs of his chair with his hands clasped together behind his head and reviewed the paltry entries, summarizing everything he knew or could assume about the three local deaths. He included the murder-suicide family and the graphic artist, both from Tunkhannock, basically a thirty-five mile radius, demographically speaking.

HYPOTHESIS

Date	Name	Age-Sex	Occupation	Death	Particulars	Interval
Apr 11	Schultz, Karl	45-M	Unemployed	Suicide	Murder/suicide Wife, 2 children Tunkhannock Hand gun Thurs. night	Start (34days)

Date	Name	Age-Sex	Occupation	Death	Particulars	Interval
May 2	Danields, Bill	45-M	Dentist	Suicide or accident	Ether, alcohol Lived alone Few relatives Silver Lake Fri. night	21 days

Date	Name	Age-Sex	Occupation	Death	Particulars	Interval
May 15	Edwards, Joe	36-M	Art,design	Accident	Fall Lived alone, Few relatives Tunkhannock Fri. night	13 days

Date	Name	Age-Sex	Occupation	Death	Particulars	Interval
May 23	Morson, Jane	46-F	Computers	Suicide	Shotgun Lived alone Few relatives Silver Lake Fri. night	8 days

Date	Name	Age-Sex	Occupation	Death	Particulars	Interval
May 28	Carpenter, Lottie	58-F	Retired	Suicide	Asphyxiation Lived alone Few relatives Silver Lake Nicely dressed House cleaned Refrig. full Wed. night	5 days

It was better than nothing, but he wasn't proud of it. What could be summarized from such an organized presentation of the facts, he didn't know. He stared and thought for the better part of an hour. A call to Mitch was in order.

"Mitch, I have a thought about the Carpenter woman. Did you hear from Doc Davis yet?"

"No, I hope he has something soon. Maybe I should call. I'm gonna call," the chief said anxiously.

"I think you should. And I'd like you to ask him to take a look at the bottom of her shoes. And if you have to, get the crime lab guys over there and have them call you."

"Sure, Pete. What do you have in mind?" Mitch answered. He felt Pete was being bit mysterious.

"I don't know. I just have something to either rule in or rule out. See what they say. I'll be right here. Let me know, will you?"

"Will do. Let me get on him."

The Endless Mountain Hospital doubled as a quasi-crime lab when autopsies like this were performed. Doctor Jim Davis was just finishing his work, his coroner's report electronically documented by tape recorder, as he went about his examination of Lottie Carpenter. Blood samples and her clothing were being sent by courier to the State Police Crime Lab in Harrisburg. Results could be expected by late Monday, maybe sooner.

Chief Mitchell discussed the exam with Doc Davis. "There was nothing other than the obvious. She did have a lump under her left breast and a scar from a previous lumpectomy next to it. This should have been operable, nothing to cause the mental distress of a suicide level. But unless it is your own body, it is difficult to judge," Doc Davis reported.

"Doc, I need you to do one thing while you're still there. Are the crime lab guys still with you?"

"Sure. They're going over all the clothing items and packaging them. They're waiting for a courier to take them to the lab. They're still here. Hold on. I'll put you on with Sergeant Mann."

HYPOTHESIS

"This is Mann," sounded the voice.

"Sergeant, Jim Mitchell. Look; do me a favor and take a look at her shoes, will ya, and tell me what you think."

"Sure, hold on." The opening of the plastic evidence bag could be heard, followed by some discussion by the two men on the other end. "Chief, just what are you looking for? They seem okay. No stains, marks, anything like that."

"Are you sure? How about the bottoms?"

"We're sending everything out for a closer exam on the scope, but right now there's nothing unusual. They're clean."

"Okay, thanks, Sergeant. Let's stay in touch."

Chief Mitchell called Pete Woodard and filled him in on the discussions. As anxious as the two were to receive the reports, they just had to wait now. Pete informed Mitch about his notes. Mitch was interested to see them and said he was coming right over.

Pete heated up some Italian tomato soup he had just made and prepared two bowls and some homemade bread for their meeting. Mitch's Jeep Cherokee could be heard on the driveway as he was laying out the dishes.

When Mitch arrived, the two of them sat with their bowls of soup and plate of bread in front of the large paper worksheet with Pete's summary on it. "Not much, but it's a start," Mitch offered.

"This thing with Lottie Carpenter, I don't know. It's not adding up at all." Pete iterated his build-up of facts. "She fills her refrigerator with fresh groceries, dusts and vacuums the house, dresses up in a nice outfit, and then proceeds to drink a large quantity of vodka and breathe in some car exhaust. What's up with that?"

"I have the same thoughts. What person would get all dressed up for her planned demise? On the other hand, I have actually read that it is a common occurrence."

"I happen to know you are right. It's almost ceremonial with suicide victims. They prepare for the event. I guess in such a state of mind that is the most important thing that was going to happen to them in quite a while."

"Well, I do know that she wasn't a customer of the liquor store in Montrose, at least. I ran down there this afternoon with her picture, and the two employees who are usually there don't remember her as a customer," Mitch added. "That's the only place in town to buy vodka. It's a small town, and they would remember."

"Yeah, but most people up here in the north end of the county run over to New York state to shop, and there are plenty of places to buy liquor there—supermarkets, private wine and spirits stores, you name it. It's only a ten-mile drive, same as a trip down to Montrose."

"You're right, but all her leftover grocery bags have Montrose store names on them. She was a local shopper, it seems. So, why would she drive over to New York just for vodka when she can get it right next to the supermarket? Anyway, let's wait 'til Monday. I'll have everything back from the crime lab guys. We'll go over it together. See you then. Get some rest."

"I might have some other info by then too. Something I'm working on. You're right, though. The vodka thing doesn't add up."

"Okay. See you then."

8

Joe Pratt's successful independent investment broker headquarters offices in Wilkes Barre, Luzerne County were a distance of fifty miles from the center of the northeastern Pennsylvania Marcellus Shale natural gas phenomenon in Susquehanna County. The majority of his investors lived in Luzerne County, and his customer base in the northern counties of Wyoming and Susquehanna consisted of a few individuals developed from referrals over the years. His approach was classic: genial, understanding, helpful, and at times, consoling. The latter was often the case in dealing with the proceeds of wills and estates among family members, actually an effective way to expand the network of clients once his personal rapport took hold.

The residents of these northern counties were always of interest to all the investment advisors in the region, in particular since the initial wave of Procter and Gamble retirees began rolling over their investments and retirement proceeds upon leaving the workforce there. P and G's largest facility had been built forty years ago just outside Tunkhannock, and continues to expand. Hundreds of employees with twenty-five to forty years service have accumulated million-dollar portfolios in company stock and retirement programs. The challenge to investment advisors such as Joe Pratt was to convince people to leave the nest egg in an investment plan and only live off the investment returns, along with any social security and pension payments for which they were eligible. This was a concept not many had given thought to, and it was a rude awakening for them. Otherwise, a dwindling base of savings would spell problems in a client's later years if they withdrew too much of their stock values.

The Marcellus Shale gas well leasing and drilling contracts promised to far overshadow any economic impact the bi-county region had ever seen for a long while to come. Pratt's entire focus was on this potential every minute of the day. Nothing was more important. His existing accounts in Luzerne and Lackawanna counties to the south offered nominal growth and few new opportunities. By contrast, a new millionaire was being created every day in and around Tunkhannock and Montrose in Wyoming and Susquehanna counties, respectively, at least until the most valuable land locations were being put under lease contracts by the gas well drilling companies. His investment products were very different from others, and he knew he offered a distinct advantage, an advantage so much better it was hard to refuse.

"Joey, my friend, how's life in the gas lane?" Senator Bob Wellman's unmistakable voice came through the phone.

"Senator, how's my favorite government official? Still trying to change all those Democrats down there in Harrisburg?" Pratt joked. Harrisburg was the state capital, located in the southeast part of the state about 120 miles south of Pratt's office.

"I can only do the impossible, and that doesn't even cut it." He sounded serious this time. "Listen; I've got another political fundraiser to do, and I think you ought to be there."

"Sounds okay to me. Same deal as always?" Pratt reminded. He'd done this with the senator before.

"Yes, it's just outside Montrose, a fellow by the name of Sam Burns, a politico type. Wants to run for state representative next time, and I'm sure he's looking for some support on my end. He's a teacher in the local high school system. Anyway, Sue will send you all the particulars from my office. It's next Wednesday. That okay with you?"

"Oh yeah, it's a priority, in fact, as you know," Pratt replied. "When you're up, we have to discuss your investments as well. Can you spare some time?"

"You know I can. Is there anything I can answer while we're on the phone?"

"No, it can wait 'til we have some quiet time."

"Thanks. See you then. By the way, I was sorry to hear about Lottie Carpenter. She had done some nice things for us."

"You're quite right. I was so sorry to hear about it. What a shame. She will be missed. I'll see you next Wednesday." Senator Wellman hung up the phone and busied himself with some research notes for his next phone call.

Joe Pratt swung back into his chair, reflecting on the surreal conversation he had just had. Senator Bob Wellman and he had been boyhood friends since the age of five. They lived two houses away from one another in Scranton. They attended the same schools right through college. Wellman was a high school athletic standout—baseball and football—while Pratt cheered from the sidelines. Wellman was senior class president at the University of Scranton, while Pratt had all he could do to maintain his grades without extracurricular involvement. They were on different career paths—Wellman, political science, and Pratt, economics—but remained best of friends, frequently sharing student life and occasions together.

Wellman enlisted in the military, where he was able to complete law school. He was away for seven years and came back as a Marine captain, degree in hand and with every aspiration to enter the world of politics. He met his wife, Kathy, and settled in Tunkhannock after a law clerk stint with Judge Wilton Horvath at the Wyoming County courthouse. Afterward, he operated his private law practice for five years before being elected Twentieth District state senator fourteen years ago. His reelection repeated every term since by a wide majority, and he now commanded the chair of the locally popular Agriculture and Rural Affairs Committee and he sat on the Appropriations Committee as vice chairman.

It was unquestionably attributed to him that the new bypass highway around Tunkhannock was his doing and his alone. This relieved the single main street small rural county seat of five hundred tractor-trailer trucks and three thousand other vehicles per day, returning the charming Victorian village to its former quaintness. He was the darling of his district—young, good looking, well respected, the promise of the future for his otherwise-forgotten hometown corner of the sate.

Joe Pratt began his career as an accountant and worked for various firms in the Scranton-Wilkes Barre area. He acquired his CPA (certified public accountant) and his CFP (certified financial planner) registrations and veered into the investment planning business when his accounting clients demonstrated a severe lack of personal financial abilities. Some of them took more time to plan their annual vacation, as the saying goes, than their entire life's finances. He was a rapid success, representing four major investment firms and two private investment consortiums with proven reserves and performances. Life was good.

Joe Pratt fell under the hypnotic influence of Senator Bob Wellman's aura. The senator knew the few influential, wealthy people in his district, and he played the game well. But it was all above-board and beyond reproach. The senator knew all too well that perception was the reality, especially in a small rural district like his. Joe Pratt, on the other hand, could benefit from his association, and he did. At every occasion, the senator would make the most important introductions and frame them with very pointed suggestions that people should benefit from a relationship with Joe Pratt, like he did. Joe was a financial genius, according to the senator. "He's not tied to just one financial dictum. Instead, he's free to orchestrate the best investment plan among all his principal investment firms. And he does a hell of a job!" the Senator would crow. Joe was good at what he did, but the senator did put him on a high pedestal, and he had to ratchet down any expectations when he first met a new client referral. It worked well, Bob's praises and Joe's humble reception.

Then one day, six months ago, their relationship intensified. During dinner with Senator Wellman and his chief of staff, Fred Campbell, Joe Pratt was informed that it was time to pay back. The potential fortunes of the three were immense, as described in the plan by Campbell. As the details were disclosed, Pratt sat in amazement at the precision of the plan. It was flawless, and it was highly rewarding. It just needed everyone to buy in and synchronize their desires with their actions in a concentration of effort within a tight window of opportunity. That window was the signing of gas well leases by the right people at the right time; in other words, there were certain parcels of land that were strategically important to a certain well drilling company. They were large acreages with commensurate gas production potential. It was essential to have them under the control of certain gas drilling interests while the other companies busied themselves signing up a few acres here and there as the skeptical landowners stepped up one by one when their anxiety boiled over and they couldn't take the self-imposed pressure of delaying anymore.

An assured method to motivate these mostly timid landowners to sign a contract was what the group of three could offer. Pratt could infer that other forces were at work here too. There must have been a very cooperative gas drilling company. The debriefing didn't divulge any other participants, but for something this big, there had to be. His part was simple. Once a contract was proposed, he would present his investment proposal as referred by Senator Wellman, and the game would be over. Anyone would see that the longer they waited, the more they would risk missing out on the limited international investment portfolio that was endorsed by the senator and other local investors who had already gotten involved.

It was a one-two punch. It sounded really slick. A property owner would be identified by the geologists at a certain gas well drilling company, and Campbell would soon approach the landowner to offer the "honor" of hosting the senator's next political discussion forum for their neighborhood. It was an offer no one could refuse. "Senator Wellman? Here, at my home? I'd be honored. When do you want to do it?" would essentially be the reply.

Within four weeks, a garden party or a tea soiree of the locals on a Sunday afternoon would occur. People were ecstatic at becoming involved. Most never considered any form of political activism. They hardly remembered to vote when it came time. But the format of the request and the assistance of Fred Campbell's office, with invitations, phone calls, even the hors d'oeuvres, was too good to pass up—all the host had to do was supply a list of neighbors' names along with a location for the event and the rest would be taken care of. This, of course, was a setup.

The host would be so impressed with the notoriety and sense of importance that they had been welcomed into this political world of the upper echelon that they were unknowingly nonresistant to any suggestions or indications of purpose made by these seemingly powerful people. Those suggestions were the only focus of Wellman's group. During such an event, Senator Wellman would use his cachet expertly, just enough to impress and not too much to separate himself from the hoi polloi. His rural agenda was always popular: schools, roads, farm tax credits, and now, of course, mineral rights provisions for dealing with the gas well drilling companies, which really hit close to home, all for fifty dollars a plate and a picture with the senator taken by Fred Campbell. Who could not feel they had a good day?

Joe Pratt's introduction was inconspicuously made to the host, and Joe made a point to spend adequate time sharing information as need be for someone considering a gas well lease, should it ever be offered. Of course, Pratt would follow up in a week or so, explaining various investments, and if it seemed that the host was confident in investing, almost immediately a landsman was at the door with a five-year drilling lease and sign-up bonus agreement. It was set up to be fail proof. Pratt wondered about the gap between when people signed up and got their check and when he would hear from them to arrange an investment contract with him. However, it had worked every time so far. There was the dentist, Bill Danields, and then the Jane Morson woman down the road from Silver Lake, and also Lottie Carpenter and a few others. He would sign up a few others who were interested in his portfolio. It was beautiful!

There was a problem, though. The investment packages were not endorsed by the Securities Exchange Commission or the Pennsylvania Insurance Commission. They were bona fide investments; however, they were all international, and none of them was registered with the Securities Exchange Commission or with any United States insurance company. Instead, they were financial annuities with almost instant returns in the form of small monthly payments and further annual stepped-up valuations. The investments from any lease arrangement were to be wired to a Car $_3$ investment fund in the Caribbean, representing the three Caribbean island entities of the Bahamas, Puerto Rico, and the Dominican Republic. These locations were touted as "Third world countries with first world emerging products." Pratt would be the US interface with any clients and would receive a fee and commissions for handling the client interface, reports, and distributions.

His concerns were few. The fund was very profitable, and Wellman was already involved in it as an investor. He would have the clients driven to him without much investment of time and energy, and the conversion ratio was 100 percent. His liability was nil and the rewards great. It was finally his turn to benefit in a big way from what little investment activities the region had previously been able to offer.

9

Chief Jim Mitchell received a copy of the Lottie Carpenter suicide report by fax from the state police Gibson station around 4:00 pm Monday. After scanning it, he called Pete Woodard and invited himself over to share the findings.

When he arrived, they both paged through it quickly, as though hoping to find some extraordinary revelation.

"It doesn't look out of the ordinary. It's just as we thought, some booze and then asphyxiation. Death occurred between 6:00 and 8:00 p.m. Friday," murmured the chief as he fanned through the sheets of the file. "There's a sketch of the garage layout, some comments about the weather, the rain that is, and no signs of struggle or anything like that. Only her prints and the kid's were on the car door and the car key and also on the phone inside."

"What about the shoes?" Pete asked anxiously.

"Yeah, it says here they were clean, the bottoms that is, except for a green fiber that matches the living room carpet. There was no dirt of any kind. I guess this helps to fix the time she went out to the garage since the rain storm early that night would have caused some mud indications on the shoes, especially the soles."

"Mitch, that's just it. Because I think if they are clean, she may not have walked out to the garage."

"Well, how did she get there?"

"She could have been carried," Pete cautioned.

"What! Do you know what you're saying?"

"I do. This information is what I've been waiting for all along. Those shoes in my mind were absolutely clean. I should have said something when they loaded her into the body bag."

Mitch was on the phone in a flash, calling the state police center in Gibson as he gasped, "Sergeant Mann, please. This is Jim Mitchell... I'll wait." After a short delay, Mann was on the line.

"Mitch, you got the report by now, I hope," Sergeant Mann answered.

"Yeah, Sarge, thanks. Listen; I need you to verify something. The question about the bottoms of the shoes, just how clean were they?"

"Clean. I mean very clean. There was that green fiber, but that was it. No mud, no dirt, nothing. Why, what's up?" Mann asked.

"Keep it to yourself, Sarge. We're working on a few things up here, and this is just a piece of it. Thanks, I'll get back to you. Hey, can you have those clothes and shoes sent back to your office for another look when we get a chance? Thanks." Mitch stared knowingly at Pete. "Pete, you're on to something. What made you think of that? Mann said the bottoms were clean."

"The ambulance crew, when they laid her on the gurney to put her in the body bag. I didn't think anything of it then, but the soles of her shoes weren't dirty. They were black and would have shown at least some dust from the driveway if she went out there before, say five or six o'clock. After six thirty or so that rain came through and lasted 'til about eight o'clock. Her shoes would have definitely been muddy for sure if she walked to the garage then. Either way, I looked in the car at the floor mat just before Grady closed the door, and it was perfectly clean too. I don't know, maybe it's nothing. Something to think about anyway."

"Well, I have some additions for your spreadsheet," Mitch announced."Let's go over a few things and do an update on it."

Mitch supplied a couple of miscellaneous facts, none of which were earth-shattering. Of the five names on Pete's list, three of them had gas leases: Danields, Morson, and now Lottie Carpenter. Both Danields and Morson had been deriving income from their investment from the lease agreements, but no drilling had yet been planned. So there was no income from the gas extraction yet. Helen and her grapevine were on the top of their game. Lottie Carpenter's proceeds had probably been invested, but it was not known for sure.

"Mitch, I know you want to keep all this quiet, but do you think we can get a look at the bank records of all five victims? Follow the money, you know?"

"Whew! Now you're asking a lot." Mitch said as he pondered the idea. "How could I pull that off? We'd need a court order. And I'd probably have to get the DA involved to do that. That'll blow the lid off all our below-the-radar approach so far."

"Is there any way to keep this quiet?"

"Let me try. I'll give Larry Larson a call and go down and see him in person. He's a good guy. He encouraged me to run for county sheriff three years ago, but that wasn't for me. I didn't retire to get involved in things like that. But I did consider it an honor to be asked by someone like him. He's well regarded by the law enforcement and the local attorneys. Let me see what I can do."

"We're going to need to get the same information on the two people in Wyoming County too," reminded Pete.

"Yeah, he should be able to coordinate that."

District Attorney Lawrence Larson was the pride of his hometown area of Silver Lake. As a young attorney, he returned to the rural town and set up his own practice in Montrose, subletting part of his office to Forbes International, an investment company owned by Joe Pratt. Pratt's phone inquiries would forward to his Wilkes Barre office, and appointments would be set up on site in Montrose on most Fridays, or anytime if need be. Larson's legal practice lent an air of sophistication to Pratt's operation, although they each enjoyed the halo effect of the perception the other's business brought to the one location in this small town.

Larry Larson had quite a bit of promise, and everyone thought so. Depending on his personal aspirations, he being a loving family man with a wife and two young sons, it was the opinion of most people that a federal Senate seat in Washington, D.C., was destined for him. He did present such an air. He was confident, brilliant, hardworking, and most of all, trustworthy. The meager county salary certainly was not enough to fully support his family, and he was not yet successful at convincing the county officials to upgrade the DA position from part-time to full-time. The work of the district attorney was, however, full-time; that is, if a conscientious effort were to be made. He also carried an increasing number of private clients, and a decision had to be made soon as to which master he would serve. He was finding both careers more difficult to pace, this year in particular.

Chief Jim Mitchell's visit was interesting to say the least. Court orders to view the financial records of the recently deceased suicide and accident victims should be easy to obtain in both counties. Larry Larson would walk right across the street to see Judge John Larson, his uncle and president judge for Susquehanna County. To address the two Wyoming County victims, a simple call to Judge Horvath, for whom he law clerked, was another easy matter. It was done that afternoon, and he personally started to arrange Chief Mitchell's visits to each of the three local banks.

The challenge now was to not raise any suspicions among bank personnel regarding the actual reason for the expanding investigation. Larson set things up by making a call to each bank to find out where some of the names might be registered as customers. He blanketed the actual names among a list of other fictitious names under the guise of an identity theft investigation. In each case he dealt with the bank manager, usually at a vice president level, and in all cases, someone he knew and who was pleased to assist. Identity theft was a serious concern, and bankers were quick to help in these matters.

Northeast Penn National Bank was managed locally by vice president Will Dobson, an acquaintance of both Larry Larson and Jim Mitchell. Mitch had been told that three of the names on his list had accounts at Dobson's bank. When Mitch visited the bank with assistant district attorney Marsha Witman the next day, he was granted a private office and three sets of records. Dobson closed the door upon leaving them alone to examine the documents. The accounts were different, as one might expect, but the large transaction histories were easy to spot. In each case there were amounts exceeding five hundred thousand dollars, which were deposited in the last six months; and again, in each case, the checks were written by Gasco, one of the prominent gas well drilling companies who had been working the Marcellus Shale exploration for two years now. Gasco International Exploration, Inc. also had local operating accounts with Northeast Penn Bank and one of the other banks with branch offices in areas not covered by Northeast Penn's branches.

It was interesting to see the financial tale of the newfound wealth, but it was almost as one would expect from conservative rural types who had little monetary desires and who valued small-town living above all else. Among the normal household expenses,

Doctor William Danields had little outstanding debt. He paid off a car loan and took a vacation both within a month of his windfall. An amount of $370,000 was sent to an investment company, FII, Inc. Jane Morson retired a small mortgage balance and some credit card debt, all amounting to less than $22,000 and then issued a $510,000 check to Forbes, Inc. Lottie Carpenter was the most surprising. She wrote only one check, and that was to Forbes International Investments, c/o Joseph Pratt, for an amount of $575,000. Chief Mitchell just stared at the three sheets of reports, each in a slightly different timeframe but with such similarities.

Larson was able to track down the bank of deceased murder-suicide victim Karl Schultz to Keystone Bank and Trust in Tunkhannock. Chief Mitchell drove down there with Marsha Witman and repeated the process. But even though Schultz was a gas lease contract holder, there was no evidence of his increased income due to such an arrangement. The graphic designer Joe Edwards, who had fallen from the Dietrich Theater's roof, had a meager savings account, a personal checking account, and a business checking account, all with the same Keystone Bank. No one person's accounts showed any unusual activity, but Mitch thought that at least Schultz's accounts should. Mitch called over to the DA's office asking for Larry Larson. "Larry, Mitch. I need to ask one more favor."

"What is it, Mitch? Anything you need," came the reply.

"I'm going to need to look at the bank records for Forbes International Investments."

There was silence on the other end. "Mitch, now you're getting into some heavy stuff. Dead people's records are one thing, and I was even warned about that from both judges. But there are privacy laws in this country, and unless someone is under intense criminal investigation with evidence to that effect, it's going to be next to impossible." They both sat silently, knowing that the first one to speak owned the situation and had to deal with it. DA Larson pretty much did all he wanted to, but not all he could. Silver Lake Police Chief Jim Mitchell had done all he could, but not all he wanted to. The silence continued.

Another stream of thought brought Chief Mitchell back to the task at hand. "Okay. Hey, Larry, I'll get back to you. But listen; I really appreciate all you've done."

"Mitch, if you come up with anything even close to suspicious that we can confirm on my end, I'll be glad to take it from here."

10

"Pete, I've got some more information for your spreadsheet," Mitch announced over the phone through the sound of rustling papers on his desk.

"Okay, go ahead." Pete walked over to the dining room table, where the spreadsheet was laid out.

"All three of the Silver Lake people had bank accounts at Northeast Penn Bank, and all three had gas well drilling leases with Gasco International Exploration. But the best is that all three had invested the money, or most of it, with a company called Forbes International Investments. Kind of coincidental, isn't it?"

"There are no coincidences." Pete was soberly attentive, scribbling notes as he spoke. "What else do we have? What about Schultz and Edwards?"

"Yeah, they both had small bank accounts at Keystone Bank in Tunkhannock. Nothing unusual there, except Shultz never deposited any of his gas lease income. I don't know how much it was, but I estimate it at about four hundred thousand dollars, with the size of his farm land and all."

"If anything, the graphic designer guy, Edwards, stands out in that he has nothing in common with the rest of these people," commented Pete.

"See, there you go again. Thinkin' outside the box. I would have never looked at it that way."

"Can we find out any more about him?"

"Let me try, Pete. I'll make a couple of calls."

"How was Larson about all of this?"

"You mean what did he think?"

"Anything. I mean, what did he have to say about your cluster theory of all these deaths in Silver Lake?"

"Well, he was very interested, but I think he was just trying to appease me. In fact, I know I used up all of my political favors and more."

"Did he want to get involved?"

"He helped to the degree he could at this point, I guess. Then he said he would look into it more when I have more to go by."

"Okay, let me fill you in on some scuttlebutt [What is this?] that I came up with."

"Go ahead."

"The dentist, Danields, and the Morson woman both had one of those political parties this past year. Right?"

"Yeah."

"Guess who else attended?" Pete paused for effect. "Lottie Carpenter!"

"How'd ya find that out?"

"My crack Silver Lake CIA agent: your wife, Helen."

"Whaddyaknow! I told you."

"I called you this morning, and she told me you would be out for a few hours. So she checked a few things for me, like who was at these get-togethers. The Lottie Carpenter name stuck out for many reasons; she didn't really socialize. You know, only the Silver Lake Ladies' Club once a month, and that was it as far as anyone knew. Right?"

"Right."

"And she didn't have a fundraiser herself, but at least she was at one."

"Yeah, but how does that connect to anything?" Mitch wondered.

"I don't have the foggiest, but it's just one more piece, you know? One more thing: it seems Nora Connely called Helen to invite both of you to a political meeting with Senator Bob Wellman at a fellow teacher's home in Montrose in a few days."

"Geez, you know more what's going on in my own house than I do."

Pete kept his somber tone. "Mitch, I know you don't like these things but I want us to go—you, Helen, and me."

"Now you're askin' a lot."

"I know, but I think we need to do it. We might learn something."

"Okay, if you say so. I'll have Helen set it up. Just for the record, what is this supposed to prove?"

"Can't tell yet. Maybe nothing. Let's just chalk it up to the process of elimination."

"I'll let you know the schedule."

"Okay, and hey, I received an invite from Nora Connely for dinner this Monday. I'm sure Helen had nothing to do with it."

"What do you think?"

"I'm not stupid. And there is the first rule."

"I know. I know. There are no coincidences. But she really does seem to need some help in deciding what to do with the land lease offers she's been getting."

"That's what she said. Anyway, it'll give me a firsthand opportunity to see what these gas deals are all about. Maybe we'll learn something there too."

"Plus, she's a really nice lady. I'm sure you'll enjoy it, and I'm sure she'll appreciate any assistance you will give to her situation."

"We shall see."

11

"Joe, it's Senator Wellman's office; a Mr. Campbell," Joe Pratt's secretary announced over his speaker phone.

"Fred, how are you doin'? Are you keeping the taxpayers happy?"

"We're trying, but that's like swimming upstream. Hey, we need to get together to plan a few things. Bob's going to be having a few more dog-and-pony shows, and I want to keep you up-to-date."

They both felt that wasn't the real reason for the meeting, or at least Joe Pratt thought he did.

"Let's do it tonight. Okay with you?" suggested Campbell strongly.

"Sure. Where and when?"

"Bob's home, seven o'clock."

Pratt's drive to the senator's home in Tunkhannock seemed disconnected from all the past dealings the two had together. The tone of Fred Campbell's brief conversation was foreboding. He didn't know what to make of it, but something was different.

The Victorian-home-lined streets were always a joy to view upon entering the small town. Throwbacks, they were, to much simpler times when lumbering, farming, and quarrying drove the economy. *Now the land will give birth to even more prosperous harvests from beneath,* he thought. *And this time, I'm going to be right in the path of the proceeds.*

He arrived at the large white early nineteenth-century-era home, one of the grandest on the street. It was built by a tannery owner by the name of Jean Falset, an immigrant from France whose family came into the area as part of an advance party to prepare a safe retreat for Marie Antoinette's escape from France in advance of the French Revolution. She never made it out of the country, as history tells of the populace revolt and her beheading. Bob Wellman was proud of the home and its history, and assuredly of his position in the community and what his goals were for the future.

Pratt arrived at the stately home and rang the doorbell. Senator Wellman welcomed Pratt and escorted him into his study. Already seated there were Fred Campbell and another man, introduced as Ron Potter. No affiliation was attributed to Potter, and Pratt didn't ask. Fred Campbell led the conversation.

"Joe, thanks for coming. We're here to discuss future plans involving the gas leases."

"I would have assumed that in any case," Pratt responded. He could sense an unusual demeanor in the air among the group.

Campbell continued. "Gentlemen, it's about Ed Wilkinson. His time has come. We'd like you to handle it, Joe."

"Me? I don't want to make a habit of doing that kind of stuff!" Pratt whispered, looking around as if to find witnesses to what was being discussed.

"It's this way, Joe. You took care of the Carpenter woman nicely, the way we said, and everyone appreciates that. We have one or two loose ends still, and this is one we need your help with," Campbell insisted. Pratt said nothing.

The room closed in on Pratt. He felt alone, anxious, concerned beyond his wits. *What have I gotten into?* he thought.

"Think of it this way. If he were coming after you, you would defend yourself, right? Well, he will be coming after you sooner or later, or at least he will be causing someone else to do so. It's just a matter of now or then." Campbell's logic failed, but Pratt knew he was in deep and certain details had to be cleaned up. This was one of them.

"Why me? Why not handle it like some of the others?" Pratt pleaded.

"You have the access, a reason to get close to him. This one's going to look like an accident. His home is in Bridgewater, outside of Montrose, and that's a relatively busy place. Lots of neighbors, traffic, things like that all times of day. His potential gas lease property is a few miles outside Silver Lake, as you know. Mr. Potter here has set up a meeting at the property on Friday, day after tomorrow. The pretense is that he is from a gas well drilling company doing subcontract work for Gasco and that he needs to get the final approval for the location of the rig and to discuss some other matters."

"So how am I supposed to fit in?"

"You are there to look out for his interests on the investment side of things. Mr. Potter will inform him that if he was expecting to consider investing in the Car 3 Fund, his payment could be made in a way to save him most, or possibly all, of his tax liability by separate wire transfers direct to the offshore account. You are there to confirm that and complete all the paperwork, and we want you to get that done right on the spot. In fact, have all the forms prepared before you arrive. That way, all we need is a signature. In a way it doesn't matter what you tell him. He is never coming back from that quarry. We just want you to get him off guard and push him off the edge."

"Well, if Potter's there, why doesn't he do it?"

"Mr. Potter will leave you two alone to discuss your financial details. Mr. Potter's task is to confirm the use of the quarry as our main water storage facility and that's all. Its geographic location has been exactly surveyed and identified with a ribbon marker in the center of the quarry bottom. When you ask him to show it to you, it can only be viewed by getting close to the east ledge. The rest is up to you," Campbell directed.

"You know I'm a part of this thing, but I feel I've already contributed more than my share. If I do this, it'll have to be my last." He sensed that if he didn't do it, his fate might be suspect anyway, but he had to make his point.

"There are only a few of us involved in this deal, Joe," Wellman added. "Believe me, we've all contributed quite a bit. I'm just asking you to do your part. The issue here is how do we keep a low profile while making personnel changes among the landowners, if you know what I mean?"

Wellman was perfectly equipped to deal with this kind of authority challenge. He was stalwart as a student of the Milgram Obedience Experiment conducted in the early 1960s by a psychologist, Stanley Milgram, who was studying the Nazi concentration camp killings. He found that even good people will do bad things when commanded to do so, as exhibited in his experiments where people were told to give increasing levels of electrical shocks to other subjects when they continued to give the wrong answers.

The controversial truth shocked the world of psychology, and the experiment was repeated throughout the world for verification. Ordinary people without any malice toward another whatsoever thought they were simply doing their jobs in the most terrible processes one could imagine, the torture of another human being. More than 90 percent of the many subjects studied were unable to resist the authoritative instructions given them, even if they were incompatible with their fundamental standards of morality and humanitarian well-being. Wellman knew this well from his military training, and to some degree, even used it in his political life regularly in influencing his staff to carry out various assignments for him, although none were of this severe level. It all came down to having the person feel that he is just an implement carrying out the authority's orders, and he at some point doesn't feel personally responsible for his actions.

They discussed their time schedule against which everything they did was measured. It was Wellman's way of keeping the pressure on. They soon had to reach certain benchmarks en route to their final goal of controlling one of the most valuable patches of ground in this Marcellus gold rush. They were almost there, and everything had to be in place before they could ease up; and that time was very soon.

The meeting ended somberly, but with all in agreement. Pratt stood up to leave with his unenviable mission in mind, and he would do it as expected. The depth of his involvement left him no choice. He would always do his part. The rewards were tremendous. Until now, the risks were minimal. This would be his last assignment, and he would make sure that was understood in the future.

"Take a gun with you, just in case," Campbell advised.

"Yeah, okay," Pratt mumbled.

After Pratt left, Wellman, Campbell, and Potter continued to discuss matters. "It appears, gentlemen, that we have a problem," Wellman cautioned.

"One thing at a time, Bob. Let's see how he handles the quarry meeting. Then we'll take care of things," Campbell said.

"The sooner the better," Senator Wellman answered.

Pratt's drive home that evening was pensive. He gave quite a bit of thought to how this might turn out overall. After reality set in, he saw his role with the investment group as one of the principal ones, but also as one in which many ways he could be expendable. As a protective safeguard, his plan was to prepare a statement that outlined everything he knew. He would store it in a sealed envelope in his safe deposit box with instructions to his Montrose office manager, Martha Hayes, to open it upon his death. If he were put in this position again, he would divulge this documentation to Wellman as a defensive measure. *It might save my life,* he thought.

12

"Pete, I've got another one," Chief Jim Mitchell announced alarmingly over the phone.

"What? Another suicide?" Pete Woodard questioned.

"I don't know. Why don't you meet me there? Route 167, about four miles south of Silver Lake at the quarry road on the right."

"What's the deal?"

"We've got a body at the bottom of the old quarry there."

"Geez, I'll see you there."

Pete turned off the electric range, where he was preparing his evening snack, and quickly changed into some clothes from his bathing suit and T-shirt. He knew the location Mitch was referring to and launched his car in the right direction. Sirens were sounding ahead, and all he had to do was drive to their source. Everyone was arriving at the same time. The narrow country road was lined with ten vehicles already, and more were arriving by the minute.

As Pete approached, he was met by a crowd of people held back a few yards from where the road was intersected by an old quarry entrance. He observed Chief Mitchell and two men up ahead, discussing the obvious matter at hand. Chief Mitchell made his way toward the crowd to separate them and allow the ambulance team to enter. He waved for Pete to come along, and Pete followed him up the road.

Ed Wilkinson lay at the bottom of the quarry, a distance of about sixty feet below the edge at the end of the entrance road. Blood was caked in his ears and on the back of his head, his body face up about fifteen feet from the east quarry wall. He was dressed in business attire, a sport coat and tie, suggesting that he came to the location during or after business hours. Other than that, there were no indications of what might have led to his demise. It appeared to be an accident, pure and simple. His car had been parked at the road entrance for two days, and his absence from his home and business had not yet become a concern over the weekend. A hiker who enjoyed fossil hunting at the local quarries discovered the twisted body late on Sunday afternoon.

Wilkinson was a fifty-year-old attorney who lived alone in Bridgewater, just outside of Montrose, and owned this land at the south border of Silver Lake Township. The quarry activities were long defunct since his grandfather died more than twenty years ago. He held onto the land for hunting, and the small amount of taxes didn't prohibit such a luxury, even though the area amounted to 310 acres.

Chief Mitchell gave the clearance for the ambulance crew to go down and pick up the body. He hesitated to do so, but darkness was setting in. After he marked the location with chalk and took some photographs, he instructed them to take the body to the Endless Mountain Hospital, where he would have coroner Jim Davis do the autopsy.

Pete observed the activities and mentally noted as many details as could. He stood at the crest of the hill overlooking the quarry void and turned northward, making a quiet observation. His

HYPOTHESIS

instincts told him that although Wilkinson's death surely appeared to be an accident, it may have some concurrent similarities with the previous deaths he and Mitch had been discussing.

Mitch taped off the location with yellow police tape, an occurrence, he thought, becoming all too common. He had to make some phone calls and talk to Helen to try to find out if there were any family members. He also called Doc Davis to alert him of the need for an autopsy rather than just a simple death pronouncement.

Pete left the scene quickly and bee-lined right home to his notes and updated his entries, adding Ed Wilkinson's accident with what he had just heard from Mitch.

Date	Name	Age-Sex	Occupation	Death	Particulars	Interval
Apr 11	Schultz, Karl	45- M	Unemployed	Suicide	Murder/suicide Wife, 2 children Tunkhannock Hand gun Thurs. night Gasco lease, 210 ac. Keystone Bank	Start (34days)

Date	Name	Age-Sex	Occupation	Death	Particulars	Interval
May 2	Daniels, Bill	45-M	Dentist	Suicide or accident	Ether, alcohol Lived alone Few relatives Silver Lake Fri. night Gasco lease, 290 ac. Northeast Penn Bank Forbes Int'l	21 days

97

Date	Name	Age-Sex	Occupation	Death	Particulars	Interval
May 15	Edwards, Joe	36-M	Art, design	Accident	Fall Lived alone, Few relatives Tunkhannock Fri night Client: Forbes Keystone Bank	13 days

Date	Name	Age-Sex	Occupation	Death	Particulars	Interval
May 23	Morson, Jane	46-F	Computers	Suicide	Shotgun Lived alone Few relatives Silver Lake Fri. night Gasco lease, 280 ac. Northeast Penn Bank Forbes Int'l	8 days

Date	Name	Age-Sex	Occupation	Death	Particulars	Interval
May 28	Carpenter, Lottie	58-F	Retired	Suicide	Asphyxiation Lived alone Few relatives Silver Lake Nicely dressed Wed. night House cleaned Refrig. full Gasco lease, 380 ac.	5 days

Date	Name	Age-Sex	Occupation	Death	Particulars	Interval
May 31	Wilkinson Ed (Lived in Bridgewater)	58-M	Attorney	Murder or Suicide	Fall, quarry Widower Silver Lake Sat. eve Nicely dressed Gasco lease?: 390 ac. (NE Penn Bank?)	3 days

HYPOTHESIS

Pete sat and stared incredulously as the information began to speak similarities. The only thing he needed to substantiate was if Ed Wilkinson banked at Northeast Penn. He was sure what the answer would be. But, on the other hand, this was a very small community, and any random grouping of people was going to have similar segmentation. There just weren't many variations one to another with the very few businesses in town.

One thing stood out: the ever-decreasing interval of occurrences, now down to only a few days apart. He knew enough about systems in his business life, including mechanical, operational, and, in particular, behavioral systems, to surmise that something was about to occur again, and very soon. They have an order, a regularity to them; that is, until a breakdown is eminent. Then, just like a bearing in your automobile needing grease, an indication will manifest itself, a squeak as in the case of the bearing. After that, the sound will repeat itself more and more frequently until it gets attention or self-destructs.

Pete was increasingly convinced now that something for sure was going on. He recognized a pattern that fell outside the harmony of life in Silver Lake ever more so with each passing day. *Actually,* he thought, *Mitch noticed the systematic disturbance in his fairy tale life here in Silver Lake when he initially spoke with me. That was the ultimate system disturbance indicator.*

One thing is clear: we are in a continuing pattern of more frequent intervals where we might anticipate when something could happen next. Indications are immediate. Something else is going to happen soon, but I need to know who and where. How can I determine those two things?

This is a behavioral system, and behavioral systems have one thing in common. They rely, knowingly or not, on feedback. That feedback tells the system to adjust and make another effort toward its end, its purpose. I need to know what that end is, and then I can look for the feedback trail. I would think there must be something organized in order to achieve some goal. I can also surmise that the timeframe is soon. I also feel that when the next event occurs, it will be within a day or two and it will be in close proximity. So far, nothing I can sense tells me exactly when, where, or who.

13

Attorney Killed in Fall at Quarry

By Mary Michelson, Staff writer

Filed: Monday, June 2, 2008
Published: Wednesday, June 4, 2008
Susquehanna County News

Local noted attorney Edward Wilkinson was found dead Sunday, the apparent victim of a fall at his property in Silver Lake Township. Wilkinson's property contained an old quarry which has been inactive for over twenty years. Silver Lake Township Police Chief Jim Mitchell reported that the body was found sixty feet below the quarry edge from which Wilkinson is believed to have fallen by John Warren, who was fossil hunting in the quarry with his son. There were no apparent signs of foul play. A state police investigation team was called to the scene. Investigators are asking anyone who may have been in the area around that time to call State Police with any related information.

Attorney Wilkinson had been in practice in Montrose for twenty-eight years and had served on many non-profit boards and civic committees. He has been legal counsel for the Montrose City Council for the past twelve years. He was a member and officer of many service organizations including Kiwanis, VFW, and Lions Club. His wife, Rose, passed away eleven years ago. Funeral services will be delayed due to an autopsy order being carried out by County Coroner James Davis.

"Pete, Mitch." The voice on the phone was unmistakable.

"Yeah, what's up?"

"I have the information on Edwards' computer, and you won't believe it!"

"Surprise me."

"It's gone. Not to be found."

"What do you mean?"

"Some guy came in and bought it, along with some of the furniture, fax machine, and odds and ends. Cash! Edwards was in business doing ads, brochures, and flyers, and things like that for years. His little office was a storefront in a building owned by his family in Tunkhannock. It was small time by any measure."

"How about files and things like that?" Pete asked.

"I can't really say. First, I'm outta my jurisdiction, and second, I didn't have a search warrant. And third, I didn't want to arouse any more curiosity than I already had. The father did say he cleaned out the office and he's got a 'For Rent' sign on the window if I want to come down."

"If I had to guess, any pertinent files or computer disks would be missing too," Pete added.

"I don't know. I asked Mr. Edwards to call me if anyone else inquired about the business. He said he would. We'll have to get down there and look for ourselves."

"Let's think about when that would be the right time, trying not to arouse suspicion and all that," Pete cautioned. "At some point, we might want to check his phone records too."

"Good idea."

"Any information from Doc Davis about the quarry accident?" Pete asked.

"Not yet; I'm gonna guess that there won't be anything."

"You never know."

"We'll see. We're on for that Sam Burns thing later today," Mitch reminded. "We'll pick you up."

"Sounds good. I'm looking forward to it."

Early that evening, Mitch, Helen, and Pete headed over to Sam Burns's political fundraiser for Senator Bob Wellman. The soft evening air welcomed such an outdoor event, and it felt good for Mitch and Pete to break away to the fresh atmosphere of the gathering. It was very well attended for a garden party, about twenty-five people, mostly teachers from the Montrose school district, including school superintendent Bill Ross, a hometown product of whom everyone was proud. His endorsement among this group of moderately influential professionals made all the effort in putting the fundraiser together worthwhile.

True to form, Senator Wellman was on top of his game. He socialized with every single individual there, eye to eye, and spoke to whatever variety of subjects was presented to him. His advantage in situations like this, where many other politicians would be on edge, was that he was a complete natural. Conversation came easily; answers to tough questions were managed forthrightly and with command. The shroud of the mysterious state legislature was lifted right before his audience's eyes, much to their appreciation. He was sincere, and most important, believable. He wanted to know his constituents' highest priorities, and he was going to discuss their merits right then and there. If it was something he could endorse, he would say so; if he was doubtful, he would explore it in further conversational debate until his petitioner would realize the difference; diplomacy at its best, and people loved him for it. A bonus that complemented his presence was his beautiful and thoughtful wife, Kathy. Her interests were well known to be involved with local charities, and she had accomplished admirable achievements in that realm in her own right. Together they were an unbeatable pair, and one in which the entire community was proud. They were royalty.

The senator's presentation to the group covered all the usual popular concerns: economic conditions, health, education support. In part, he touched on the gas well drilling influences, including environmental impacts, contractual fairness, and local revenue spinoffs. His time seemed well spent. Everyone was a supporter by the end of the meeting and gladly accepted the courteously distributed donation request cards to fill out after he left.

Helen circulated among some acquaintances, and when she came back to join Mitch and Pete, she possessed an amazing amount of information. Sam Burns and his wife, Ann, hardly had to lift a finger to orchestrate the event. They were only asked to establish a call tree in which each of a few people promised to call a few other people to attend the event. Everything else, including the appetizers, drinks, chairs, and tent were brought in that morning. It really was interesting to be a small part of politics like this, and everyone in attendance was made to feel important as such.

The majority of the other people attending were ostensibly in support of the senator's comments. For example, Sam Burns, Nora Connely, and her sister, Carol, discussed their landholdings with a Gasco representative named Frank Potter. The same trio was in a slightly larger group conversation with the Forbes International representative about investment and tax strategies for leaseholders' income; in particular, the consensus was that tax rates would be higher after the presidential election, and it could be advantageous to acquire the income this year rather than wait.

HYPOTHESIS

"You learned all of that! While I was here feeding my face!" Mitch exclaimed when Helen finished.

Pete said nothing.

"Not only that. Senator Wellman's wife, Kathy, is the niece of that lawyer who died in the quarry, Ed Wilkinson," Helen added. "The funeral is on Saturday."

Pete immediately turned to Mitch and said, "We need to talk, tonight!"

Mitch nodded. "Let's go."

"Helen, can you join us? Mitch, is that okay?" Pete asked.

They both agreed.

"Let's go to my house. I've got something to show you."

On the way home, the threesome discussed the night's happenings and offered their individual take on the dynamics at work during the fundraiser. It was fascinating.

They sat at Pete's dining room table with a view of the moonlit lake through the hemlock trees. The evening cooled, and Pete closed the door facing the lake. It was usually open, but tonight proved to be uncomfortably chilly. Pete poured hot water for their tea, and the work session they were about to begin seemed incongruous with the beauty and relaxed surroundings of Silver Lake at night. Mitch and Helen sensed they were in the presence of someone other than the Pete Woodard they thought they knew.

"Well, let's have it, Peter me boy!" Mitch requested as he stirred his tea. Helen sat quietly.

Pete smoothed out his wrapping paper worksheet, simultaneously leaning forward, using both hands pressing downward on it in an outward arcing motion a few times. "There, let me see now," he started.

Pete drew a sketch in one corner of the sheet and labeled the figures.

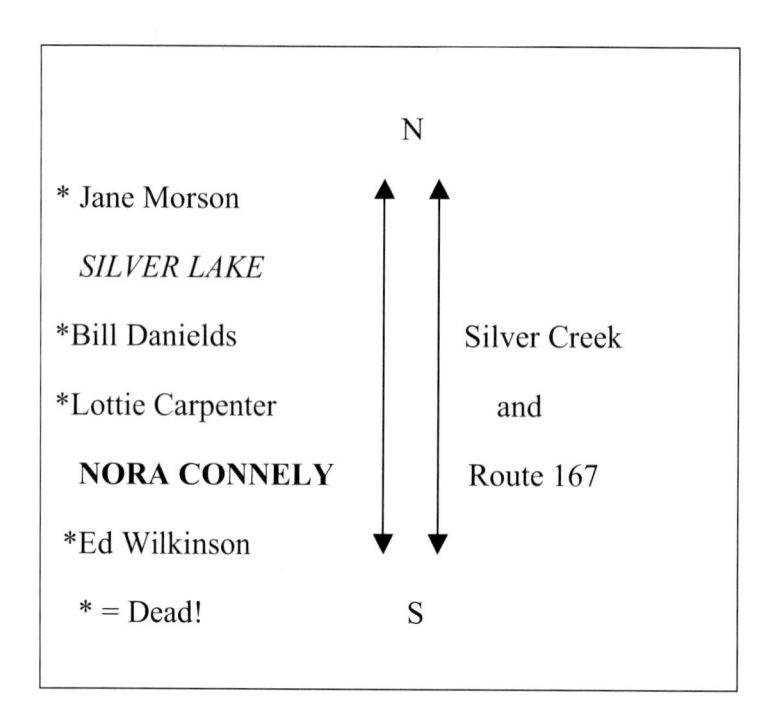

```
                        N
                        ▲ ▲
* Jane Morson           │ │
                        │ │
   SILVER LAKE          │ │
                        │ │
*Bill Danields          │ │   Silver Creek
                        │ │
*Lottie Carpenter       │ │   and
                        │ │
  NORA CONNELY          │ │   Route 167
                        │ │
*Ed Wilkinson           ▼ ▼
                        
 * = Dead!              S
```

The three sat and stared, the obvious possibility stated silently. "They don't all live here in Silver Lake, but they all so far have a property tie-in along Silver Creek and Route 167, either along or below the lake itself," Pete stated purposefully. The creek ran parallel to the road.

"Petey, me boy!" sounded Mitch.

"Does anyone know where Sam Burns's other property is?" asked Pete.

"No, but I can find out easily. It should be in the Platt Book," said Mitch, referring to the recently published map of all county properties showing owners and amount of acreage.

"I'll run over and get it," volunteered Helen as she rose and took Mitch's car keys from him and hurried out the door.

"While she's gone, I want to ask you something. It's pretty obvious to me in looking at this chart that Nora Connely may be in danger, to say the least. Would you agree to allow Helen to help us while we look into this further? And I want to add, I believe this is dangerous," Pete emphasized.

"She wouldn't want it any other way. What do you have in mind?"

"First, let's get Nora over to your house tonight for a day or two until we settle on what we will be doing. When Helen gets back, let's explain everything to her and have her call Nora to pack some things and wait for you to arrive. It's after nine o'clock now, but I don't mind bothering her at this time of night, under the circumstances."

Pete made the latest entries on his worksheet, adding details with Mitch's help. When Helen returned, they explained their concerns to her and she made the call to Nora, simply notifying her that she and Mitch were coming over within a few minutes.

"Mitch, before you come back, ask Nora a couple of questions for me, will you?" Pete requested.

"Sure, what do you want to know?"

"Find out everyone she spoke with at Sam Burns's fund raiser tonight—names, affiliations, whatever you can get. Also, ask her where she does her banking."

"Got it; I'll be back as quick as I can."

"Mitch, be sure to make it as quick as you can. I mean it. We've gotta nail this down fast." Pete motioned for Mitch to come closer so he could whisper. "Can Helen use a gun?"

"I already thought of that. I'll go over my Glock with her before I leave."

Mitch and Helen left together. Mitch planned to return within an hour, as soon as he transferred Nora to his home. Pete found his Pennsylvania topographical map book that he used for hiking and opened it up to the local grid. It showed the full length of Silver Creek, and how it meandered through Silver Lake Township on its way to Salt Springs Park in Franklin Forks. He thought, *Sam Burns's property must be along it somewhere. I'll wait for the Platt book to see exactly where.*

Date	Name	Age-Sex	Occupation	Death	Particulars	Interval
Apr 11	Schultz, Karl	45-M	Unemployed	Suicide	Murder/suicide Wife, 2 children Tunkhannock Hand gun Thurs. night Gasco lease, 210 ac. Keystone Bank	Start (34days)

Date	Name	Age-Sex	Occupation	Death	Particulars	Interval
May 2	Danields, Bill	45-M	Dentist	Suicide or accident	Ether, alcohol Lived alone Few relatives Silver Lake Fri. night Gasco lease, 290 ac. Northeast Penn Bank Forbes Int'l Wellman fund raiser	21 days

Date	Name	Age-Sex	Occupation	Death	Particulars	Interval
May 15	Edwards, Joe	36-M	Art, design	Accident	Fall Lived alone, Few relatives Tunkhannock Fri night Clients: Wellman Forbes Keystone Bank Computer missing	13 days

Date	Name	Age-Sex	Occupation	Death	Particulars	Interval
May 23	Morson, Jane	46-F	Computers	Suicide	Shotgun Lived alone Few relatives Silver Lake Fri. night Gasco lease, 280 ac. Northeast Penn Bank Forbes Int'l Wellman fund-raiser	8 days

Date	Name	Age-Sex	Occupation	Death	Particulars	Interval
May 28	Carpenter, Lottie	58-F	Retired	Suicide	Asphyxiation Lived alone Few relatives Silver Lake Nicely dressed Wed. night House cleaned Refrig. full Gasco lease, 380 ac. NE Penn Bank Wellman fund-raiser	5 days

Date	Name	Age-Sex	Occupation	Death	Particulars	Interval
May 31	Wilkinson Ed	58-M	Attorney	Murder or Suicide	Fall, quarry Widower Silver Lake Sat. eve Nicely dressed Gasco lease?: 390 ac. NE Penn Bank **Wellman's wife's uncle**	3 days
	(Lived in Bridgewater)					

Date	Name	Age-Sex	Occupation	Death	Particulars	Interval
N/A	Connely, Nora	53?-F	Teacher	N/A	N/A Widowed Silver Lake Gasco lease, 517ac. NE Penn Bank? Wellman fund-raiser	(soon?)

Date	Name	Age-Sex	Occupation	Death	Particulars	Interval
N/A	Burns, Sam	50?-M	Teacher	N/A	N/A Married Silver Lake land Along Silver Creek Wellman fund-raiser	(soon?)
	(Lives in Bridgewater)					

In a corner of his worksheet he made a list of everyone they spoke about recently.

Contacts:
    Al Dorrance, Montrose Police Chief
    Jim Davis, Coroner
    Sgt. Jim Mann, State Police
    Cpl. Carl Grady, State Police
    Larry Larson, DA
    Judge Larson, Susquehanna Cty
    Judge Horvak, Wyoming Cty
    Bob Willis, Bank Mgr. Northeast
    Nora Connely
    Helen Mitchell
    Mr. Edwards, Joe Edwards' father
    Josh O'Neil, Lottie's gardener

When Mitch returned, he gave Pete an update. "Nora's safe and sound. Her sister stayed over after the Burns political party, and she feels she can go over to her home in Waverly for a few days until school is out and she will be all right there; but they are scared out of their wits. I didn't know what all to tell her, so I asked her to wait 'til tomorrow."

"Well, I'll be over there tomorrow after school to discuss the gas leases with her anyway, so she should be all right for another day. Then I'll insist that she leaves for her sister's when we finish."

Pete found the Pratt listings for Sam Burns's properties: one for his home in Montrose where they attended the political event, and the other in Silver Lake Township, along Silver Creek about two miles farther to the east just before Salt Spring State Park. It fell into line somewhat with the others, but it was quite a distance away. He would include it, though, as part of the analysis.

"Let's review. I updated everything, but there's no question a lot is missing," Pete reported. "Think about it. If there is a connection, then who is to gain from these deaths?"

"If you leave out the graphic designer, Edwards, then everyone else who died had a Gasco gas lease except Wilkinson. If you then leave out Schultz in Tunkhannock, everyone else lived alone, attended a fundraiser for Wellman, and has property connected to the others in Silver Lake, and, by the way, has some investment dealings past, present, or future with the Forbes company," Mitch concluded, as Pete thought he might.

"See who stands to benefit, you once said, Pete. That's what we need to do."

"You are absolutely right! We need to find out if Wilkinson can be connected to Gasco and Forbes and also if he has a bank account at Northeast Penn, which I'd bet he does."

"But what does all this prove?" asked Mitch.

"Well, for one thing, look at the intervals of occurrence. It has been decreasing steadily to only a few days, likely indicat-

HYPOTHESIS

ing another incident soon. I'm guessing Nora Connely or Sam Burns. Notice if you start at Schultz's death, the intervals are in a decreasing sequence, but what is really coincidental—and there are no coincidences—they form a Fibonacci sequence except in reverse, where the difference between the two previous intervals predicts the next one and so on. Watch; I'll do it for you. Starting at Schultz's death as an interval of thirty-four days after some related event, the interval before Danields's death is twenty-one days, and so on, in a decreasing interval sequence of 34, 21, 13, 8, 5, and 3 with all the rest of the victims; so, 34 minus 21 is 13, 21 minus 13 is 8, 13 minus 8 is 5, 8 minus 5 is 3, and most important 5 minus 3 is 2 and 3 minus 2 is 1, which is tomorrow and the next day! If I were to believe this number theory indication, I would think something, and more than just one thing, is going to be happening soon.

"Holy guacamole! That is amazing, Pete!"

"I don't think anyone is following a formula or trying to be cute or psychotic about this or anything like that. It's just a natural progression of the systematic occurrences we are looking at. It's found all throughout nature, like in the spaces between the ribs of seashells or ripples of water, you know, things like that. It's everywhere in everything we do. No real explanation for it other than nature, or human nature in this case."

"Pete, that's amazing. I've heard something about that but never realized."

"It is, in my mind, however, a fairly confident... I won't use the word proof... but a fairly confident indicator that these deaths are some kinda progression, a progression toward an end, a schedule... something that's going to happen or has to happen. I don't know what, but something."

"What do you think it could be?"

"At the very least, there are some suspicious suicides and accidents that could be pronounced as suicides and which, under the proper scrutiny, might not be so, and the flow of dollars from the gas leases goes to Forbes Financial probably, my guess is under some insurance policy that will not pay out for a suicide. Now that I think of it, Schultz's lease payment may have been made directly to Forbes. Maybe that's why there was no bank record. At the very least, that's what's going on! Nora's the obvious next victim, unless I miss my guess."

"Where do we take this from here?" Mitch questioned. "I'm hanging it out now as it is. I can't very much nose around anymore without raising suspicions. I really don't have the resources to do much more without bringing someone else in. Besides, something like this can go deep, if you know what I mean."

"I know. Whom can you trust to discuss this with? Someone who'll do the right thing without jeopardizing you if we're all wrong about this. No repercussions," reminded Pete.

"I've gotta go to the county, straight to the DA, not the sheriff or anybody else," Mitch said.

"Sounds good to me, but my suggestion is to just tell him as little as possible while getting the point across."

"As little as possible? We don't really have a lot to begin with anyway!"

"Oh yes, we do. Think about it. We can link all Silver Lake property owners' deaths to Gasco, Forbes, Northeast Penn, and possibly, when you think about it, Senator Wellman. That's four heavy hitters, and there could be more to this! I suggest mentioning just the Silver Lake and Forbes connection and see what transpires from that."

"All right."

"We can always kick in with some more guidance if need be later on."

"I see what you mean. I'll visit with Larson tomorrow," Mitch concluded.

The two continued to stare at their notes, wondering what they might be missing. Was it as simple as the Forbes thing? It seemed so.

"By the way, there were two more deaths in the area this week. One down at the nursing home in South Montrose, and the other was a car accident out on the interstate highway, Route 81."

"Do they live around here or have land here?"

"Neither one; I just felt I should mention them. Not leaving anything to chance."

"Let's keep a separate file on them and note the occurrences. But I would put them in the category of normal death activity, which we will always see. I think to include them would cloud our thinking right now."

"Agreed."

14

District Attorney Larry Larson sat in quiet astonishment as Mitch unveiled his story. Five—and possibly seven—deaths got his full attention. He knew Mitch for all of his years as a police chief and admired his community achievements. He lived in the same town of Brackney in Silver Lake Township and saw firsthand what Mitch was all about. Larson's recommendation that Mitch run for election as county sheriff, his immediate legal emissary, was the most privileged association a law enforcement official could have with a district attorney. He trusted Mitch's judgment, and Mitch felt the same about him. Yet, somehow Mitch's theory was lacking in total credibility. Mitch did not mention Pete's involvement, or that Helen had any in-depth knowledge. He did acknowledge that Nora Connely was cautioned about staying at her home for fear of her getting caught up in the progression of the thing.

"Mitch, you've got a tiger by the tail on this one," Larson summarized. "If I've got this right, you are saying that this Pratt guy from Forbes is selling investment plans of some sort to landowners who have recently entered into an agreement with Gasco International. Then, for some reason, they end up dead by suicide and the investments, which probably have some sort of insurance component, are going to be negated. Or, worse yet, all of the investment money might disappear entirely."

Mitch hadn't thought of that "money disappearing entirely" aspect, but it amounted to the same thing.

"Wouldn't people entering into such an arrangement be interested in an annuity, a monthly investment return? From what I gather, most of these landowners have been doing it that way with the investment brokers. Wouldn't they have beneficiaries who would have to be paid off anyway?"

"I imagine so," said Mitch.

"So what would be the connection from Forbes to their deaths?"

"This is where I have to speculate. If they have insurance policies, there would be little or no payout in the case of suicide. It's possible there are more people involved than just Forbes. I have my thoughts in this area from indications so far, but I hesitate to involve anyone else. That is why I'm here to meet with you."

"I'm glad you brought it to my attention."

"You have the resources to investigate this above-board and out in the open. I don't want to be an alarmist. I've just been concerned about some of our local citizens and the safety of two who are still alive, Nora Connely and Sam Burns," Mitch instructed. "All I ask is for you to take a look at things. See what you think and let me know. I'm convinced, but I need you to be convinced also. The best way for that is to come to your own conclusions."

"I'll need to involve some people on my end, the sheriff and some others," Larson advised.

"That's why I'm handing this off, so that you can take it to another level."

"Are you the only one to know about this?" Larson asked.

"Yes," Mitch lied.

"All right, let me start by crawling all over Forbes and see what they're all about. Let's plan to talk in about two days."

"Okay," agreed Mitch. "On my way back, I'm going to stop at the quarry where Wilkinson died. I want to get a good look around in the daylight. Probably nothing there, but you never know."

Mitch drove up Route 167, heading north out of Montrose about six and a half miles to the quarry entrance road and did a U-turn, parking in front of the entrance gate just a few feet from the road. He walked in about a hundred yards to the edge of the quarry pit. It was an impressive sight, about the size of a football field, except in a bowl sixty feet below the surface where he stood. There was an accumulation of standing water at the far end, which sloped even deeper from the main floor of the imposing edifice.

He walked to the edge and gazed down, looking for the orange surveyor tape he had seen attached to the floor the day of Wilkinson's death. It was not visible, and he walked even closer to the edge to find it. This, for the most part, proved the point about Wilkinson possibly doing the same and getting too close to the edge in doing so. He actually felt uncomfortable in getting closer, and it had not yet come into his view.

He studied the ground around the area presumed to be the place from which Wilkinson fell, even covering a wider scope by walking into the brush behind him to a depth of about twenty feet. Nothing was obvious. So he decided to walk down the entrance road along the south edge to get to the quarry floor. It was a quiet afternoon, but as he made his descent, he felt even more insulated from the sounds of the surrounding woods; not even a breeze could be felt.

The old roadway was overgrown, and other than the recent foot traffic during the Wilkinson incident, there was no sign of activity. He remembered that it had been abandoned more than twenty years ago. As he looked back toward the wall where he had stood, he could see why the orange surveyor tape was difficult to view. From this vantage point it was obvious that the edge was angled upward there and didn't provide a clear downward viewing angle.

When he reached the bottom, he walked to where Wilkinson's body was found. He gazed thoughtfully at the chalked human outline. There was some rubble that probably fell from the wall on a regular basis; in fact, there was rubble all around the entire circumference of the floor of the pit. He made a sketch for his file and took some measurements of the body's distance from the wall before leaving this vestigial landmark behind. He felt there was nothing more to be learned.

From another vantage point two miles upslope to the north, Pete Woodard and Nora Connely were enjoying the same view, except of a southerly panorama in which the quarry was lost among the beautiful countryside in the far distance. He had arrived for dinner and conversation about the land leasing and gas well drilling arrangements Nora was troubled with. The view to the south was the first part of her tour for any visitor, and by far, it was the most delightful. The scenery appeared to be that of another dimension, with its mountain ranges unfolding one behind the other into the golden haze of the early evening. Not a scant indication of human habitation was within the view except the faint wail of a siren in the distance. She felt fortunate that the land had stayed that way and promised to continue to be so for the foreseeable future.

Nora led the walking tour through the old barn and itinerant worker quarters and then over to the ancient farm equipment, only because Pete expressed a particular interest in the workings of the machinery. "When I was a teenager, I used to drive this one to cut the hay. Then after two or three weeks, once it dried out on the ground, I would drive the same tractor with the hay baler attached. My father and sister would follow and bring the bales to the barn, where my mother would meet them to help unload. The whole family was involved. We had long, hard days getting it all in before we went in for dinner," she recounted. "Then the cows had to be milked before we went to bed. In the late summer, the itinerant workers picked the corn, and we sold it to the grocery stores in New York and Pennsylvania."

"What a tough life!"

"Actually, you know, we didn't think so at the time. We worked very hard and were busy all the time. All our neighbors were doing the same. It was all we knew. It leaves me with the best of memories. We worked together as a family, solved all our own problems, and were proud of the accomplishments in our own way. It was a loving life."

"You seem to almost miss it."

"It made a living for our family, got us through school, and then back here to let Dad retire after Mom got ill before she passed away. Sort of like a social security succession plan for the elders in the family," she stated with a touch of emotion in her quavering voice.

"All's well that ends well, I guess."

"Let's have a look at that pot roast and see if it's ready." Nora led the stroll back to the house while wiping a little moisture from her eyes.

They were greeted by the pleasant aromas of the roast upon entering the house. Pete was embarrassed by all the preparations she had made, but he looked forward to the first home-cooked meal he had had in over two years, and this one promised to be spectacular.

"How can I help?" he asked.

"Everything is almost done. I just need to mash some potatoes and make the gravy while the roast rests for ten minutes. Then we can sit and enjoy."

The screen door breathed in the soft evening breeze, carrying scents of fresh spring growth from its travels as he watched her deft movements throughout the familiar workings of the kitchen. *It is a comforting thing to be able to see a woman enjoy doing something for someone else the way she moves about,* he thought, *and it is obvious that she feels good about it as well.*

This was one of the few complete home-cooked meals she had made since her husband died. She was savoring every task, reveling in memories of good feelings from having done them so many times in the past and enjoying the fruits of her labor with someone who would be more than appreciative.

They exchanged thoughts so naturally. She was personable and had a smile in her eyes that was very engaging. Conversation came easily, sharing old times from their childhoods back and forth. They couldn't have been more different—he, a city born and bred, polished jock type, confident, intelligent, and accomplished at everything he tried, and she, a country farm product with a humble presentation but not lacking at all in personal achievements. They both ended up as equivalents of some sort but got there by totally different means. The beauty of the fellowship emerged as something that could not have been better if it were planned, and they both felt the weight of this otherwise simple encounter, all this in a friendly little dinner meeting.

"Can I at least cut the roast? That's something I can handle without getting in the way."

"Sure, the knives are in the top left drawer there. Be careful."

The scene of domesticity didn't strike either one as unusual, although it was the first time they had been in each other's company alone. Standing side by side, unrealized by either one of them, they were absorbed in a moment reminiscent of their former happy family lives and the surrogate situation they were experiencing. It was titillating to have met someone like this, they both thought, each sensing feelings welling up that hadn't been experienced since their youth.

The ring of the phone snapped everything back to reality.

"Hello?" Nora's expression changed to gloom almost immediately. "Oh my God, how is he? He's right here. Pete, it's Helen. Mitch has been hurt."

Pete grabbed the phone. "Helen, Pete." He listened for an agonizing minute.

"I'll be right over. We'll go right down."

"Nora, I'm really sorry. Someone ran into Mitch along the highway by the quarry. I'm going to take Helen down to the hospital. I can't tell you how much I appreciate what you've done tonight. Can I take a rain check?"

"Of course; go! Please call when you have some news."

The shift in emotions was stark for Pete as he drove away en route to pick up Helen. *What in the world is going on?* he thought. *Right now, I just want to make sure Mitch is okay.*

15

The small hospital was somber. Police Chief Jim Mitchell was a universally loved community member, even to those who had never met him. His command and small-town exploits had carried the respect of everyone from as far away as Montrose, where the hospital was located. In these small rural towns, personal accomplishments are enjoyed by all as though they were their very own achievements. More so, personal tragedies permeated the spirit of the communities in the same way. Now it was the latter. Everyone felt helpless except to pray, and that is what they did.

Endless Mountain Hospital is a quaint twenty-nine-room facility with all the necessary basic services and a very talented and dedicated medical staff. News of any patient emergency arrival traveled quickly throughout the small building, but today's arrival was especially noteworthy.

Helen and Pete had waited six hours for any kind of news. Sympathetic smiles came their way with encouraging comments from the staff as they passed by them in the waiting area. Every emotion was coursing through them: nervousness, sickness, disgust, revenge, sadness, inadequacy.

It was after midnight when Doctor Art Sheehan finally came to the visitor's lounge. He looked exhausted after tending to the ordeal all evening, but forced a smile and consoled Helen with a hug. "Mrs. Mitchell, he's going to be all right. I want you to visit him, but only for five minutes. He's heavily sedated and probably won't know who you are. But any encouragement is a help. He will need it," he advised. "He will come through this, but recovery will be long. The broken hip is one thing, but the massive bruising and damaged muscles are going to dictate a delicate recovery."

"Oh, thank you, Doctor. You are wonderful! I prayed as much for you as I did for Mitch. Thank you so much!"

Helen and Pete entered Mitch's hospital room, not knowing what they might see. It was not encouraging. The lighting was dimmed, and the glow of the electronic instruments added to the eeriness. Mitch was not conscious, his lower body was in a cast, and his leg was slightly elevated in a sling. Plastic tubes transferred oxygen and liquids, electronic monitor wires were attached, and a nurse was in attendance full time.

Helen clung to Pete and sobbed. "Mitch, my Mitch! I love you so much! What did we do to deserve this? Pete, he helped so many people. How could this be?"

Pete was visibly moved, but silent. His thoughts were the same as Helen's. His reality check needed updating. *This was not a coincidence,* he thought. *We are in the middle of something big, really big, but what in the world is it?*

They watched Mitch quietly, and once in a while, Helen offered a word of encouragement: "Mitch, you can do it." "I love you." "Rest easy and get better." "I'm praying for you."

"Mrs. Mitchell, I'm afraid that's all the time we can give you today," Doctor Sheehan murmured as he indicated the way to the door. "We have your number. We'll give you a call tomorrow to let you know if there is a change. We'll take good care of him."

"Thank you, Doctor. Please let me know as soon as possible when he wakes," Helen pleaded.

The drive home was sullen. There were two ways to return to Brackney, and Pete took the longer one along Route 29 up to Lawsville Center and over Laurel Lake Road, which did not pass the scene of the accident. Neither spoke for a long time, Helen knowing and appreciating Pete's sensitivity in taking the longer route. "Helen, are you going to be all right tonight?"

"I'm sure. I've got the animals to look after. That'll keep me busy."

"I'm going to ask Nora to stop by if that's all right with you," Pete suggested.

"I'm fine. Don't go through any bother."

"Helen, I insist. Nora's a good friend, and I'm sure she's waiting to hear how Mitch is doing and how you're holding up." They arrived at the farmhouse, and Pete walked her to the door. Helen nodded approvingly and walked in slowly and sank into the sofa. She was exhausted. Pete looked up Nora's number in the directory and called. It was 2:00 am.

"Hello."

"Nora, Pete Woodard. Sorry to wake you."

"Oh, you didn't wake me, Pete. How's Mitch? I'm so worried."

"Well, we just left him. He's in guarded condition on a lot of sedatives. It looks like a broken hip and quite a bit of lower body damage. He was not conscious when we were there. We could only see him for a few minutes."

"My God, I've been up all night worried sick!" Nora exclaimed. "What can I do?"

"Glad you asked. I wonder if you could spend some time over here with Helen before you leave for your sister's in Waverly, just to make sure she's holding up all right. I plan to make her a little breakfast. Maybe you would like to join us."

"I will, Pete. You go right ahead with breakfast. I'll be over in an hour. I'll bring a few things."

"Thanks. Take your time. See you in a bit."

After Nora arrived, the three of them sat in the kitchen, somewhat comforted by the smells of toast and coffee. Appetites were absent, conversation meaningless, but necessary. Pete felt he should ask Helen to lie down for a while, but she insisted on feeding her small herd of farm friends first. Pete and Nora agreed that it would probably be therapeutic but warned her to heed their advice for some rest. Nora assured Pete she would stay through the day instead of leaving to stay with her sister as he had suggested. He left his number and said he would try to get some rest for a few hours. He knew, however, that he would not.

Pete's thoughts went to Mitch's accident. When he left Helen and Nora, instead of driving home to the lake, he drove south on Route 167 to the accident scene. There were scuffmarks and some indications of an incident on the road, but only if you knew where to look since there were no skid marks. What interested Pete was that Mitch's police car was parked off the road right at the entrance to Ed Wilkinson's quarry when it was hit. Pete wondered if Mitch may have gone back there for some reason to examine the Wilkinson accident scene. It would be hard to determine if he were getting out of or into his car when he was hit. His right hip was broken, so Pete assumed he must have been facing the oncoming car while standing with the door open. More than likely, Mitch was getting back into his car and turned to face the oncoming traffic. But this was just a guess.

Pete parked his car safely off the road in a small clear area farther ahead and walked back to the quarry road. The sun was just rising, and the early morning mist lifting from the woods glowed in streaks of light through the tree limbs and was almost enchanting, although his task reminded him that it was not. He stood at the edge of the quarry, where Ed Wilkinson must have done the same before his fatal moment, and couldn't help looking around behind him, allowing for the possibility that Wilkinson may have had some assistance in his fall. There really were no conclusions to be made other than the fact that it would be very difficult to be victim of a fall, since one would have to either get very close to the edge and have the rock face give way, which it appears did not, or be pushed.

The quarry itself was bowl shaped and quite formidable in appearance, fortress-like and in contrast to the beautiful forest surroundings. He had learned from Mitch that it was sixty feet deep, and it appeared at least that. There was one entrance about thirty feet above the floor of the bowl that opened to a ramp that circled along the sidewalls and descended to the lowest level. Some orange surveyor tape was attached, probably by nailing through it, to the stone quarry floor at what appeared to be the inscribed center of the bowl. This seemed unusual since there was no other apparent activity here. The roadway to the ramp entrance sloped downward from where he was standing and was grown in with bushes and some small trees in spots. Other than the orange tape, it had all the characteristics of any one of the hundred or more abandoned quarries in the county.

He decided to walk down for a closer view. The main road circled southward in a downward slope before arcing back to the entrance ramp. An old building appeared along a path in the woods to the south, straining to stand upright but fallen in on itself from neglect and the toll of time. What appeared to be an old outhouse behind it had already fallen and was partially overgrown. No recent traffic was evident. Some construction garbage had been dumped at the entrance in years past, but otherwise this location of a once-active business venture was just a remnant of its interesting past.

He walked down the ramp to the center of the carved-out edifice. It was awe-inspiring, like being in the center of an amphitheater. The surrounding walls were every bit six stories high, trees and shrubs growing from cracks in the walls. He estimated the diameter to be about one hundred yards. It was peaceful, but disquieting at the same time. He tried to imagine the amount of material removed to create the void, and it was staggering. It represented years upon years and thousands upon thousands of man-hours pecking away at the rock to extract one of the east coast builders' prized materials, Pennsylvania bluestone. It was a fairly soft and easily worked material, yet it was a durable stone for home and building trim and walkways.

The eight-inch-long orange ribbon was indeed nailed into the bedrock of the floor. It seemed to be recently installed, not having any weathering effects from water or sun. There was a number "five" handwritten on it as though with a felt-tip marker. *Is this what Ed Wilkinson came to see?* Pete thought.

He looked up to the infamous edge from where Ed Wilkinson must have fallen. It did seem that a person would have to get close to the edge to be able to see this marker. That appeared to be the only thing of interest as Pete made a walking tour of the quarry floor. When he looked for the location where Wilkinson's body was found, a chalk outline and some residual bloodstains marked the spot. It was 6:45 a.m., and he was now feeling very tired; exhausted, actually. It was time to catch a few hours' rest. After that he would call the hospital to get an update on Mitch and then see when it would be possible to have Helen visit again. From what he saw of Mitch lying there at his early stage of recovery, it could be a few days before that were possible.

He walked up the ramp, enjoying the vista northward, recognizing the hills to the west as the same ones aligning Nora Connely's property. He thought, *That must be her home on the crest of the faraway hilltop about a mile north. What a view that is from there!*

HYPOTHESIS

Silver Lake Police Chief in Hit-and-Run Accident

By Mary Michelson
Staff writer

Filed: Tuesday, June 3, 2008
Published: Wednesday, June 4, 2008
Susquehanna County News

Silver Lake Township Police Chief Jim Mitchell was found lying in the road early Monday evening by a passing motorist. The apparent victim of a hit-and-run driver, Chief Mitchell is in guarded condition at Endless Mountains Hospital in Montrose. Len Miller was driving north on Route 167 at 5:00 pm when he came upon the scene at a quarry entrance a half mile south of Silver Creek Road. He flagged down another motorist who drove to a nearby home to call for help. The Silver Lake ambulance responded, along with the state police. Trooper John Haden commented that the driver's side door was torn off Chief Mitchell's police car, as though he was hit when exiting the vehicle. There were no skid marks. Mitchell was found ten feet from the front of his vehicle.

A state police investigation team was called to the scene. Investigators are asking anyone who may have been on the roadway around that time to call State Police.

Chief Jim "Mitch" Mitchell is a highly regarded community official and has been the local law enforcement officer in Silver Lake Township for the past eight years. He lives with his wife, Helen, in Brackney. He has undergone surgery, and his condition is listed as guarded.

16

"Helen, it's Pete; how are you holding up?" he asked when she picked up her phone on the first ring.

"Oh, fine, I just want him back home," she sighed.

"Well, listen; we're going down to see him this afternoon. I called Doctor Sheehan, and he says he's awake and in good spirits, I guess as well as can be expected. Apparently the car door must have taken the direct hit and he only got a glancing blow, as hard as it must have been," Pete reported with as much positive news as possible. Mitch still had a long recuperation ahead of him, and both of them knew it. "Now, the doctor wants to limit the visitors. So can you make an apology to Nora? I know she would like to go along."

"I will. Actually, she planned to run over to her house for the mail and a few things later this afternoon. So everything will work out."

"Good, tell her to get right back and not to talk to anybody. I mean anybody. I'll be over at two o'clock. See you then."

Pete needed to find out from Mitch what was discussed with

Larry Larson and how much or how little he had told him. He hoped as little as possible. *This Forbes and Gasco thing has to be connected,* he thought. *After the deaths of five people, Mitch visits the DA for some banking information that indicates Forbes as a common denominator for four of them, and he gets no further help. Then there is another death in a quarry accident. After that, Mitch visits the DA again, and Mitch is run down right at the scene of the quarry accident. The Wilkinson death in the quarry is tied in somehow. Wilkinson is an attorney. Maybe there is a common thread with him. If that's the case, then there really are no coincidences.*

There were no instructions from Dr. Sheehan to limit the number of visitors. Pete just needed to talk confidentially with Mitch if he was able to, and he didn't want Nora there. He would ask Helen if he could have some brief private time with Mitch, and she would understand.

They arrived at the hospital just after Mitch had a fresh change of bedding and a new hospital gown. He was understandably tired with all the jostling about, but this is the kind of activity the nursing staff encouraged in order to get a patient like Mitch moving around, blood circulating; and even his complaints were a welcome form of mental exercise and a sign he was getting back to his old self.

He did look very well, alert, rested but with greatly weakened strength, which was obvious from his paltry handshake. Pete stepped outside the room to give Helen some time alone with him. He found Dr. Sheehan, and they discussed Mitch's progress. Nothing was much out of the normal expectations. His stay would be at least one more week, and then if all went well, he could be sent home for extended bed rest and a daily exercise regimen and physical therapy.

When he returned to Mitch's room, he and Helen were in an embrace; at least, she was trying to lean over and caress him. There were tears in her eyes, even though she promised herself that would not happen. Mitch's words were slow in coming, actually, very relaxed, much unlike his normal pace. Pete was sure it was the medications, particularly the painkillers, that were the vocal influence. It became obvious that Mitch wanted to speak with Pete. Helen said she would bring back some magazines, and she stepped out.

"Pete, they almost got me," Mitch gasped. "I'm sure that truck was aiming for me. Believe me." Mitch spoke softly, keeping his head straight forward, not making a motion or gesture.

"Mitch, I hate to say it, but I figured the same thing. It's been gnawing at me, and now I'm able to confirm it with you directly. Can you describe the vehicle?"

Mitch spoke slowly and almost in a whisper. "Yeah, sure, but what good would that be? This thing goes deep. To me, if there was ever a professional hit, that was it. That truck was damaged, of course. It's probably on a farm someplace in a million pieces. It could never be identified."

"Tell me about your talk with the DA." Pete needed to get as much information as possible from Mitch before his sedatives kicked in and he went off to sleep.

"Like we discussed, I went over the deaths with him and our—by the way, I didn't mention you—our suspicions about Forbes and Gasco and that maybe there's a connection. He was taken aback, especially when you add in the two deaths in Tunkhannock... if they're connected, you know."

"I mean, was he shocked, excited, what?"

"Oh yeah, he got it loud and clear. He listened very intently. He seemed to ask all the right questions."

"Back to what you said before: did you tell him you were the only one who knew about this?" asked Pete.

"Actually, he asked me if anyone else knew."

Pete slumped back in his chair. He knew of the relationship Mitch had with Larson. "Mitch, I believe you are still very much in danger."

"I'll be safe in here. There're no trucks comin' through as far as I can tell."

"What made you go back to the quarry?"

"I just wanted to get a good look around in the daytime."

"Did anyone know you were going there or see you go in?"

"No, just Larson."

"What!"

"Yeah, I think I mentioned it to him when I was leaving."

"Mitch, I don't trust anyone at this point. Let's just keep anything else to ourselves until we figure a few things out," Pete cautioned.

"What about Nora? How's she doing?"

"I'm not so concerned about Nora staying at your house. After Lottie Carpenter's funeral tomorrow, she's going to move in with her sister over in Waverly, according to Helen. It's the end of the school year, and she only has to drive in to class for two more days. Then she's able to stay in Waverly. Helen told her that you want her to have her mail held with no forwarding address until this thing gets sorted out. They were my instructions, but she doesn't know I'm involved. She thinks they were your instructions, and I want to keep it that way."

"The Township has arranged for temporary police coverage, Helen mentioned; a guy named Wayne Thomson. I know him. He's a good man. He's helped out before," explained Mitch.

"Again, I'm not trusting anyone."

"You're right. I'll mention that to Helen."

"You look bushed. We better let you get some rest. I'm going to work on a few things. I'll call you tomorrow. You can take calls, can't you?"

"I can, but I can't reach the phone. So make sure you let it ring or tell the operator to get someone to help me."

"See you soon."

"Thanks, Pete."

17

Nora's visit by Joe Pratt from Forbes Financial had been set up a few days earlier, and she looked forward to his arrival. It was late afternoon, and the sun-baked farm fields surrounding her farmhouse emitted an aroma like nothing else on earth, she thought. Hay-like, musty, and manure-based, believe it or not, was an aromatic that coalesced to satisfy the senses far beyond what would be imagined, given the source of emissions. It was country life at its taken-for-granted best. She relished the day. It brought back memories of farm activities, preparations for the first hay harvest, and work 'til dawn embedded in her makeup from childhood days raised on the farm. You could not buy such a sensory experience by way of the most lavish vacation in any exotic location she could think of. Her day was complete already.

Melancholy soothed her mind and relaxed her body with anticipation and understated excitement. The school year was approaching an end, and she and Carol would plan some travel, this time actually out of the state, to New York City for a week of plays and sightseeing, dining, and shopping. She had a few details to take care of, and this visit was one.

Joe Pratt's SUV floated through a cloud of dust and arrived at the end of the driveway. His smile and exuberance exited the vehicle almost before he did. They sat on the porch, each enjoying the view and the pleasantness of the afternoon. They had become friendly acquaintances, more so than just the financial business at hand would normally produce. When it came time to review some figures, they moved to the kitchen table, a business forum much familiar to those of country persuasion. It was enjoyable.

Nora's newly minted portfolio would be derived from her initial gas lease contract, amounting to $1,292,000. The money was already transferred to her bank, Northeast Penn, and she just needed to finalize the Forbes paperwork to initiate her investment. It was projected to grow at the rate of $5,900 per month at a minimum, and in addition, an annuity guarantee of $5,418 per month for life was an option upon additional endorsement whenever she wished to enact it. Further, a paid-up insurance policy of $2,800,000 was locked in at initiation. Her life would be cast financially without a care. Along with her teacher's pension and social security, she could plan a complete retirement without worry. All of this good fortune was explained by Joe Pratt, referring constantly to the paperwork and brochures that outlined this financial smorgasbord.

Nora served up a slice of apple pie for each of them along with the obligatory cup of Barry's Irish tea, a traditional blend of Kenyan and Indian teas. It was a good portion stronger and bitterer than what Pratt might be used to, she warned, but it cut through the sweetness of the pie in a perfect balance, cleansing the palette with each sip, readying the mouth for the next explosion of flavor. Her pies were her secret, and if it were not for her frequent purchases of Endless Mountain honey, one would never discover her envied special ingredient.

When they finished, Pratt packed up his things and said he would get back to her in a few days. Pratt's car crawled away down the driveway with headlights glowing through the dust and the dusk. It slowed at the roadway entrance, where a vehicle and two men met him. They talked for a minute, and Pratt slowly slumped over in his seat, his face contorted slightly in pain, and then there was no breathing. Without saying a word, they moved him to the passenger seat, and one man drove it away, followed by the other.

Nora turned out the porch light and walked out onto the porch for a breath of air. She sat in her favorite rocking chair, her pulse racing as she thought about her meeting. Now her future would change in ways she never dreamed.

18

Natural gas drillers' problem: millions of gallons of wastewater

By Mary Michelson
Staff writer
Filed: Tuesday, June 3, 2008
Published: Wednesday, June 4, 2008
Susquehanna County News

Recently, one natural gas drilling company pumped and recovered more than 4 million gallons of water to develop just two Western Pennsylvania gas wells for Houston-based gas and oil company, Gasco International. The problem of how to handle millions of gallons of wastewater is one of the biggest challenges emerging in the rush to extract natural gas from the Marcellus Shale.

Hydraulic fracturing is the process of blasting cracks in the mile-deep shale with pressurized water, chemicals, and sand, and it is the essential process to be used in extracting the natural gas held within the layers of rock. It is one of the industries' single largest costs, both from an economical and environmental standpoint. In order to release the gas from the wells, the water concentrated with salt, metals, acid, and naturally occurring radioactivity must be piped back to the well head and afterwards remediated from the toxicity it acquired during the pressurized process. Only four wastewater treatment plants in all of Pennsylvania currently exist which are specifically designed to treat such industrial wastewater. There is only one such facility in nearby New York State. To make matters more strained, none of the processing plants are located close by. The nearest is in St. Mary's, over 200 miles away from the center of Northeast Pennsylvania drilling in Susquehanna County.

Municipal wastewater treatment plants do exist locally, but very few can accept the extra flow of water because of capacity and technological processing constraints. In order to vie for the available business of accepting waste products, any municipal plant is now required to obtain approval and develop a testing plan to assure proper remediation of this new waste composition according to Pennsylvania Department of Environmental Protection spokesperson, Edward Helsley. In other states where similar gas well drilling is carried out, the wastewater is pumped underground to holding wells; however, Pennsylvania's underground rock formations are not similar and such practices would be hazardous to wells, streams and rivers even at great distances from the wastewater source. The lack of this processing resource is predicted to very quickly develop into an insurmountable restriction as the number of wells increases almost on a daily basis. For example, one Marcellus Shale operator has forecasted that its demand for water disposal would overload the existing Pennsylvania facilities in two to three years, said John Orsen, a marketing manager with Water & Process Technologies, Inc., which is developing techniques to recycle the wastewater. "And that's only one producer," he said. "So somebody has to do something."

Treatment of the wastewater is necessary because of its high toxicity. In order to facilitate the fracture of the shale, gas well drillers add chemicals and acids to the water which are proprietary additives the operators do not have to disclose publicly because it is considered intellectual property information. As the water flows through the rock, it gathers salt, metals and natural radioactivity. When it comes to the surface, it can be eight to ten times saltier than ocean water. "The Marcellus water is the worst on the planet," Mr. Orson said. "It's going to be a tough challenge to remediate."

The Pennsylvania Department of Conservation of Natural Resources has cautioned drillers that they are not staffed for this increase in licensing-related reviews and that they will, however, take every precaution to preserve the environment, even if the process is slowed down to levels not anticipated by the exploration companies. They fear that the possibilities of pollutants being released into drinking water and agricultural water supplies are very real and increasing dramatically with each arrival of a well permit application. "Drinking water supplies can be dramatically affected by only a small amount of errant wastewater flow," according to Bryan Swistock, Executive Director of DCNR.

In order to meet the demand, the industry consensus calculates that a new wastewater treatment plant would have to come on line every few weeks. The approval process for one plant can be as long as two years. The new plants would also have to possess unprecedented capacities of around 500,000 to 700,000 gallons per day. Compatible locations must be identified first, and then engineering studies completed for each particular site. The regulatory process comes after that, and the individual reviews can be a tedious process.

The biggest challenge to operators is the cost of transporting wastewater to the treatment plant. A typical Marcellus well returns between 2 million and 3 million gallons of water from hydraulic fracturing, and most of it has to be trucked off site. That amounts to about 600 tanker trips for each well.

Operators also are not giving up on the idea of sending the dirty water deep underground into disposal wells, a method that has been criticized in Texas because of dangerous incidents of leaks and spills. The Pennsylvania Oil and Gas Association is trying to identify appropriate geological formations in the state to accept the wastewater. "Right now the technology is not persuasive enough to guarantee fail-proof disposal including contamination of water supplies, soils, and the danger of leaks and spills throughout the management process. One spokesperson from Gasco International said that although Pennsylvania has not often been able to use disposal wells in the past, that's not to say it couldn't happen in the future."

Both the independent gas operators in the state, and the national companies, like Gasco, hoping to explore the Marcellus, have formed industry study groups to solve the water restrictions before extensive drilling begins. The national group, called the Marcellus Shale Water Conservation and Management Committee, has been meeting regularly to discuss technology and innovations near at hand that could alleviate the situation. The member companies are compiling information about how best to use and treat the water in this shale in a way that is both economically and environmentally responsible.

One of the most promising ideas of particular interest to all involved is technology to recondition the hydraulic fracturing water so that it can be reused in well after well. Professor John Nordstrom, Houston State University, is collaborating with a local manufacturer of paper mill equipment and a local municipal engineering company in Tunkhannock to reduce the amount of freshwater extracted from the environment for hydraulic fracturing. He said two products in particular, a thermal evaporator and a crystallizer, show promise for treating the water used to fracture the Marcellus Shale. Depending on the quality of the wastewater, the evaporator can turn it into 70 percent distilled water, which can be used to fracture the next well, and 30 percent concentrated brine, which is disposed of like normal drilling wastewater. The crystallizer turns the brine wastewater into 98 percent distilled water and two percent solid salt. The processes, he said, are also built to work in conjunction with one another. "In many places, long term, that's probably going to be the solution," he said." Effectively, we should be able to recover over ninety-five percent of the initial water used."

The two companies also are working on the portability of those technologies, so parts of them can be moved between areas of concentrated shale drilling. The goal is to be able to eliminate a fair amount of the trucking to and from the well sites.

Regardless of how industry plans to deal with the shale's dirty water, a DEP spokesman emphasized that it is not the regulatory agency's problem to solve. "Our challenge is to enforce the law, and industry's challenge is to abide by the law," he said. "We'll help them any way we can, but it's not our job to find them a place to dispose of their water," he added. "It's their job to make sure they do it right." Contact the writer: mmichelson@susqnews.org

19

Man Found Dead in Car

By Mary Michelson, Staff writer

Filed: Friday, June 6, 2008
Published: Wednesday, June 11, 2008
Susquehanna County News

A man was found dead this morning, the apparent victim of a heart attack. Joseph Pratt, President of Forbes Financial International, Inc., was found in his car, parked at the Forbes Financial International offices in Montrose. Employees entering the building noticed the body just before 8:00 am. An autopsy will be carried out by County Coroner James Davis.

Forbes Financial is headquartered in Wilkes Barre and has had an office in Montrose on Maple Street for the past few years.

"Pete, have you heard the news?"Mitch's call from the hospital was very much unexpected.

"No. What's up?"

"They brought Joe Pratt in here this morning, dead as a doornail."

"You are kidding me! How did he die?"

"Looks like a heart attack. Now what? We lost our star suspect," Mitch complained.

"I can't believe this! Let me think for a minute. You know, on one hand, it probably almost doesn't matter. More than likely, he's just a small cog in a big wheel. But he sure would have been our easiest connection to figure out what's going on with the investments these people had. What do you think Larson is going to do?"

"I don't know. He was in here to see the body. He stopped to say hello and said he might have something relating to our conversation."

"Did he say what it was?"

"No, but he said he is going to be busy on it for the next few days. Then he'll stop by. He seemed pretty sure of himself, and he spent a lot of time confirming the details I gave him."

"I'll bet he did. What timeframe? Did he say?" Pete asked.

"No, but it sounded like it could be soon. I have a feeling two or three days. Why?"

"I don't know. We'll see, I guess." Pete wanted to think some more about these latest developments. "Look, I'll give you a call. You don't worry about a thing. Just get well. I want Helen to visit her sister in Philadelphia for a few days. Did she tell you?"

"Yeah, what's with that?"

"Just for safety's sake."

"What about the animals?" Mitch asked.

"We've got that covered. Rich Haywood's son, Bill, is coming over twice a day. You've done the same for them on different occasions, and they were more than willing."

"I know. Nice people. Make sure Helen is taken good care of."

"You know I will. This is the best thing for her." Pete was in effect "whistlin' by the graveyard," and Mitch knew it. They both did. With Helen's and Nora's safety accounted for, the forces at work would now only have to deal with Mitch, and maybe Pete, if they were really smart. Mitch knew he was a sitting target, and his conversation with Pete never mentioned it. But he knew he had the best ally in Pete, and the unsaid confidence was evident in their conversation's negative space; that is, they talked about everything but what was really on their minds: Mitch's vulnerable status.

"Pete, the ball is in the DA's court. Let's just wait a few days until we see what he does."

"Okay, but I want to put the ball in *our* court. We have to control this thing, or it will control us, whatever it is. I don't want to wait a few days. Let's see if we can get something accomplished in the meantime."

"What do you have in mind?"

"I want to save your butt, number one. I'm going to have you transferred out of that hospital. Doc Sheehan will have to agree. I won't tell him any of the details but enough about the danger you may be in to motivate his cooperation. You game?" Pete wasn't going to take "no" for an answer anyway.

"Wow! All right, if you say so. Where to?"

"You'll find out when you get there. I'm coming down to see Sheehan right now. We'll have you out of there in two hours. I'll feel a lot better, and you'll be a lot safer."

Pete made a few phone calls, and within a half hour had also discussed the matter with Doctor Sheehan. He had to agree. Pete made all the arrangements through an outside party. No one, not even Doctor Sheehan, was to know Mitch's whereabouts. Helen would be told of the change in plans as soon as Pete could confirm Mitch's arrival at his new location.

20

Pete stood at the hospital ambulance entrance with Doctor Art Sheehan as Mitch was loaded into the waiting unmarked ambulance. Doctor Sheehan gave the ambulance crew Mitch's medical records, along with an explanation of his recovery status. It was premature to move him like this, but under the guidance of Pete's cautions, it was definitely the lesser of two evils. The new attending physician would of course consult with him as needed, but only by way of a phone contact through Pete directly. The ambulance left quietly and made its way out of town.

"Doctor, will you let me know if anyone calls regarding Mitch? I mean anyone. You will be put on the spot when they want to know where he is. You obviously don't know, but we'll have to have an answer for them so that we can keep you out of this. Any suggestions?" Pete asked.

"Yes, I can simply say he's been taken to specialists at Hansen Medical. Hansen is a private hospital with no access by the public. Celebrities, politicians, and the like go there. There's no way anyone can call or visit without being on a guest list, and there's no way any outsider can find out who's there. It's a securely guarded facility, very safe and confidential."

"Sounds perfect." Pete had to widen his circle of trust by just one more person in discussing this to any degree with Doctor Sheehan, but he would find out for sure where the connections lay among the local cast of characters. "Believe me when I say this, Doctor: your cooperation is vital. I haven't told you much to protect you from any unnecessary involvement and for your own safety, but you can bet something is up; and we will know for sure when Mitch's absence is noted. By the way, my involvement is not to be mentioned."

"You are certainly mysterious, Pete. I hope this gets cleared up soon."

"It might be a while, but our mission is already a success; keeping Mitch safe, that is."

Pete handed the doctor a slip of paper. "Here are my cell and home numbers. Please call me when you get either a call or a visit regarding Mitch. And I mean right away. And I also mean no matter who it is, the very first person."

"Good luck, Pete."

"Thanks, Doc. And thanks for your help today. You may have saved a life."

Pete drove to one of the few pay phones he knew of in the small town. It was located in the Price Chopper supermarket, a few blocks from the hospital. He called Helen and explained everything. She was shocked, but grateful, once she had the full explanation. She too was asked by Pete to remain incognito. "Do not call anyone. Don't worry about the animals or the mail. Everything is being taken care of. The best thing you can do is remain quiet and out of contact." His admonition was very stern. "I will check on Mitch every day and call you. You are not to call me under any circumstances. There is no reason for you to talk to me. Do you understand?"

HYPOTHESIS

"Yes, but what if—"

"Helen, there are no *what if's*." Pete's tone was loudly intolerant of her question. "Do you understand?"

"Yes," she answered meekly.

"Helen, this is a matter of life and death: Mitch's, yours, Nora's, and mine." He absolutely hated to talk this way with Helen. It hurt him more than her, but it was necessary. He could hear crying on the other end. He felt absolutely lousy. "Is your sister there?" he asked.

"Yes."

"Can I speak with her?"

"Sure; Gina, Pete wants to talk to you." Helen handed her the phone.

"Hello Pete."

"Gina. How are you?"

"Fine. Thank you for all the wonderful help."

"Listen, I want you to take Helen's cell phone and remove the battery. Then put it away and don't ever use it. I want your landline number and your cell number. When I want to call Helen, I will only contact her through you. And I will only precede my conversation with a code number that you and I will now decide upon. Do you understand?"

"Yes."

"I suggest your birth date, month and day."

"April 30."

"Then its 430, understand?"

"Yes."

"How about giving me your phone numbers? I will use the cell primarily, but give me the home, too."

He wrote down the numbers and said, "I'm hanging up now. You can be sure that Mitch is safe. It is your job to do what I just said to keep Helen safe." He hung up without further conversation, not even able to imagine what Helen and Gina must be thinking.

He knew that anyone tracing Mitch's phone records could easily determine the two or three most commonly occurring calls, of which one would be Gina's. The only reason he felt secure about it was that Gina and Helen were not actually staying in Gina's Philadelphia home; instead, they were at her summer place on the Delaware shore. It would be a stretch to locate them there, at least for a few days.

Pete felt he had accomplished an awful lot, all in one day. Now he was free to be proactive. He might even be in control; of what, he did not know. He picked up some groceries in the store and returned to his car. His cell phone rang. It was Doctor Art Sheehan.

"Pete, you wanted to know if anyone inquired about Mitch."

"Yes, Doc, who was it?"

"Well, I don't know if it would be important, but Jim Davis talked to me a few minutes after you left. He's on staff here, and he's the county coroner, you know."

"Yeah, I'm aware of that. Interesting. What did he want to know?"

"He was just mainly curious why I would allow him to leave so soon. He knew how bad Mitch was. And he, of course, wanted to know where."

"What did he say when you told him?"

"Well, I had fine-tuned my answer for such a question from a medical peer after you left, and I told him that I felt some titanium screws were needed in the pelvis break as a result of a consultation I had with a doctor at Hansen, an old classmate of mine. That part is true, the classmate being there, I mean."

"You're great, Doc." Pete felt he finally had someone who could be trusted.

"Wait. There's another thing. A few minutes later I received a call from Larry Larson, district attorney. He said he had some information for Chief Mitchell, but he understood he wasn't here and wanted to know how to reach him."

"What did you say?"

"Same thing; I said it was not even possible for me to contact anyone there regarding a patient once he is enrolled. And as far as I'm concerned, he's enrolled."

"What happened then?"

"He wasn't too happy, but he didn't challenge the procedure."

"Was that it?"

"Yes. He thanked me and hung up."

"Thanks, Doc. You've been a big help."

Pete immediately thought of the ambulance, quietly ambling away in the opposite direction of Baltimore, Maryland, where Hansen Medical was located. His diversion was already at work.

21

Pete Woodard was clear to think things through now that he had all his birds in their nests, as it were. Mitch and Helen were in good hands, and Nora was safely out of town with her sister. His thoughts swam in a continuing swirl, passing the facts through his mind with each revolution. He loved puzzles, but they were never life and death exercises before; possibly his very own death. The added dimension was unnerving but exhilarating at the same time.

He had few resources at his command except for his own mind. Oddly enough, he felt he had an actual advantage. No one knew he was working on these details. He had the ability to orchestrate things as he had done earlier today. Best of all, his business negotiating skills had always been predicated on thinking about any issues from the other party's point of view. He mentally put himself in the other person's shoes, "on the other side of the table," he used to say. He never ceased to think about a situation in the other person's terms. It was what he did. He was an excellent mediator of differences as a result. He accomplished much in his day using this method. Now he would see how well this worked according to his growing suspicions.

HYPOTHESIS

Confirming first what had happened to date since Mitch initially reached outside of his small-town world for information, he thought out loud, *"Mitch goes to the DA for help with banking information; he gets limited help; he returns to discuss even more deaths and the Forbes connection, possibly with Gasco involved, and he gets run over by a truck on a clear day in plain view of any passing vehicles, and Larson was the only person who knew he would be there. The day after that, the subject of Mitch's conversation with Larson, Pratt, is found dead of a heart attack. Mitch lies in the hospital recovering for two days, and almost to the minute of removing him to the other location, two people inquire as to his whereabouts: the coroner who had pronounced the four Silver Lake victims dead, and the DA who was working on Mitch's information, but who had little time to confirm anything. Pratt, Larson, Willis, maybe Gasco—any one, or all, could be involved."*

He surmised, *The plan was to take advantage of the leaseholders by getting them to invest their recent wealth with Forbes. Senator Wellman could have at least helped that happen for some sort of political favor from Forbes. Then, by having each death appear as suicide, the insurance doesn't pay the insured amount to any heirs, and probably there is at least a major decrease in the value of the investment as far as any heirs would be told. Or the money isn't available at all for some reason. The investors' beneficiaries, who would probably be uninformed in these matters, would settle with little or no questions about the policies. Possibly some small amount would be allocated to placate heirs. However, and a big however, any heirs would be dealing through an attorney, and that attorney should be a safeguard to question the validity of any such scheme. So what's going on here? Unless ... there is only one possibility: the victims all have attorneys who are in on this.*

If I were the one doing this, I would have an attorney in on the deal. That attorney might have been Ed Wilkinson, but maybe he really did have an accident in the quarry. No, there are no coin-

cidences. It wasn't an accident. He was killed for a reason. What could it be? I should try to find out the attorneys for each of the victims and if they have a will, beneficiaries, relatives, or special arrangements. It will be difficult, but all that information is on file at any courthouse and is public information. However—and a big however, again—I could go to Wilkinson's office and start there. I could ask straight out if he handled the victims' wills and legal affairs; that is, if his office is still open ... probably not. Besides, that would just bring another person into the picture, and I'm not sure whom I can trust.

I have to lay low. So I can't do it myself. How to do this? This could be the key to the entire picture. Doc Sheehan! I can trust him. He's already been a help. Let me see if I can work it through him. He's got possible reasons to do some investigation like that as someone who may have been involved with the victims when they were processed at the hospital. No, I'll have to find another way. I'll save Doc as a backup in case I can't get it otherwise. Let me try something else.

Pete felt he was on to something. *I need to ... that's it!* He would call Sam Waterman, his lawyer in Michigan, and have his office contact the county clerk's office for information about the deeds on file.

His fingers couldn't dial the phone quickly enough. "Sam Waterman, please ... Pete Woodard calling. No, I can't wait. Tell him I need him on the phone now. It's an emergency ... thanks."

It seemed like an eternity until he heard back from the secretary. "Mr. Waterman will be right with you, Mr. Woodard. Thank you for holding."

"Pete, how have you been?" Waterman's high-pitched voice came across with exceptional clarity. He had done wonders for Pete in the past. They respected one another greatly and enjoyed working on matters together. Sam was the best of the best.

"Fine, Sam. Listen; we can catch up later, but I have an extremely important thing to get done today."

Sam knew that when Pete said something like that he wasn't exaggerating. Waterman was great at running with the ball with very little guidance. They were a good team. "Go ahead."

Pete gave Sam the short version of the situation with Mitch. Sam knew about Mitch's work with Pete on the Saunders murder a few years ago, so he engaged seriously with what Pete had to say.

"I need to have you call the county clerk's office and the register of wills in Susquehanna County, Pennsylvania and get everything you can for all the people involved. I need a copy of their wills, their attorneys' names, and the deeds to any properties they may own."

"That's a tall order for any courthouse. They don't exactly move too quickly, even for the local lawyers."

"We'll have to do the best we can. There's no way I can expose my involvement in this small town. The news would be all over the place in minutes, and I believe it would be dangerous."

"I know how it is." After a brief delay, he added, "Let's see; I have the name of a courier service out of Binghamton, New York, here in my listings. They are bonded and typically used in out-of-town situations. I'll set them up to go down there and personally wait for all the documents. I'll call the courthouse myself and get things started. I have a Larry Larson listed as the DA. Can he be of any help?"

"God no, I'm not sure if he's trustworthy enough! He could be implicated, from a standpoint of receiving political favors at the very least. Maybe not, but I'm not trusting anyone at this point."

"How can I get ahold of you?"

"You have my cell, but that's not reliable in this neck of the woods. I'm calling from my home if you can see that on caller ID."

"Got them both. Let me get on this. I'll get started today, but even tomorrow will be a minor miracle to get this done."

"Thanks, Sam. Just do the best you can. And, Sam, in case anything happens to me, you'll know about this and what to do."

"I already thought about that, Pete. Be careful."

Pete was not one to sit and wait. He thought, *There must be something I can do.* He brought the Forbes Web site up on his computer, and while it was interesting, it looked typical of any one of hundreds like it. The products included the standard stocks, bonds, money markets, and funds of all sorts with familiar-sounding names. The emphasis was undoubtedly on emerging markets in third-world counties, China, India, and Indonesia hardly being able to be referred to as third-world countries anymore. Life was changing quickly, and the products offered by Forbes Financial International, Inc., were sophisticated in their presentation, at least during the initial reading.

Pete thought, *Not much to be learned from the Web site. Let me click through on the links to the investment companies to look at the details.* Usually brokers such as Forbes relayed the details this way.

The first link didn't activate, nor did the second. The rest did not either; only the Forbes International Funds—there were three of them—had some linked information. Performance figures from previous years and fund manger data, the usual things. His impression was that maybe the links were terminated after the announcement of Pratt's death. But he still had offices in Wilkes Barre, and his office in Montrose was still open, although only with one employee.

He dared not inquire at that office now; maybe at a later date. *Not much to be found out on the Forbes Web site. Wait a minute!*

In a small corner of the home page he saw something startling as he closed out the window. He waited as it came back on the screen. When it did, it just about took his breath way. It was a small icon with the words, "Web design by Edwards Design, Tunkhannock, PA." He thought, *Again, there are no coincidences.*

So Edwards designed the Web site sales pitch and probably any brochures, forms, and sales documents used in the Forbes deals. I'm sure all those materials could stand some extra scrutiny by a professional in the business to see if they are legitimate. My guess is they are not. That's why Edwards was removed from the picture. More than likely, he knew too much. Now that we have a solid connec-

HYPOTHESIS

tion to Wyoming County, I wonder where Schultz fits in down there. Maybe not at all, but time will tell.

Pete decided to look for Edwards Design's web site and it came up on his screen immediately. It had the typical bio, products and services list, and a client list consisting mostly of local businesses. As Pete read through the names, he spotted the Forbes listing and another one that almost took his breath away, Senator Robert Wellman. He thought, *Senator Robert Wellman. It could mean nothing. But, there are no coincidences, period. Who would have thought this info could still exist by way of a back door like a dead guy's web site. I'll bookmark everything and make a printout right now before this disappears like his computer.*

Pete's dead time waiting for either Sam Waterman or Larry Larson to do something was fruitfully occupied. He felt very productive and relieved. He felt in control, and that is a powerful place to be. He thought, *I'll have to get samples of Forbes' literature firsthand. How can I do that now that he is dead? His Montrose office is under a microscope by the DA's office by now. Maybe I'll have the Wilkes Barre office send me what information they might have, but I don't know what to ask for. Nora would know. She probably has everything I would need. Let me think about that. I still want to remain in the shadows, and as far as she is concerned, I'm just here on vacation. I think for now I want to leave it that way. I'll ask Sam to request literature for the international funds when he calls back. That's it!*

Okay, what else can I do from my little hideaway here in the woods? One thing I better do is get a decent meal into myself and then get a good rest. Tomorrow is going to be a busy day. He drove over to the Tall Pines Players Club golf course and restaurant. The Wednesday night feature was prime rib marinated in a Greek-style garlic sauce. He fancied himself a prime rib aficionado, and this was one of his two favorite restaurants of all time. The owners and staff were the best, and he enjoyed visiting two or three times a week.

Nightfall and fresh sheets couldn't come soon enough. He was drained.

22

Forbes Scam Exposed

By Mary Michelson, Staff writer

Filed Tuesday, June 10, 2008
Published: Wednesday, June 11, 2008
Susquehanna County News

An investigative team headed up by District Attorney Larry Larson and Sheriff Ken Petersen has uncovered an alleged illegal investment scheme by Forbes Financial International, Inc., and its founder, Joseph Pratt. Pratt was found dead in his car three days ago at his Montrose office, the victim of an apparent heart attack. The Forbes company is a financial planning and investment organization headquartered in Wilkes Barre, specializing in international portfolios. According to District Attorney Larson, materials were discovered indicating illegitimate companies along with false brochures, investment forms, and web site programs linking funds transfers to the Cayman Islands, Bahamas, and Curacao.

Forbes Financial International is a privately held company founded in 1981 by Joseph Pratt. Until recently, its business was mostly conducted in Luzerne and Lackawanna Counties; however, recent investment activity relating to the proceeds from the Marcellus Shale gas well drilling encouraged Forbes, as well as many other investment firms, to open offices in Susquehanna County. Coincidently, Forbes' Montrose office was located in the same building as District Attorney Larson's private practice. "It was shocking to learn that such gross criminal activity was planned and conducted right under our very noses," said Larson. "Millions of dollars are involved and indications are it will hurt a lot of good people. We believe most of the funds may be unrecoverable based on the intricate off-shore transfers made. In particular, the backbone bank of the whole operation has indicated the institutions and accounts it transferred funds to don't exist anymore along with certain of their records."

State Senator Robert Wellman expressed his concern. "Forbes was one of the most highly regarded financial firms in the region. I have a personal stake in this company for some of my investments, and I thought I knew these people well, but apparently not. I caution everyone to be very guarded about both the familiar and newly established investment firms in our communities. Be sure to check with the State Attorney General's office to verify the legitimacy of any firm you are dealing with."

The full extent of the operation is not known. Forbes is an independent firm representing major brokerage and insurance companies. It is expected that only a portion of the firm's clients will be affected. The State Attorney General's office is currently conducting an audit of both of Forbes' facilities. Any investors with questions or information pertaining to Forbes or any of the funds it represents are asked to contact the Attorney General's office.

Pete was incredulous as he read the article. *How could Larson get so much information so quickly? How did he know so much in such a short period of time? Is there more to this than meets the eye? It looks like the case is solved. Is this all there is?* He thought about making a round of calls to Mitch and Helen. His plan was to drive to a payphone across from the firehouse a few miles from the lake. He needed to find out how Mitch was doing and relay that to Helen anyway. Mitch would appreciate hearing the news about Larson's incrimination of Pratt and the Forbes organization. He would tell him about the Edwards connection as the Web site designer for Pratt.

Mitch was resting when Pete called. "Mitch, how are things with you?"

"Actually, Pete, I really do feel great. Must be the drugs. They had me walking down the hallway this morning. I couldn't believe it." This was music to Pete's ears.

"Don't overdo it now. We need you back here, but only when you're at least your old 50 percent."

"Was I ever even that good? No kidding, though, I'm really feeling pretty good. I get tired easily, you know. It's the healing process, I guess. How's Helen holding up?"

"Just fine; I'll call her after I finish our conversation. I told her I'd call every day, and I will. While I think of it, do you need anything?"

"No, but thanks; just get me home as soon as you can."

"Well, that might be sooner than you think. It looks like Larson has confirmed your claims about Forbes and Pratt's financial dealings; I mean publicly, in the newspaper."

"Already? Either he works very fast, or he knew something all along...he knew something all along. I know he did. He had to."

"That's what I thought too. There wasn't a lot of detail, but it did indicate that they had a good amount of information. I mean, they must have in order to make such a statement. When you met with him, did he mention to you that he had other complaints or suspicions?"

"No, he just listened carefully and said he would get right on it. I guess he did. The quick timing is unusual, though. Don't forget that Pratt rented office space right in the same building as Larson's private office."

"Yeah, maybe so, but... oh, by the way, Larson was looking for you... almost right after you left in the ambulance. He told Doc Sheehan he had some information for you. Maybe that was it."

"Maybe he got Pratt's secretary to fess up."

"That's another possibility."

"Where did Doc Sheehan say I went?"

"He's a pretty smart guy. He said you were transferred to a private hospital where a specialist would put some screws in your pelvis, Hansen Medical in Baltimore. Sheehan said he was out of sorts about not being able to contact you. Hey, also, the coroner, Davis, asked about you too, right before Larson called. What do you think?"

"It's crazy. I'm with you. I'm not trusting anyone until this gets settled."

"Listen; I have my lawyer in Michigan doing some digging for us. I want to see the deeds and wills and anything else on public file for all of our victims. Let's see what that brings up."

"Good idea. The out-of-town-lawyer connection is perfect cover."

"Another thing: Senator Wellman was a client of Forbes. It seems like he's expecting a loss of his investments too. And guess who did the design work on the Forbes Web site?"

"If you tell me Edwards, I'm a believer in your 'no coincidences' philosophy."

"You are right on the money. Wellman had work done by him too, probably political things, but still there's a string of connections."

"Sonuvagun!" Mitch was flabbergasted by all the news. "You've been one busy guy."

"Well, if you're up to it, we can talk about the next step. But I don't want to interfere with your rest."

"Are you kidding? I'm going outta my skull here."

"Okay. I mean, I've gone about as far as I can go undercover. I think somehow we need to have you contact Larson to see what he had on his mind the other day or what might be developing. You know, just to keep the pot stirred a little bit. Or maybe we can find out if that's the end of things. I mean, are they also connecting them to the deaths, or is the Forbes thing isolated all on its own?"

"I still should maintain my cover, don't you think?"

"Oh yeah, you'll need to use a cell phone from a different area code. Can you get one?"

"No problem. There's a guy here from Florida. I heard him in the lobby earlier. It's the only place he was able to get a cell signal here, something to do with the wireless system around here, I suppose. I'll see if I can find him."

"That will be perfect. Give him twenty bucks for his trouble, make the call, and then tell him to turn the phone off when he leaves. He is just visiting, right?"

"He is. That's why I thought of him. He's leaving for Florida right from here."

"Perfect. Don't forget to put the call blocker on."

"Standard procedure, Pete."

"Okay, I suggest just calling Larson to see what he wanted you for. Then we'll see how it plays out after that. He should want to discuss the suicides."

"I'll do it right away."

"Remember, there are no outside calls allowed, so to speak. So you'll have to gin up a reason why you can't take a return call. Actually, just say, 'No calls, doctor's orders.'"

"I'll think of something. Sounds good just like you put it." Mitch felt as though he was back in the hunt.

"All right, I'll call you tomorrow."

When Pete arrived back home, there was a message from Sam Waterman. It said that he was sending the courier directly to his home with the information he requested. He should be there by four o'clock, which was fifteen minutes from now. The code number was the usual, which Pete knew were the last four digits of his social security number, 0627. They had used this system before a number of times.

Pete's attention was still on Mitch's safety. He felt there never could be an end to his concern for Mitch no matter what Larson found. It certainly was more than Mitch bargained for as a small-town policeman.

The knock on the door broke his thoughts. The courier left a stack of envelopes, along with her business card. He quickly got to work.

First, the Wilkinson files. He was anxious to see how a lawyer's affairs were organized. There were two deeds. One was for his home outside Montrose, three acres purchased in 1988. The other was for the 390 acres transferred to him, presumably upon his father's death in 1987. This one had the quarry on it. His will was recently updated; in fact, last year. The update referenced a landowner's organization agreement in the addendum. The beneficiary of his property in Montrose was St. Mary's Catholic Church, Montrose, Pennsylvania. The other beneficiary named for the 390 acres was the E.L. Rose Conservancy, a land conservation organization in Susquehanna County with properties in Silver Lake and other townships.

The addendum in the update superseded the Rose receivership in that it explained the property's membership in an organization with first claim as the Sow and Reap, Inc., consortium. Sow and Reap would inherit the property as part of the organization's members' commitment to one another for a mutual benefit involving a gas well investment the members made as a group. This partnership agreement was to be in effect for six years—which was February 2, 2013—at a minimum, or if the group disbanded by mutual consent, whichever came first. His successor in case of his death was a niece named as Kathleen Wellman, Tunkhannock, Pennsylvania. Pete remembered that Senator Wellman's wife was mentioned at Sam Burns' fundraiser as being Wilkinson's niece. Then the beneficiary receivership would revert to the original E.L. Rose Conservancy as a long-term commitment. It seemed as though Wilkinson was working in cooperation with some other people for their mutual benefit and that each party wanted certain long-term guarantees for their monetary commitments, whatever they may be.

The addendum contained a copy of the Sow and Reap Agreement, which described an investment arrangement among—and Pete stammered as he read the names aloud, talking to himself as he was prone to do—*Jane and Henry Morson, John and Charlotte Carpenter, William Danields, Nora Connely, Edward Wilkinson, and John Nordstrom.* It further included "their successors or assigns." Wilkinson appeared to be the author of the agreement, as was noted in one of the clauses and agreed upon by all participants as not having any conflict of interest. Officers were listed as Nora Connely, President; Professor John Nordstrom, Houston, Texas, Vice President; Jane Morson, Treasurer; Edward Wilkinson, Secretary. The description of the organization's purpose was "to collaborate on a mutually beneficial mineral rights extraction process to be funded in part by the members and in part by a grant that was seeking both state and federal approval." The rest of the document was general in nature, but Pete was able to at least infer that the participants, as a group, were to be committed to one another for a period of six years, after which time any previous beneficiaries would be considered unless the agreement were extended by unanimous participation.

Pete was dumbfounded. *Is this literally the smoking gun? What God-awful inferences can be made from this? My God!*

HYPOTHESIS

The next envelope had to be Nora Connely's. She was so close to Mitch, and Helen and never said a word, which, as he thought about it, was no one else's business, he had to admit. Her deed was still listed as including her late husband's name. Her will was recently updated to name her sister as primary beneficiary; obviously this was done after the recent death of her husband. The will also had an addendum similar to Ed Wilkinson's, naming her sister, Carol Wherthing, as the beneficiary and partner in the Sow and Reap agreement unless the agreement terms were vacated. This meant, essentially, that Sow and Reap was in control of the property as a consortium until it ended its authority over the land, including the home, but that since her sister was planning to live at the home soon, she would be a successor to Nora's claims. The will was filed by attorney Edward Wilkinson. Now Pete felt there was something to be considered among all these facts.

It was a toss up which envelope to study next. He chose Jane Morson's. The property deed was listed as owned by John and Jane Morson. Beneficiaries in their joint will were the E.L. Rose Conservancy. Again, like Wilkinson's will, an addendum was filed explaining that the Rose Conservancy could only exercise receivership after a six-year minimum or upon vacating of the agreement by the Sow and Reap members. Another attorney had filed the original will many years ago as a basic document, but Wilkinson had filed a new will with the Sow and Reap addendum last year.

This is getting more and more interesting, Pete said to himself.

Bill Danields had deeds on file for the building that housed his dental office in downtown Montrose and also for his home on Nasar Road in Silver Lake. He appeared to not have a will prior to his membership in the Sow and Reap consortium. Ed Wilkinson had filed a simple will on his behalf, primarily assigning his property in Silver Lake to the consortium and then afterward to the local Community Foundation of Susquehanna County. His home and his business assets were both assigned to the local community foundation as primary beneficiaries. He had no relatives named in the will. Pete thought, *What a lonely statement of a man's life this is.*

The last envelope contained the details of Lottie Carpenter's life. Hers was the simplest of all. She had named, of all people, Nora Connely as sole beneficiary of her estate. It was a recent will, updated just two years ago, initially naming Nora Connely as beneficiary and then updated a year later by none other than Ed Wilkinson by adding the Sow and Reap addendum.

"Talk about following the money," Pete said out loud to himself. "My God, this is a straight road to Miranda Rights time. What in the hell is going on here?"

Pete had a lot on his plate, all in a matter of forty-five minutes of reading. *We have four local Silver Lake people dead and two others who could be somehow related. We have Nora Connely, who seems to turn up in the geographic center of everything I look into. We have a dead financial planner who sold investments to future dead people as a way to just about guarantee their deaths. We have a quick-draw DA who seems to know what is going on before it even happens. And we have a nosey coroner who pops up on a more-than-normal basis. I'm calling Mitch.*

"Mitch, Pete. Have you connected with Larson yet?"

"No, they've been sticking needles in me since I got off the phone with you, and to tell you the truth"—he paused—"I'm feeling really drowsy right now."

"Hang in there. Do you feel like talking?"

"Sure. I'll be all right. What's up so soon?"

"I got all the courthouse records, the deeds, wills, and a real surprise, an agreement among all the Silver Lake victims." Pete went on to tell Mitch the details of his find.

"Nora Connely has an agreement? With all those people? And Wilkinson to boot? Five people in an agreement and four of them die recently? Now I'm really concerned for her."

"Well, maybe, maybe not," Pete advised. "I still have to think about this, but would you agree that there is still a lot missing? That Larson still must not be at the bottom of this whole thing?"

"You're right. What's on your mind?"

"I still would like to see what comes of your conversation with Larson, but don't call him until I can check out a few more things, probably tomorrow. I'll let you know when."

"All right, whatever you say."

"Mitch, for now, just get some good rest, and I'll be in touch."

23

County Sheriff Ken Petersen had been in office for almost two years. His military police background and thirty years of tough international government service, although known to all, was not the least evident by way of his mild manner. Assuring and commanding, he gave the impression that the job would get done, period. Laying much below his capabilities, the daily responsibilities of a rural county sheriff rarely went beyond the typical court ordered foreclosures and trial summonses. However, Susquehanna County is over eight hundred square miles comprised of all small towns connected by a network of two-lane roads, making just the travel time to and from locations needing attention a formidable task for him and two deputies. Overall, it was enjoyable work, rewarded in little recognition other than when running for reelection, a component of the position he thought of as demeaning. He was not a big fish in a small pond, but rather, as he viewed it, one of the biggest small fish in a very small pond.

HYPOTHESIS

District Attorney Larry Larson had called Sheriff Petersen to meet solely to discuss their next approach for the Forbes mess. Larson intended the sheriff to take the lead on the matter, knowing full well that the state attorney general, the State Insurance Commission, and the FBI would soon become heavily involved. He wanted to gather as much factual information as possible, as soon as possible, and establish a direction that could be easily followed up and straightforwardly resolved. Most important, he wanted Petersen to handle it without his involvement.

"Larry, I welcome the change of pace, but to track this thing down much further is going to take a lot of time and expertise that I simply don't have right now. I think we've done enough," Petersen began.

"Our job is almost done already anyway. But this little crime spree can be good for both of us. You and I are both employed politically by the voters. I think we're in good shape in that regard, but I don't want to leave anything to chance by passing up this once-in-a-lifetime opportunity to make hay, if you know what I mean."

"I do, but I guess I don't care about it as much as you. You're the younger guy on his way up. I'm just glad to do the community some service and have a comfy little second career before my golden years."

"That's just it. With a little effort, and I mean very little, we can set this up to be a coup for both of us. Let me be clear. I really want to do a good job on this one: thorough, no loose ends, and a professional handoff to the state—and probably the feds, the way this is looking."

"Yeah, I hear what you're saying."

"Mitch had it mostly figured out about all the deaths involved, and he pretty much linked the investment scam with each one before he had the accident. The least we can do is pick up where he left off. We have some resources. I guess the question is: do we have the interest?"

"We have the interest; I can assure you that. But what more do you think we can handle? The guy did it, and that's that, isn't it?" asked Petersen.

Larson felt he had turned the corner and gotten some buy-in from the sheriff. "We have already established the financial wrongdoing by following Mitch's lead and simply talking to Pratt's secretary, Martha Hayes. I want to structure any further information along these lines," he began. "First, among the three or four normal deaths each month around here, Mitchell noticed a higher than normal number and that more of them were suicides than ever before. Second, he identified three suicides and one accident victim, Wilkinson, in Silver Lake alone, and another suicide by a guy named Schultz in Tunkhannock. All of them had benefited from a gas lease. Third, Forbes was involved in some sort of investment package with all of them except Wilkinson. Fourth, since all of the Silver Lake suicide victims' properties were connected with one surviving resident, Nora Connely, he felt her life may be in danger too. That, I don't necessarily agree with, especially now that Pratt is dead, but we can look into it. Finally, he determined that Pratt may have had something to do with all the suicides and maybe the Wilkinson accident. I tend to agree, and the info you got from Pratt's secretary after his death leads me to believe he had this well orchestrated."

"Pratt wasn't the only one involved," Petersen added.

"You're definitely right. This stuff goes international. Who knows where it ends? That part is beyond us. Do you think there is anyone else involved locally?"

"It's hard to say. So what more can we can do?"

Larson sensed an opportunity, but he wanted Petersen to figure it out for himself. "That's why we're here today. We have a search warrant. Let's make the most of it."

"Well, I guess we can just go in there and talk some more with Martha. I can go through his appointment book and travel records, maybe credit card history, to establish a record of what went on for, say, the last year."

Larson was ecstatic. Petersen had taken over. It was his discovery. Any further discoveries, and Larson was sure there would be more, would find authoritative endorsement from Petersen. "I'll get you whatever you need from the courts. When do think you want to start to finalize it?"

"I'll handle it with Martha this afternoon, and I'll bring some help from my office to catalog things as we go along."

Larson felt if he could let Petersen work one-on-one with Pratt's secretary it would be more productive. They would both convict Pratt and implicate someone out of the county, if not out of the country, by discovering the evidence where Martha probably already knew to find it. They would do it independently of his direct involvement and in a convincing way.

"Let's plan to meet again tomorrow before the end of the day. This way I might have something for the AG and the press. They've both been hammering me for more info."

After Petersen left, Larson continued combing through every detail of each victim's death. He had police reports and coroner's reports on each one. They were all different, no similar modus operandi, but they were mysteriously premature suicides regarding age, social well-being, and, in particular, the wealth of a substantial gas lease payment. The other common thread was their Forbes investment that was derived from a Gasco International lease payment. The sheriff's work was sure to reinforce that. After a few hours that same afternoon, and much sooner than he expected, he received a call from Petersen. "Larry, are you coming back to your office today?"

"I can. What do you need?"

"I'm right next door in Pratt's office with Martha. She told me everything. Can you come right over?"

"I'm on my way." He walked the short city block from the courthouse to his office. Sheriff Petersen was sitting in Pratt's office with Martha, who was crying uncontrollably.

"Martha and I just had a little chat," announced Petersen. "It's pretty emotional for her, as you can see."

"Martha, we're not here again to make you feel uncomfortable," Larson said, although that was a lie. He wanted her to feel the full strength of the two legal representatives she was facing. He needed to extract all the facts available as soon as he was able. "We just want you to help Sheriff Petersen as he goes through these things, and you are the best person under the circumstances." She continued to cry without saying a word.

"She already has," Petersen answered. "We started examining the list of alleged investment victims, and almost as quick as we began, Martha volunteered some suspicions about the international funds."

"And?"

"Well, if I got it right—and, Martha, you correct me if I'm wrong—Pratt was dealing with offshore funds in the Caribbean, Bahamas, Curacao, those sort of places, and all the people we are looking at who came up dead one way or another invested in them. That's not all. It seemed to Martha that the investment documents, the brochures, the contracts didn't come from those fund managers like their other funds."

"What do you mean?" Larson prompted.

"Hold on; there's more. The monthly investment reports that were mailed out to their clients weren't sent by the funds themselves, as with all their other funds. Instead, Pratt prepared the report on forms that were sent to a mail forwarding service in Philadelphia. He said it made them look more professional."

"But most of this we know already," Larson said.

"The best is yet to come. You all right, Martha?" Petersen directed his look to her. She nodded. "Martha has indicated to me

HYPOTHESIS

that possibly all the literature, forms, contracts, and reports were produced locally by a graphics company down in Tunkhannock, none other than Edwards Design."

"Edwards is that other guy who fell off the roof of the theater a few months ago."

"Or did he? Fall that is," Petersen added.

"So what you're saying is Pratt was selling investments using documents that he created himself. Then he was issuing monthly reports that he created himself rather than a legitimate fund manager. So are we saying that he was a lone eagle on this whole deal? He sent the money offshore. He must have had some outside help."

"Probably so; here is a file of his bank record for the last twelve months. It shows deposits from Northeast Penn, care of Forbes International Investments, Inc., to a Forbes account."

"Okay, I see that. But it now has a $920 balance, even though it appears like roughly three plus million dollars in deposits were made," Larson observed as he studied the document.

"Three million four hundred and twenty-seven thousand to be exact," added Petersen.

"So where did it go?"

"That's just it. It was wired supposedly to an international fund named Car 3, but it seems that such a fund doesn't exist, at least according to Martha. She has been nosing around little by little over the past two months, but Pratt handled all those transactions. She handled everything else. Car 3 stood for Caribbean Third World Emerging Markets Fund. That, apparently, was a specialty of Forbes; third-world investments, that is."

Larson was waiting for the connection to the deaths, but nothing was happening in the conversation to indicate further information. "What else?"

"Well, here's the bombshell. Martha and I have pulled the phone records for this year back to January. That includes office landlines and Pratt's cell phone. We also have Pratt's appointment book for the same period. Now watch this. We also have investment proposals for all of the five suicide victims and Wilkinson, and we have four signed agreements. Wilkinson had never signed before he died. We have lined up the dates of the proposals, the dates of the signed agreements, and the dates in Pratt's appointment book."

"I can guess that they all match, right?" Larson concluded.

"Au contraire, monsieur," Petersen anticipated quickly. "They don't match at all."

"What?"

"Exactly! Wouldn't you think that someone who was booking upward of a half million dollars worth of investment contracts at a time would have some record of his calls and his personal visits to these people? In fact, it's just the opposite. There is absolutely no record of appointments. There are no phone calls. The only date record we have is what Mitch found out at the banks when he was able to see that the checks were written to Forbes. In each case, when you look at those dates, they were all the same as the investment contracts, at least for three of the four victims, Schultz being the exception. Schultz's money must been wired directly to Car 3, according to the payment notation in his file."

"This is still all circumstantial," Larson summarized.

"I knew you'd say that," Petersen answered. "Now for the coup de grace."

"You mean there's more? You two have been busy." Larson was trying to calm Martha down. "You okay, Martha?"

"Better, Mr. Larson," she finally spoke while continuing to wipe her tears. "It's been difficult."

"It seems like Pratt's work in developing the brochures and forms didn't have much of a paper trail either. The only way Martha knows about Edwards Design is that he delivered some brochures personally one day and then had a closed-door conversation with Pratt. There are no invoices or check ledger records of payments to him. She assumes it was all a cash deal. When he heard of his death, it didn't seem to affect Pratt. You would think that someone he did business with would deserve some sort of comment, but there was none."

"Do you have any of those brochures here?"

"That's another thing; nothing is here. There is nothing to be found!" Petersen claimed.

"Sounds fishy to me. Can we get a copy from the Wilkes Barre office?" Larson requested.

"Sure, I'll call down and ask," Martha answered.

"Well, you both have had a very productive afternoon. But, Ken, I'm afraid it's still all circumstantial. On a civil trial basis, there is probably plenty of proof. But criminally, we have nothing."

"I know the law, but this isn't about a trial. The guy is dead. We need to put this thing to bed as best we can and move on. It's over," Petersen officially pronounced.

Larson enjoyed hearing that. "You two have done an admirable job." Larson, concealing his patronization as much as possible, but still wanting them to feel as though they were accomplishing these discoveries on their own, added, "But we still need a tighter connection."

Martha finally spoke, and she spoke with a vengeance. "He said he loved me, and now I know he was just out for himself."

Larson and Petersen were taken aback at the turn in her composure. "He killed them. I'm sure of it, and I'll tell you why."

"Go ahead, Martha. We're listening," said Petersen.

"Joe was a wonderful, loving man." Now she began to get misty eyed. "He said we would retire to the Caribbean together, and I believed him. But as this gas lease thing evolved so quickly in the last few months, he paid less and less attention to me. He was in another world. At first, I thought it was just business. He was a very hard worker, you know. But he began to have a lot of closed-door conversations, more than normal. He never used to close his door. I listened in a few times when we would receive a call from the Bahamas. All I can tell you is that they were transferring funds without reporting it to the federal government.

"At that point, I became worried and he became more distant. He said it was the strain of the gas lease prospects. If he didn't work quickly, someone else would get the business. I understood that, but I could tell something mysterious was going on. This all started after Mr. Schultz died. There were more conversations after Mrs. Morson and Dr. Danields died. Then after Mrs. Carpenter died, I was sure there was a connection. The reason I know it is that on the day of her suicide, she called here to confirm her appointment with Joe that evening. He had already left for the day. So all I could say was that if she didn't hear to the contrary from him, then he would be there. Two days later, she too was found dead. So what I'm saying is that I can place him at the death of Mrs. Carpenter from her own words over the phone. How do you think I can do that? As she was talking to me, she said, 'Oh, here he comes up the driveway now.' He must have been late, and that was the reason for her call. It was quarter to five when she called."

"I'm afraid it's still all circumstantial, but you know, Larry, you're not in a trial mode here. You're just trying to establish a basis for others to finish up with, and I think we've done our job," Sheriff Petersen commented. "We have a ribbon and a bow on this thing, and we are almost finished, at least for the major items. We can connect the financial scheme. The suicides, accidents, murders, whatever they were, are probably part of it. We can wrap this up whatever way you want, but I'm convinced Pratt is the local kingpin. Whatever he had going on internationally will have to be handled by the feds. What do you think?"

"You're right. I think it can be wrapped up right there. Martha, go home and get some rest. We really appreciate your help. Are you going to be all right?"

"Thank you, Mr. Larson. I'll be fine. I just need to take a few things with me." She was crying and having trouble catching her breath, gasping loudly.

"Martha, if it's all right with you, we'd rather leave everything as it is," Sheriff Petersen requested.

"Oh sure, I just have a few personal items, nothing important."

"Can we give you a ride home?"

"No, thank you, Sheriff. I have my car. I'll be all right." She left.

"Ken, what do think?" Larson asked.

"We have as clear a case as we are going to get. The financial side is backed up with everything we need. The deaths are tied in as best as we can determine. We have an open-and-shut case."

"Give me your report as soon as you can. I plan to issue something to the press tomorrow based on what I heard today. Are you okay with that?" Larson asked.

"I'm fine as long as you agree."

"Yes, and I'll start on my report to the attorney general. The financial side is ironclad, I feel. We still need to lock in more facts on the deaths; you know, motive, means, and opportunity. I'm seeing all three to some degree, but I don't think we'll ever put Pratt at the scene of any of the deaths, other than maybe the Carpenter woman."

"I think it's the best they can expect. If the feds want to chase down the international side, then they've got a good start. For my guess, they have bigger fish to fry."

"Let's call it a day," Larson sighed.

24

Forbes probe may include six killings

By Mary Michelson, Staff writer

Filed: Monday, June 16, 2008
Published: Wednesday, June 18, 2008
Susquehanna County News

Susquehanna County Sheriff Ken Petersen has brought forth further information today allegedly connecting the deaths of six local residents to the Forbes International Investments firm, with headquarters in Wilkes Barre and offices in Montrose. In a report to District Attorney Lawrence Larson, the morbid scheme included the sale of fraudulent investment plans from non-existent Caribbean firms known as the "Car 3 Fund," Caribbean Third World Emerging Markets Fund. It is alleged that Joseph Pratt, who died recently from a heart attack, acting as CEO of Forbes, profited from falsified sales of investments and insurance policies issued by "Car 3" and transferred investments out of the country to foreign banks.

HYPOTHESIS

Of significant note, five investors' deaths have been connected to Forbes and investigations are continuing. Another death may be related due to extenuating circumstances. Clients of the investment scheme were all recent recipients of gas well lease proceeds from Gasco, Inc., a Houston, Texas, energy exploration company. Forbes, Inc. specialized in international third world investments, and it is alleged that many of Forbes's clients were assured of double-digit returns from this investment segment.

District Attorney Lawrence Larson has submitted a comprehensive report to the state Attorney General's office describing the recent events and offering his opinion as to how to proceed. It appears that with the death of Joseph Pratt a week ago any local prosecutions are suspended, and that each of the victim's deaths will be reconciled with the county coroner's offices in Susquehanna and Wyoming Counties. Further investigations are expected to be handled on a state and federal level as they may relate to international trade and monetary exchange regulations.

Investors in the alleged scheme have been identified as Robert Schultz, of Tunkhannock; Jane Morson, Charlotte Carpenter, and Dr. William Danields, of Brackney; and attorney Edward Wilkinson of Bridgewater, all of whom had been previously judged to have died by suicide or, in the case of Dr. Wilkinson, an accidental fall. Another possibly related death in the scheme is Joseph Edwards, of Tunkhannock, who was a vendor of marketing materials to the Forbes firm and who was previously presumed dead of a fall from the roof of the Dietrich Theater in Tunkhannock. The unusual occurrence of extreme deaths came to the attention of DA Larson from Brackney Chief of Police Jim Mitchell. Chief Mitchell is recovering from a hit and run auto accident along Route 167, and is said to be rehabilitating strongly. His diligence is noted by DA Larson and the community is much in debt to his service. Larson expects state and federal agents to reconcile the events which have international implications.

In further news of these events, the Wilkes Barre headquarters of Forbes International Investments, Inc. and its Montrose office have been seized by FBI agents for extended investigations. Any questions that investors may have are requested to be addressed to the State Attorney General's office in Harrisburg.

District Attorney Larry Larson leaned back in his reclining office chair and folded the newspaper neatly to crop the Forbes article before laying it on his desk to view. He read it over and over, critiquing each and every detail for its accuracy and the sense of direction it would give the feds now that they had assumed the case. The press release appeared just as Larson had written it. His slate was almost clean. Any further notoriety would deflect the workings of the case from his involvement to Sheriff Ken Petersen, just as he had intended. Petersen's work with Pratt's secretary had been perfect in establishing a barrier between him and anything to do with Pratt. All was well as far as he was concerned.

25

"Hi, Pete; mission accomplished," Mitch's phone call announced.

"Tell me one thing and one thing only. Other than 'How are you feeling,' what else did he say?" Pete knew what to expect from Mitch's talk with Larson, although Mitch had no idea why he asked the question the way he did.

"He said two things, actually."

"Just give me one."

"He wanted to know when I was coming back."

"I thought so. Just for the record, what was the other one?"

"He praised Petersen's efforts in digging up the details."

"That's to be expected, I guess."

"What next, my friend?" Mitch asked.

"You're coming back tomorrow, and Helen will be back too, I suppose."

"Right."

"You probably should tell Nora that it's okay to return."

"Oh, she's back already. She only stayed a few days. Just

enough time to get away and relax a little, she told Helen. Now that Pratt was dead, she figured everything was all right."

"Really? After all our planning and worrying about her?" Pete wondered. "Mitch, I'd like you and Helen to stay with me for a while. For one thing, my house is all on one level and that would be easier on you than those stairs at your farmhouse. Second, it will be safer for all of us until we are satisfied that the Forbes thing is all wrapped up. I've got lots of room. So that's no problem. And it will give us some quality time so that we can work out a few more details that are still bothering me. What do think?"

"It's fine with me if it's okay with Helen."

"Mitch, it's not up to Helen."

"Oh, I see. Then... we'll do it."

"Here's what we'll do. I'll come over to pick you up. Little did anyone know that you're only a few miles away at the Addison House, the best bed and breakfast ever, nurse-owner included with the deal."

"We owe 'Nurse Ratchett' a lot," Mitch answered. . "She has me walking and exercising whether I want to or not. The food's not bad either."

"I'll be over for you tomorrow around 10:00 a.m. I think you should call Helen yourself on Gina's cell phone and let her know that you're doing well. She'll be glad to hear from you personally after all these days. See if she wants to come home, and if so, she will be coming right to my house. We'll have someone pick her up."

"Will do."

"Another thing, Mitch: tell her I checked on the animals myself yesterday and they are all fine. They're being well cared for."

"I think she's more worried about them than about me."

"See you soon, my good friend; I have some things to do before you get here. For one, I need to get a real food order from the market. We won't survive on what I keep around here."

"Pete, do me a big favor. Will you make your lentil soup? We love it."

"For you, anything."

"Well then, I'd like to add—"

"Never mind, one request at a time."

Pete knew that Mitch was going to request his delicious butter rolls, which he would also include as a surprise. *It is time to kick back and relax a little,* he thought, *and this is the perfect occasion.*

26

The next morning unveiled a glorious Pennsylvania day, one that epitomized the reason Pete came back to visit each summer. He adjusted the passenger seat in his car to the rearmost position and went into the Addison House bed and breakfast to pick up Mitch. Victorian antique décor was the dominant theme, so much so that you could forget what century existed outside in the real world.

'Nurse Ratchett', Holly Evans, insisted on some breakfast for the two of them before leaving. Her prognosis was good in that she would give Mitch a clean bill of health in another two weeks if he kept up his exercises. The scale of her small size next to the hulk of Mitch while she warned him to take heed of her advice was a heartwarming Norman Rockwell scene. She really cared about him, and he respected all she had done for him, and it showed both ways. Actually, she was prepared to discuss Mitch's care with Dr. Sheehan, whom she had been in constant contact with at his home, the one leap of faith Pete allowed in trusting someone, and it seemed to have paid off.

HYPOTHESIS

Mitch buried Mrs. Evans in the biggest bear hug ever, to the point where she couldn't even be seen in the envelopment of his arms and embrace. Pete loaded Mitch and his bags into the car and came back inside to discuss compensation arrangements with Mrs. Evans before leaving. She was more concerned for Mitch than any monetary considerations and would not hear of such talk. Pete wrote a very handsome check and said he would handle any balance through Dr. Sheehan. He bent low to give her a kiss of recognition for her compassion, and he felt that she truly thought it alone was to be enough for her services.

She smiled through watery eyes and waved to them from the picketed porch as they backed away from their parking spot and began the five-mile drive to Pete's home at Silver Lake. Once there, they were greeted by the smell of ham hocks, vegetables, and lentil beans simmering in the soup pot as they opened the door.

Mitch maneuvered fairly well, but with a pronounced limp of the right leg. It was still in the cast, and he wore oversized shorts with a slit up the outside so that he could get into them. They made their way to the landing overlooking the lake and took in the view. It was one where words did not need to be spoken, for a few moments at least. Silver Lake was one of the most beautiful places on Earth. Everyone who has ever been here agrees. Peaceful, idyllic, quiet natural surroundings under eighty-foot-tall hemlock pines drain the anxieties and stresses from the body and replace them with sedative effects that can almost make the body go limp. *This is just what Mitch needs after his ordeal,* Pete thought. He would do his best to help his best friend recover and regain the strength of his former self.

"Relax with your feet up. Take a nice nap when you want. I'll make us some tea and be right back," Pete offered.

He returned to find Mitch asleep, and when he turned to leave him, he heard, "Not so fast, partner! When are we going to talk about the case?" Mitch was on guard, even when he was sleeping.

"Now, if you want. I have lots of questions and no one to bounce them off of," Pete replied.

"Me too; I've had a lot of time to think, and maybe I'm crazy, but I think there's still a loose end or two."

"Or three or four," Pete added. "I have some things that don't fit, and you know I don't want to try too hard to force them into what we already know. They may have another home. You know what I mean?"

"I do. Let me start with a couple of things," Mitch began. "For one thing, Larson found out an awful lot of facts in a very short period of time. Granted, he has the resources with the sheriff's department and all, but still it was a minor miracle to wrap that thing up so fast."

"I thought the same thing," Pete added.

"Another thing: Northeast Penn Bank had to cooperate in wiring that money, especially if there was no reporting."

"Agree." Pete was enjoying seeing Mitch back on his game. *It has to be good for him,* he thought.

"Here's another thing. Larson said he received a call from the feds who were at the quarry when they called. I know that is a cell phone dead spot even along the highway at that location and of course, down in the quarry."

"I didn't know he said that. But you're right. I remember that they had to go for help during your accident. The guy's cell phone didn't work."

"It's just got a lot of loose ends, hard to explain as far as I'm concerned," Pete added. "The other thing I noticed, mainly because I had my ear to the ground listening for something, was that a few people were unusually interested in your whereabouts and your return, namely Larson, Doc Davis, and of course, Nora."

"Well, they are all people who are friends, and it's probably natural, you know."

"I mean, it can be expected. These are your friends, and they care about you. I'm probably reading too much into that, but I wanted to mention it."

"I think I need to get in front of Larson just to see for myself if I feel good about this thing being over. I somehow have to put it behind us. You know what I'm saying?"

"I do, and I think what you just suggested fits into something I'm thinking about. Why don't you call Larson and let him know that you're back home? Call him from your cell phone so he doesn't have a fix on your whereabouts. He'll assume you're at home. If he wants to have a meeting, tell him it might be a while until you are more mobile and can get down to his office. But if he wants to meet sooner, it can be at your house early next week. Tell him to call on your cell phone because you can't get up to answer the house phone easily. This way when he calls, you can answer it here."

"What do we do when he wants to come to the house?" Mitch asked.

"I can drive you over and leave you there for the meeting."

"What are we going to accomplish by all of this?"

"For one, you are letting him know you are home, or at least he will think you are there. Also, you can just drop those questions on him about the quick discovery period, the bank wires, and the cell phone call from the quarry. Another thing: we can find out who else is working on this."

"Well, why don't I make the call right now?" Mitch suggested. He dialed Larson's direct line from the phone's memory list, and Larson's answering machine took Mitch's message. "Larry, it's Mitch. I'm home now, and I promised to call as you requested. Let's plan to get together when convenient for you. Sometime early next week is best for me; afternoons are better than mornings." As ended the call, Mitch remembered that DAs were usually busy in court and with appointments in the mornings.

"I really want to see you cross this hurdle before Helen returns. Then maybe we can all relax and put this to bed. Mitch, I have some people—" Pete halted his conversation when he saw that Mitch was dozing off in the soft sunlight beaming through the pine branches above. He knew the wondrous intoxication of it all, having fallen victim to it many times himself. It was just as well. He had some arrangements to make, and he wanted some time this morning to get them set up.

There was nothing in the world like it. You could lose two hours of your life dozing off in the late afternoon sunlight of Silver Lake. The soft northwest breeze wafted over the lake, hypnotizing anyone relaxing on the eastern shoreline in its path. It was soothing, calming, more than could ever be imagined—a relaxing opiate, it is simply something that cannot be described; it has to be experienced.

27

Evening settles in around Silver Lake in late June with a pronounced change in temperature. The golden glow from the west transforms the fields through a kaleidoscope of soft colors as the evening breeze is sifted through tall grasses and gently billowing trees. The muted sounds of birds become silenced with the approaching darkness. All signs of day are held at bay, waiting for the symphony of night creatures that are free to express themselves without reserve.

Stillness comes first, followed by periodic rustling of small creatures along the floors of the fields and forests. As if by rehearsal, an amphibious curtain call of frogs, toads, and crickets harmonizes in a chorus of melodious mating sounds in synchronous rhythm. As light fails, the quartets resonate into an orchestral strain interrupted only by the occasional passing of a nocturnal mammal: a deer, raccoon, or other such travelers of the night. The traffic is quiet and purposeful, each seeking sustenance in its own special way of survival.

As dusk transitions to full darkness on the moonless night, the décor of the sky is dominated by a spectacular glitter of luminance such that is only experienced in rural desolation. The occasional lament of coyotes' bays can be heard in the distance, sometimes in chorus as yips and yells typical of family groups warning of their territorial holdings. The entire orchestration is surreal when viewed firsthand and primal in its essence. Rural life is seen by many but experienced only by a few.

Police Chief Jim Mitchell's home sat in a lightly wooded meadow cleared for a distance of about seventy-five yards on all sides and surrounded by a forest of deciduous and pine trees. First-growth hemlocks were prevalent; maples, oaks, black cherry, and others strove to reach upward among them. The simple clapboard style with large porch was typical of the farms in this northeast region. A small barn sat to the side, once housing the machinery that kept the pulse of the site alive; but now it was a simple reminder of its former life and the home of two horses, two cats, a barn owl, and visitors of all types from time to time. A foundation of fieldstone sat behind it, indicating the large number of dairy cows that were housed there in years past. Next to the house stood an old well, complete with a covered pulley and rope system and even a satisfactory level of water at most times.

As night enveloped the quaint homestead, the lights downstairs dimmed and a bedroom light radiated from the upper level. An occasional shadow indicated movement and the lights diminished, and a soft glow from the kitchen remained as a lone faint beacon in the void.

The surrounding vegetation teemed with quiet activity with the cacophony of life striding in place, going nowhere, but in a hurry. Darkly shrouded human forms hunched over and made their way toward the barn. The cadence of crickets on this summer evening was true to form with a *ratchety-ratch* sound of a constant background concert, and then they stopped suddenly in deference to the visitors in their midst. Everything was quiet for a while, and then the opus began anew. Viewing this scene and the human movement was a third person watching from a prone position just inside the tree line bordering the west field section. One short radio communication confirmed everyone's position.

The night watch began for the second day in a row, with all participants vigilant for the slightest extraordinary activity. Bushnell night vision binoculars scanned wide angles of the topography from the two posts. It was tedious work given to boredom and the infinitesimally slow passage of time than what seemed to have lapsed.

The two figures in the barn counted twenty-five cricket chirps in fifteen-second intervals and added forty to estimate the temperature at 65 degrees. It seemed cooler, dampness always a factor in these wooded areas. Talking was forbidden, so hand signals sufficed as best as could be seen at close range. No eating, smoking, chewing gum, or even a bar of soap when bathing today was allowed. The fragrance of any one of these pleasures would not fit with the musky environment and would drift noticeably for a distance on such a still night. A slight chill set in, and the moisture-laden air dropped a slight dampness onto its visitors. They waited.

There were only the two horses and two cats in the barn. The two dogs had been brought to a nearby location for the evening because they would have given alarm to anyone approaching. The cats were interested in their visitors and cuddled to keep company, a slight respite from the task at hand. The horses stood still with only small motions, seemingly to never sleep or even close their eyes. Rest must come to all, and stillness eventually fell into place. Suddenly, there was a commotion! It zoomed overhead with a flap and a flurry and was gone before it was detected! Heart rates soared in the two vigilant sentinels, and they became even more keenly aware of their surroundings. The barn owl had been watching them all night and had now taken his turn at his natural evening activities without the slightest announcement of his intentions. They wondered what else was sharing their country habitat and when it might make its presence known.

Night grew on under the revolving stars, somewhat occluded by clouds but visible enough at times to introduce some sort of diversion from the task at hand. Body numbness set in, and only very minor shifts in position were permitted; however, they were hardly a relief and in fact, were useless after such a length of time. Sleep was not an option. This was reserved for another time, but the body did not know that. Even so, dedication fell victim to recurring nods, and the eyes closed to regain strength. Concentration was difficult. It was only midnight.

Over four hours had passed, and there may be another six to go. Thoughts went to Mitch and Helen, two of the most highly regarded people anywhere. It gave the assignment a purpose, but now the observers wondered if they were up to the task.

The night continued, and were are no signs of intruders. By all measures, any such assignment would have been "deep sixed" by now. However, no one would succumb to the forces against success, each held ground to offset any such attempt and each well beyond his individual capability, but each bolstered by the others and hung tough. Hours continued to pass. Another evening watch must be planned for tomorrow.

A small light flickered outside along the west wall of the house, unseen by any of the lookouts. It was steady and at about a level of four feet above the ground. The northwest breeze fanned the flames into a bloom of fire around the electrical service entrance box before it was observed. Radio communications crackled into action. "We have a fire, west side of house. Alpha 1, douse the fire! Call it in! Alpha 2, hit the lights! Bring the car!"

The parked car in front of the house blazed its lights in the southwest direction, behind the house, calculated to be the most probable approach. The fire helped the visibility, but moreover added a ghostly aura across the landscape. A 911 call went out, naming the exact description of the location as prepared in advance. "Fire at Chief Mitchell's house, fire location 26, Section 5!" State police corporal Carl Grady scanned the field to the south for intruders. Nothing appeared. Officer Sheila Gooding roared across to her location in the Ford Bronco, stopped to take on Grady as a passenger, and sped off in the direction of the logging road at the south end of the property behind the farmhouse, greeted by dust rising in her headlights. She powered through the rutted road, Grady calling out on the radio, "All officers, vicinity of Silver Lake, suspect heading south on Route 167 toward Montrose, in pursuit, may be armed and dangerous; need assistance! High-speed vehicle! Be on the lookout!"

Officer Gooding was well suited for the pursuit. She drove scary fast, and Grady hung on. She knew how to *drive.* They lurched out onto the paved road, following the trail of dirt just pushed onto it by the escaping vehicle ahead of them. She cranked the steering wheel to the left, then right, sliding in a controlled forward direction, heading south. The twisty Route 167 was a challenge on a Sunday afternoon cruise at thirty-five miles per hour, and she was slipping sideways in the darkness at seventy miles per hour with bursts of speed upward of that. In no time she was on the bumper of an SUV, dark in color; it was hard to see the type on the unlit country road. They passed the quarry road where Mitch met his fate recently, and rolled and swerved over the contours like someone with a death wish. "Do you want me to take him out?" she yelled.

"Do it!" shouted Grady.

Gooding powered expertly behind the right side of the rear bumper and gave it an extra nudge with the left side of her bumper, spinning the vehicle in front of her across the oncoming lane, off the road, and on a downward trajectory into the woods. She slammed on the brakes, backed up, and jammed the SUV into park. Before Grady could react, she was already out of the car with flashlight in hand and gun drawn. The escape vehicle lay lazily on its side, wheels spinning, engine running, lights on, and otherwise motionless. "State police! Come out with your hands up!" she commanded. There was no response.

Sirens sounded in the far night, coming from both the north and the south. Gooding and Grady stood their distance until the other officers arrived. The sounds of the Silver Lake fire engine and ambulance could be heard in the background, responding to the fire at Mitch's house. The Montrose police car and a Pennsylvania state police car arrived at the scene from different directions. Only then did Grady feel confident in approaching the overturned vehicle. All lights were focused on it as he approached in a crouched duck walk. "Police! Throw out your weapons!" he yelled.

No response.

Grady thought, *There is no percentage in approaching the vehicle and taking a chance of getting shot. On the other hand, someone could be injured and may need help. What do I care? These scumbags are not worth getting killed for.*

The group of law officers now numbered eight, an accumulation of everyone who heard the radio broadcast from a fifteen-mile radius. The flashing lights and occasional radio squawks created a surreal scene. Grady remained in charge and periodically commanded the suspects to throw out any weapons and get out of the vehicle.

Daylight was breaking, although it was still difficult to see into the overturned vehicle for signs of life. More support had arrived, and the small two-lane roadway was now blocked off to passing traffic. It seemed that whoever may be in the vehicle probably was incapacitated, but Grady was taking no chances. It was time to go, and his plan was to surround the vehicle and get a look inside with himself as the lead in command and two others in firing position.

He crawled to the side of the vehicle and did a quick bob of the head up to the windowsill and back down. It appeared that one person was slumped into the airbag, motionless. The other did not see him, but appeared to have some motor abilities. There was only one way to tell. He crawled around to the driver's side of the vehicle and yelled, "Drop the gun!" The occupant turned and raised his weapon; a shot rang out from the front of the vehicle and punched a hole through the windshield. Officer Gooding walked away, pistol still held by both hands. It was over.

The two occupants of the vehicle had no identification. The Chevy SUV was registered to a business in New York state, listed as stolen two weeks prior. Fingerprints of the bodies would be taken for further analysis, but more than likely would result in two flunkies unconnected to the real mission.

Mitch was still in danger.

The farmhouse suffered very little damage. Lighter fluid was used inside and around the electrical box to start the fire, which on a nice, quiet evening in this somewhat remote, or at least private, location would have engulfed a good amount of the house on the windward side before anyone sleeping on the leeward side would have known it. It was well planned for maximum effectiveness. Grady thought, *I can't help but think that Mitch and his wife will never get a good night's sleep in that house for as long as they live.*

Arsonists caught in Silver Lake

By Mary Michelson, Staff writer

Filed: Monday, June 23, 2008 Published: Wednesday, June 25, 2008 Susquehanna County News

Two unidentified arsonists were apprehended on Monday morning at 5:45 a.m., fleeing the home of Silver Lake Township Police Chief James Mitchell and his wife, Helen. Pennsylvania State Police Corporal Carl Grady engaged the pair in a chase after the alarm was called in to the Silver Lake Fire Department. The escape vehicle made its way south along route 167 before running off the road five miles north of Montrose killing the driver. A standoff ensued, which ended when the passenger was shot as he took aim at officers on the scene. Neither of the victims carried identification and the vehicle was reported stolen two weeks prior from a business in Binghamton, New York.

The Mitchell home sustained little damage thanks to the quick response of the fire teams. No motive was available for the crime. State police are conducting an investigation. They ask anyone with information to contact Sergeant John Ames at the Gibson State Police Barracks.

28

The ring of Pete's doorbell later that morning after the fire at Mitch's house signaled the beginning of the end in the Forbes case, and not the end, but only Pete knew it. Corporal Carl Grady and state police captain Dean Evers greeted him as they entered. There were no smiles or satisfaction of a completed mission, just concern and anxiety for what more had to be done.

This was a solemn, unenviable moment for everyone present. Pete had enlisted the help of the only person in the local outside world he felt he could trust, state police corporal Carl Grady. The watchdog assignment at Mitch's house was organized secretly by Grady with three of the most recent graduates from the state police academy. All were highly regarded, top of their class, especially officer Sheila Gooding, who graduated number one. She was her widowed father's daughter, and although every bit a lady, she was well prepared for anything that came at her. Grady and his team shifted their schedules and personal lives around to be able to help Pete on their own time. No one, not even Mitch, knew of their plans, and it paid off. At least, it seemed to.

"But now where does this thing take us with two unidentified arsonists and nothing else to go on?" asked Mitch as the group sat down.

Pete began, "Carl, first of all, thank you for the fine job. And thanks to your team members. I understand they are all on duty or sleeping for their next shift?"

"That's right. But you know they would do it again tonight if they had to. What a great group of young officers! I am proud we could help," Grady responded. "I'm still not sure if Captain Evers here is okay with it all, but he said we'll talk at the end of the day."

Evers was definitely not pleased. But there really was nothing he could do about four off-duty police officers helping a friend. Grady knew there would be some hell to pay, but his agenda was righteously inspired, and Pete believed Evers would hold no sway on the situation once all of the facts surfaced.

"Let's hear some more about this, Pete," Evers commanded brusquely. He was a no-nonsense guy and appeared to have absolutely no sense of propriety whatsoever. His physical presence and demeanor were domineering, and his attitude abrasively authoritative. At six feet three, and with a solidly built frame of at least 280 pounds, he projected control and a serious attitude right from first glance. His bedecked captain's uniform and holstered pistol enhanced all of this and added a fear factor to his overall appearance. Ruddy facial characteristics gave evidence of the many situations his line of work must have encountered over his career, leaving a cemented somber expression and a need for few words to get his point across. Grady had his work cut out for him in that respect, but Pete felt things would change in the next five minutes.

Pete proceeded, "Let me start with some facts. We pretty much all know about the suicides and accidental deaths here in Silver Lake and what part Mitch has had in identifying that cluster of unusual occurrences. Well, DA Larson agreed with him and got right to work on it, ending up with the accusations and evidence discovered against the Forbes International Investments company headed up by Joseph Pratt. Pratt was found dead of a heart attack in his car a short time before that outside his office in Montrose, another death to add to the list, in effect. Mitch's own hit-and-run accident is another incident to add to the list, as well as the arson attempt last evening."

"So far we're all with you, Pete. Where is this going?" Evers growled impatiently.

"Bear with me for a minute, Captain. All of Pratt's clients had Gasco gas well leases, and all of them seemed to have been influenced to invest their proceeds with Forbes by recommendation of Senator Bob Wellman. He himself apparently is also a victim of the Forbes scam. I mention this only because the senator may be instrumental in helping us."

"Help us do what?" Evers added.

"There's more. Mitch here had been recuperating at an undisclosed location for the last few days, and only I and one other person knew where he was. Once Mitch returned here to my house, he told DA Larson that he had returned home. He did it on a cell phone, and every indication would be that he called from his house.

"Before that, both Mitch and I independently observed that Larson had taken an extremely short time in more or less solving the Pratt's Forbes scheme once Mitch put him on to it. Sheriff Petersen was supposedly a big help, but he would have had to have been psychic to have made so much progress in such a short period of time. Also, Larson has private offices right in the same building as Pratt; in fact, he was Pratt's landlord. Circumstantial, I admit, but a fact. Another thing: Larson was a little more than casually interested in Mitch's whereabouts and return than normal; again circumstantial, but a fact. He did mention he received a cell phone call from the quarry where Mitch's hit-and-run occurred, but we know for sure that is impossible in that it's a dead zone for cell service.

"Here's the reason you are here, gentlemen: Larson was the only person who knew Mitch had returned from his hospital stay. He was the only one Mitch communicated with; not even Mitch's wife knew." Pete watched for a reaction, but there was none.

Evers said, "Well, you knew too." Pete didn't answer and let that wiseass comment float right back in Evers' face.

"What are you asking us to do? Arrest the DA on what you told us?" Evers' sarcasm was evident.

"That's exactly what I'm suggesting," Pete quickly responded. "Here is my hypothesis. Larson is one of the kingpins in this scam. I know we are going out on a limb here because he is politically the fair-haired boy of the county, and everyone loves the guy, including some in this room. I'm just stating facts so we can push through the bull here. My guess is that he and Pratt had this investment scam organized, which included the untimely deaths of some of the clients—suicides, accidents, and the like. The attorney who would administer all of their wills was also one of the victims. I would also guess that any heirs would be told that the suicides would preclude any return on the insurance side of the investments and that the net value of any investments would be a very small percentage of the original value due to market conditions or whatever. All the funds were shipped out of the country. So there is no recourse whatsoever. Pratt was the fall guy and was taken out once his job was done."

"But you said it was a heart attack," reminded Evers.

"I said he was pronounced to have died from a heart attack by coroner Jim Davis, the same person who pronounced all of the other victims dead, even one of the two deaths in Wyoming County, where he has no authority but was assisting in the Schultz murders. I suspect Davis has to be involved in this too. My thought is that the Schultz family deaths could have actually been a murder-suicide and that prompted the idea for the rest of the investors to be scammed and taken out. The Edwards accident—falling from the theater roof—was too coincidental, in particular, since he did all Pratt's website work and printing of the false brochures and documents."

"Holy God, Pete!" exclaimed Mitch. "These are people I've known pretty well for a long time."

"Apparently not, Mitch. I'm saying that given all the facts, this is the only explanation. And I'm saying, gentlemen, that this thing goes higher than you can guess right now. That's why I asked Corporal Grady to help. I didn't know where to turn with Mitch out of the picture," Pete announced to the group.

"Here's another thought. I suspect there must be a connection at Northeast Penn National Bank because of the ease in transferring funds into accounts and out of the country. I could be mistaken, but it should be checked out."

Captain Evers sat quietly, considering his options. On one hand, he could believe all the facts presented and come to the same conclusions. On the other, he had nine more months to go toward retirement, and he dreaded getting into something that was definitely going to tear away some of the political armor he had accumulated over his career. Pete Woodard's catch-22 was set up well. If he did nothing, Grady would be compelled and well-justified to go over his head. And he knew Grady well enough that that would happen. Alternatively, he would suffer greatly as a result if this deal proved to be true. If he went ahead and launched an investigation based on what he heard here today, chances seemed fifty-fifty that he would survive it even if he were correct. He thought, *There must be another way.*

Pete's old salesman approach was in full force today. Now he would go in for the kill. He knew how to ask the closing question. "Captain, is there any reason you don't want to take this to conclusion?" Pete was a master at sales, and he was prepared for an objection. The easy answer was no, and that meant Evers would do as Pete suggested.

Evers had never been put in a battle of the minds like this before. He was a front linesman, ready to bully his way through any situation, and always to his liking. Today the court of consideration was waiting for him to do the right thing, and he knew it. Little did he know that he had no other alternative. Pete was in total control, no matter what was next said.

"Let me think about it, fellows."

Pete knew that answer was coming, since it's a natural human reaction when someone can't make a decision.

"What is there to think about?" Pete answered quickly. "I presume you would want to go ahead if there was no price to pay; that is, if there was no political fallout. Am I right?"

"I never worry about that," Evers bellowed, trying to intimidate with his loudness. Everyone in the room knew otherwise. "I just think we need more proof."

"What are you waiting for, another murder? With all due respect, sir," Grady blurted. Grady had blatantly put himself in opposition to Evers. "It *is* the right thing to do."

"He's right," Mitch added. "We have reason to expect that one or more of our neighbors are in danger: Nora Connely, and possibly Sam Burns."

"Nora fits the profile of the modus operandi," Pete added. "Her property is right in the middle of the land owned by the other victims, and if there is a connection to Gasco for some reason, she could be on someone's hit list. I think Larson knows who's on that list."

Evers just listened.

"Another thing," Pete began. "We know for a fact, Mitch and I, that there is absolutely no one else to discuss this with, and I mean no one else." Pete deftly let Evers know that if he didn't buy in, he would suffer the consequences. "We can't talk with anyone in county law enforcement or anyone at the state attorney general's level. And we can't talk with any of your superiors. There is no

State Crime Commission anymore; budget cuts a few years ago took them out, leaving the AG in charge of everything. We're here in this room pretty much on our own. We don't know really how far or how deep this thing goes. Do we have your support on this, Captain?"

There was silence. Pete knew that the first one to talk owned the situation. The few seconds of silence were profound; no one uttered a word. Mitch indicated he was about to add something, and Pete motioned for him to stay quiet with a quick side-to-side shake of the head and a slight wave of his hand, while not taking his eyes off Evers' reaction. Pete viewed this uncomfortable situation as just part of the decision-making process. He was simply helping Evers come to a conclusion. They continued to wait. It did not actually matter what Evers's answer was because the scheme was going to be exposed today anyway. It had to be. There were lives at stake. It would be nice if Evers bought in, but not absolutely necessary. Evers continued to avert his eyes while mulling things over. Pete sat back in his chair.

After thirty seconds, which seemed like an hour, Evers lifted his head and spoke. "How do we know where this thing stops?"

Pete wanted to answer, but he was done talking, and Evers had to figure that out for himself. Pete would let Evers come to whatever conclusion it was going to be all by himself. Pete was in control, and he was letting Evers feel the pressure and conclude that either he cooperated or he was going to be suspected himself of something. There was no third position.

Evers continued to fill in the conversational void. "We can do this, number one. But I'm going to need some time."

"Today!" Pete answered sternly.

"It'll be tough, but maybe we can do this today. What I need is an arrest warrant from the state level. I need to contact a judge in the state capital who is one of the few guys I can depend on, Judge Joe Harman. He and I go way back. As a young magistrate, he sponsored my application to the state police more than forty years ago."

Mitch started to speak, and Pete respectfully motioned again for him to remain silent. This was the ultimate close, control over a state police captain who was not used to being told what to do. Pete handed him his cell phone and suggested, "Make the call. We have a fax machine here, and he can send it right now. Here's the fax number." Pete wrote down the number on a piece of paper.

There was no question as to what was supposed to happen in the next few minutes. Everyone in the room had his eyes and expectations on Captain Evers. Grady walked into the kitchen to make a phone call to verify what manpower resources would be available to them that afternoon. He had to discuss the situation without too many details. News like this could spread, particularly among those in law enforcement, and this information had to be kept secure.

Pete showed a handwritten piece of paper to Mitch with the names of the primary suspects on it. Included were Larson, Davis, Dobson, and Sheriff Petersen, along with a mention of Pratt, post mortem. He also composed a brief description of their findings and the reason they could not take this claim deeper for fear of the involvement of others in the position of authority. It read very clearly. Mitch handed it to Evers as he was waiting to contact Judge Harman in the state supreme court in Harrisburg, the state capital.

The convoluted series of phone connections failed, and Evers had to contact his office for help with a direct phone line, something he tried to avoid for security's sake, but it was unavoidable. Judge Harman was not to be found so easily. In desperation, Captain Evers was in the zone now, and he was going to make this happen. A phone call to another judge, Judge Larson in Montrose, was out of the question since he was DA Larry Larson's uncle. His only other immediate choice was Judge Wilton Horvath, District State Judge for Wyoming County. The judge was well regarded, a straight shooter, and a friend of the law enforcement community. Evers had testified in a trial more than ten years ago involving drugs, murder, and a parentless family as a result. He was awed by the way Horvath handled everything with sensitivity, precision, fairness, and compassion. Horvath was a role model for modern justice in everyone's eyes.

Judge Horvath was having lunch in his chambers when Evers reached him. After a full explanation, the judge said he would issue the warrants and wished Evers the best in his work on the case. "Watch your fax. They'll be coming through within the hour," Judge Horvath advised.

The noon hour and the damp rainy day called for some of Pete's soup as the group of four waited for the warrants to arrive. Pete directed the group to the kitchen and presented bowls of lintel soup, butter rolls, and tea; in Mitch's mind, food of the gods. Everyone relished the treats as they waited for authorization.

Evers made another call asking for two more officers and their state police attorney in attendance. He didn't explain the details but simply ordered everyone to stand by for further orders. Everyone would meet in Montrose at 3:00 p.m. outside the Montrose Library, which was within view of Larson's private offices, where he normally could be found in the late afternoon.

The fax machine seemed as though it would never activate. It was 2:10 p.m., and the group had waited two hours, but nothing had come through yet. Pete called the fax number, using his cell phone, just to be sure it was working. The fax rang and went through its motions and hung up. It seemed to be working properly. Finally it activated, and a stream of documents emerged as promised, much to the delight of Evers, who grabbed each one and helped it exit the machine by guiding it with his hands. Everything was in order.

Evers called Grady outside by their car and ran through the procedure with him in advance of the actual arrest, a simulation with expectations for the worst and what to do if they occurred.

Two backup officers would be stationed at the front and rear of the building. An open microphone would be employed in case reinforcements were needed. Those reinforcements would be put on notice now but would only be told the location ten minutes before entry to Larson's office.

It was a go. Evers and Grady drove the ten miles to Montrose. In a separate car, Pete and Mitch followed. When they arrived, they were met by two state police cruisers a few yards down the street.

The team members coalesced in front of the library, and after a five-minute briefing, made their way to Larson's office, weapons drawn. In a small town like Montrose, this was an attention-getting event. Nearby businesses and neighbors appeared on their porches and in their yards peering toward the unexpected activities. "Please get back inside," one of the officers appealed. "This could be dangerous. Get back inside, I said!"

Evers and Grady made their way through the entrance and into Larson's office. His secretary greeted the men and asked if she could help. "We're here to see Larson," Evers boomed. "Is he in?"

"Yes, but he's been on the phone. Let me see when he will be finished." She walked to his door, knocked, and tried to open it and peer in, per established procedure. "The door's locked. He never does that."

Evers and Grady moved purposely to each side of the door, motioning her aside and to the outside entrance door. "Larson, open the door, state police!" Grady shouted as he knocked and tried the knob.

There was no answer. "Larson, open up!" No answer again.

Grady backed up and kicked the middle of the door at the knob once, twice, three times, and it burst open. No one was to be seen. "This is Grady! Suspect is on the move! Be on the watch!" he yelled into the radio.

They slinked into the office, Evers in the lead. He lowered his pistol and walked behind the desk. He felt the neck of the crumpled body for a pulse. There was none. An empty bottle of medication labeled "Tramadol" lay open on the desktop, apparently used to induce the death. The pills were crushed for fast effect, indicated by the dust on the desktop. A water glass lay on its side, water spilled onto the desktop.

Corporal Grady called for backup resources. Two more state police cruisers were on their way from Gibson. ETA was fifteen minutes; not soon enough. He was now anxious to move to the sheriff's office. Although not a prime suspect, Sheriff Ken Petersen worked closely enough with DA Larson that the obvious connection needed to be examined.

Grady secured the scene at Larson's office by leaving one officer in charge, and the group moved down the street to the county courthouse where Petersen's office was. It resembled a scene from a Wild West movie.

They waited for the two reinforcements to arrive before entering the otherwise-quiet businesslike building. One officer kept arriving visitors outside while the three others passed through security scanners with weapons holstered so as not to cause confrontation. Once through the scanners, the security deputy was advised of the planned operation and asked to surrender her pistol and step outside. She did so without objection and was escorted by one of Grady's men, who stayed with her. Evers was directed to Sheriff Ken Petersen's office, and he was on the phone when he and Grady walked in.

"I just heard," Petersen volunteered.

"Heard what?" Evers replied.

"About Larson."

"Sheriff, we're here to ask you to come along with us for some questioning. Will you cooperate?" Evers requested.

"Yes, what's this all about? What's going on?" Petersen asked.

"You have a right to remain silent. You have a right to an attorney, and one will be provided if you can't afford one. Anything you say may be held against you. Do you understand?" Evers recited.

"Yes, but—"

"Save it, Sheriff. This is just as hard on us, believe me, as it is on you," Evers advised. "Do you have a weapon in this office or on your person?"

"Yes, in the desk drawer."

"Is that the only one?"

"Yes."

"Can I trust that you will cooperate without handcuffs, Sheriff?" Evers asked, respecting the professional relationship.

"Yes, thank you. I appreciate that. But what's this all about?"

"Corporal, take him to the car," Evers directed as he motioned for the two to lead him out of the room.

"Yes sir." Grady motioned for Petersen to lead the way.

With that unenviable task out of the way, Evers assembled the three remaining state troopers and walked the half a block down Public Avenue from the courthouse to Northeast Penn National Bank. Will Dobson was in his office on the phone, and when the officers walked in, he hung up without saying a word. "Gentlemen, can I help you?"

"You can, Mr. Dobson. You are under arrest for questioning in connection with the Forbes International Investment incident. You have the right to remain silent. You have the right to an attorney, and one will be provided if you cannot afford one. Anything you say can be held against you. Do you understand?" Evers recited.

There was no response.

"Mr. Dobson, are you carrying a weapon, or is there one in this office?" Evers asked.

"There is a pistol in my drawer on the left."

"Thank you," said the officer as he frisked Dobson."Sorry, sir; procedure. I have to put these cuffs on you. Now follow the officer out the front door." The four of them left the building and walked back up the street, where they sat Dobson in a police cruiser with one of the officers.

By this time a crowd of more than one hundred people had formed on the street despite the possible danger. Evers and the remaining officers got back into a car and drove the two blocks to the Endless Mountain Hospital. They entered and asked for Doctor Jim Davis. He was not in his office, so they had him paged to come to his office. When he arrived, his demeanor sunk to a level that needed no explanation. "How can I help you, officers?"

"Doctor Davis, you are under arrest for questioning related to the Forbes International Investments incidents. You have a right to remain silent. You have a right to an attorney, and one will be provided if you can't afford one. Anything you say may be held against you. Do you understand?" Evers recited for the third time today.

"Yes, but what's this all about?" Davis answered.

"We'll have plenty of time to discuss that down at the barracks," Evers answered.

The accompanying officer advised, "Sorry, Doctor, I have to pat you down. Are there any weapons on you or in this office?"

"No, my God! This is a hospital, for God's sake."

"I'm going to have to put these cuffs on you. Please follow me to the car," the officer asked. They all left in queue.

Captain Evers walked the two short blocks back up the street to Mitch and Pete, who were standing in front of the courthouse with the crowd of over one hundred people now. He motioned them over to where Pete's car was parked, and they got in. "What a freakin' day this has been!" Evers declared. "I need a vacation!"

Pete and Mitch let him talk.

"Okay, Chief. You're gonna back me up on this, right? I need all I can get right now." The big, tough man was obviously nervous. They all knew that the Pennsylvania State Attorney General's office would be brought in on the case within the hour as a priority-one issue. The FBI was already working with Larson on the Forbes scam, and they would want to become the lead agency now that all these facts connected to their case.

The cat is now out of the bag, and the chips will start to fall where they may, Pete thought to himself.

"No problem, Captain. You did a fantastic job! It was amazing. In one hour you wiped out the entire law enforcement of Susquehanna County," Mitch commented.

"God, you're right! We'll have to post some temporary control at the courthouse, at the very least. I'll make arrangements. Let's go over to the courthouse, and I'll talk to Judge Larson and the deputies before leaving."

29

Honeymoon is over - Natural gas companies rescind lease offers

By Michell Bayless, Staff Writer

Filed: Friday, 20, 2008
Published: Wednesday, June 25, 2008

Many northeast Pennsylvania landowners have been informed that their gas well drilling leases have been revoked and their offers rescinded. The Gaylord Consultants, representatives of industry gas exploration firms with previous interests in the region, stated in a recent letter that its clients are refocusing their oil and gas efforts and are scaling back their leasing pledges. It said further that this change in their plans is due to regulatory issues and current economic conditions. Efforts to reach a Gaylord spokesperson were unsuccessful today.

According to natural gas industry representatives, Gasco and other companies have been challenged by a drop in natural gas prices and increasing state regulations which appear almost on a daily basis. It seems that, once the realities set in regarding water availability, waste water processing restrictions, increasing regulations, and funding needed to deal with all the various aspects of setting up a burgeoning industry all at once, even the highly capitalized leading companies are resetting their business models.

Industry participants feel that financial constraints of a tightened credit market due to recent faltering economic conditions, along with, in their words, "a barrage of new permit regulations from week to week" it has been unexpectedly difficult for the industry to work with the state Department of Environmental Protection.

Recently instituted regulations require companies that want to develop wells in the Marcellus Shale to submit a Permit Application Addendum to DEP, as well as a permit application for gas well development. Some changes to regulations have been made in the last several months and DEP says it has made a continuing extra effort to get the reviews done quickly. However, DEP is attempting to do a "balancing act" between protecting the environment and the potential economic benefits of natural gas drilling. There is no question that DEP must perform its duty and it seems that its processing capacity also has been strained with all the recent activity.

DEP spokesperson Mark Clayton said, "It's been like a gold rush and although we knew it was coming, no one expected the whirlwind of activity we've seen to date. The area of the Marcellus Shale well development is very rural and a lot of people depend on their wells for drinking water and water for their livestock. It is of utmost importance to do things right and take the proper time to protect our environment and the safety of our citizens, and in particular, those downstream of these northeast region projects."

HYPOTHESIS

For now, natural gas exploration companies must resort to relying on cash flow from the existing well operations to fund future leases, causing the buy-in and leasing process to slow down by to probably one-fifth of the former planned development pace. The fast changing market can always dictate a future adjustment upward, and the consensus is that exploration financing will err on the side of conservatism for a while until credit markets are more favorable.

Contact the writer at: Mbayless@susqnews.com

30

On the return drive from town after all the arrests, Pete drove directly to Mitch's house so they could survey the damage. A gathering of cars and trucks met them along the driveway, and when they drove around to the west side of the house, they found a crew of neighbors who had already begun to make the repairs. Silver Lake Township had more independent contractors and can-do people per square mile than anywhere else in the world. Rural towns work that way. Mitch stayed in the car; his injuries were talking painfully to him after all the activities of the day. He was visibly moved. "You guys are something else," he spoke, barely though, emotions overwhelming him.

The electrical service entrance box was completely replaced and rewired, and a few new pieces of clapboard siding had been replaced underneath it and were already painted. Inside, there was no damage. Mitch was relieved at the prospects of getting back into his house and having Helen return from her sister's home.

"I can't tell you what this means to me," he stammered. He tried to say more, but it wouldn't come out. He put his head down and scratched his forehead, covering his facial emotions. He was visibly moved.

"Just get well, Mitch; we need you back!" a voice yelled from the rear of the crowd.

"You can bet on it," Mitch stammered in return with a wave.

"Gentlemen, I need to get him back for some rest; doctor's orders," Pete announced. "Thank you for everything. We'll take good care of him." Pete and Mitch had some details to discuss now that they had almost singlehandedly disembodied the entire county of its innocence.

They returned to Pete's home on Silver Lake and sat on the dock overlooking the calm evening water with celebratory cold beers in hand and a feeling of accomplishment, although anxiety still accompanied them. Mitch took a few pain pills to offset the throbbing that had set in from all the activities that afternoon. They were both anxious to hear details about the questioning of the suspects. With Larson dead, most of the facts would be missing, but even if Petersen, Davis, or Dobson were complicit, they might not have information as to the higher-level workings and how things were organized.

Mitch called Helen and explained some of the events, not mentioning the fire at their home. She would be transported home by one of Grady's state police team in two days.

"What a long day!" Mitch sighed. "We are almost home free."

"You could say that. I hope it's true. My guess is that it's a busy place down there at state police headquarters right now."

They relaxed for a while, watching the comings and goings on the lake. Then the phone rang up at the house, a distance of thirty yards from where they were relaxing. "I wonder if I should get it. All right, here I go." Pete hurried along the fieldstone walk through the hemlocks up the steps and into the house. He picked up the phone after the fifth ring just as the answering message began. "Hello, this is Pete."

"Pete, Grady, thought you might want to know. Davis spilled the beans."

"What! Give me details... wait. Let me take the portable phone down to the dock so Mitch can hear too... hold on."

Pete returned to the dock at lakeside where Mitch was sitting. "Go ahead, Carl." Pete held the phone facing the two of them with the volume turned up so they both could hear.

Corporal Grady continued. "Well, it wasn't two minutes after he arrived at headquarters that he started talking. They took his statement while he was being assigned a lawyer. Apparently, Wilkinson was his lawyer too. It sounds like he must have been in on it from the beginning with Larson and Pratt."

"What about Sheriff Petersen and Dobson?" asked Pete. Pete continued to hold the phone away from his ear so Mitch could listen in.

"Petersen had nothing to do with it. He only got involved after Mitch brought out all the details with Larson. It sounds like Larson was just using him. Dobson, on the other hand, had only a minor role in looking the other way when some of the wire transfers were processed."

"You know, I'm really glad to hear about Petersen, and Mitch is shaking his head here in agreement. He is a really good guy and a fine sheriff," Pete responded.

"We all feel the same way. Davis, on the other hand, is a basket case from what I hear. I guess he got involved when he assisted doing autopsies in Wyoming County for the Schultz family murder-suicide thing earlier in the year. He was approached by Larson and Pratt to more or less rubberstamp some suicide pronouncements. It sounds like they looked like suicides to Davis anyway, but when he got suspicious, Larson wanted to make sure he was on board. His role was minor, so to speak, but he was involved no matter how you look at it."

"What about Dobson and the bank dealings?" asked Pete.

"Nothing so far; he's quiet as a mouse."

"All right. Thanks, Carl. Get some rest, will ya?" Pete advised and hung up. "You heard the details. How do you feel about going back home?"

"Pete, my boy, you have done it again. I'm sure we'll hear a lot more from the feds when they jump in on this. I'm okay with everything. We can finally get back to normal, whatever that is around here anymore."

"I hope so. Your bride will be home day after tomorrow. Let's plan a get-together and enjoy the rest of the summer."

The two friends relaxed, enjoying the view and chatting about the details of the recent events, each hoping that was all there was to it, at least locally.

Pete was the first to break their contemplation. "I'm going to rock your boat again, Mitch."

"Ah, here we go again! What now?" Mitch bellowed.

"Listen; what do you think about this? How did Larson know? I mean, how did he know we were coming? Think about it."

"Well, maybe he didn't know."

"He knew damn well. You remember the first law?"

"Yeah, there are no coincidences."

"Right, the only person who knew about the arrest outside of the group in my house was Judge Horvath. And remember how long it took to get the warrants? I think he contacted Larson to warn him."

"Do you damn well realize what you're saying now?"

"I do. What do you think?" Pete answered.

"If it's true, we're almost back to where we started. This thing could be big, really big. I mean, *who isn't involved* would be a better question."

"If Horvath did call or otherwise let Larson know ahead of time, then we could have a far-reaching set of circumstances here.

For example, who can be trusted? I'm mainly concerned for your safety; yours and Helen's. There have been two attempts on your life, and a third is not an option as far as I'm concerned."

"You know, I don't feel comfortable dealing anymore with Evers on this either," Mitch confided.

"I know what you mean. I don't either. Here is my suggestion. Why don't we get ahold of the fed in charge of the Forbes thing and talk with him."

"The agent is Tom Chambers. I met him once on the Saunders case. He was supposed to be in touch with me, according to Larson, but I never heard from him. There's been a lot going on. I'm sure his hands are full, but what we have to say could break this thing open a little further. I'll call him. Let me run up to the house to get the phone book and make some calls."

"Don't run on that leg. Walk. While you're up there I'm going to break out two poles and we'll give some worms swimming lessons," Pete offered. He did want to see Mitch relax.

Mitch was gone for over a half hour, and when he returned, he advised, "Get ready for a visitor. Chambers is on his way. He's coming from Scranton. He's in the middle of dinner but he'll be here in less than two hours."

"What did he think?"

"The brief overview I gave him made some sense," he said. "But he didn't want to talk over the phone."

"Well, let's have some dinner ourselves before he gets here. The fish can wait." Pete led the way back to the house, and they each thought about the continuing mystery and whether it would ever be over.

31

FBI Agent Tom Chambers was very much understated, especially arriving after nine o'clock in the evening dressed in a T-shirt and blue jeans. The bulge in his sport coat betrayed the presence of a weapon in a shoulder holster, a necessity in his business, even on a friendly summer evening visit.

"Agent Chambers, Pete Woodard. Come right on in."

"Gentlemen, glad to make your acquaintance," Chambers said as he held out his identification. "FBI Agent Tom Chambers." He had the look of an accountant, but he presented himself in an energetic manner, which complemented his trim and fit appearance. "Mitch, how are you doing? Sorry to hear about your accident."

"Thanks for coming, Tom. I'm doing fine. Let me introduce officer Carl Grady, Pennsylvania State Police." Pete thought it wise to have Grady present for a number of reasons best left unsaid at this point. "Officer Grady is off duty but has been a great friend in helping us."

"I understand," Chambers assured. "Let me first say that it's a real pleasure to be here. Your reputations precede you. You've done some great things."

"Thanks," Mitch returned. "We don't go looking for these things, but they seem to end up in our laps once in a while. Our analysis on this one is lacking because we don't really have the resources to go much further. As I said on the phone, we figure you're running with the ball as lead agency anyway, and we have some thoughts that maybe will help you."

"I appreciate that. One of our agents did want to talk to you anyway. How would you like to proceed?"

"Well, you're up-to-date on the arrests in Montrose, I presume," answered Mitch.

"Yes."

"We have some observations."

"Go ahead."

Mitch explained about Judge Horvath being the only one to know in advance of the arrests and also the time lapse in getting the warrants from him. The situation looked like there could be some higher involvement beyond just DA Larson. "We just don't have the resources to verify things at our level; you know, phone records, bank dealings, security tapes, witness interviews, whatever."

Chambers sat in amazement. "You fellows have done very well so far. And, I might add, you are not far off track at all. I *can* tell you that we've been involved with Judge Horvath for some time now. So this isn't a surprise to us. I can't tell you any details. I hope you understand."

They all acknowledged silently.

"But I will say that we believe Larson and Horvath were somehow connected to Forbes and Joe Pratt's investment scam. It goes back to the beginning of the year with the Schultz family murder-suicide down there in Horvath's hometown, Tunkhannock. Mitch, as you correctly pointed out to Larson during your visit with him, Schultz was a real suicide after he shot up his family. When the estate went to probate, there was nothing left but a run-down farm and two personal loan claims on the estate from the local bank. There was nothing to be found of the funds he received from Gasco. They were wired directly to an offshore investment fund, Car 3. A brother of his from downstate, near Lancaster, made a complaint to the attorney general about getting no support from the local authorities, including Judge Horvath and the appointed lawyer, Edward Wilkinson, who was handling the case. Then, later, when you started putting two and two together, we began connecting the dots on our end, and they led up in your direction. It's like a puzzle with pieces missing from the middle."

"Do you think it ends there?" Mitch asked.

"We don't," Chambers said solemnly. Pete noted that Chambers always spoke in the plural. Chambers went on. "We believe there is at least one other connection. Here is what we know. Phone records show your call from this house to Horvath earlier today when Evers requested the warrants. We show calls on Horvath's end about an hour later, just routine local legal contacts as far as we can tell. We also found the fax call to this location an hour after that time. So our guess is that if he made a call, he used a payphone or an unregistered cell phone, or it could be that another person made the contact for him."

"What calls did you find on Larson's end?" asked Mitch.

"That's just it. Nothing. Apparently, his secretary left the office around 1:30 or so, and when she returned after 2:20, she saw his extension was lit on her phone. She assumed he was on a call with the door closed, something he did quite frequently. But there was no record of a call on his line or his cell phone. Later, at 3:10 or so, the state police came in, and you know the rest."

"Are you saying that he didn't receive a phone call whatsoever from anyone at any time?" Pete asked. He was now turning this over in his mind.

"That's the way it looks. The phone was just off the hook, lying on the desk."

Chambers took a breath and sat forward. "Now, we have another possibility. And I want you to know I've already told you too much, but we need your help." He paused to collect his thoughts. "We pulled the videotapes from the county courthouse security system today for the two hours before Evers and Corporal Grady went into Larson's office. There are two cameras that scan the street. One of them barely takes in Larson's office, which is a half block away. We think a vehicle drove up to a parking lot on the other side of Larson's parking lot at 1:50 p.m. from the other direction. It's out of the line of sight, but it appears that a car drove slightly into the left edge of the camera view and turned into the direction of the lot, as indicated by the right rear fender of the car. That car backed out of the spot about two o'clock and went off again in the other direction."

"Can you tell anything about the make, color, or driver?" asked Mitch.

"It looks like a gray-colored late model, possibly a General Motors full-size sedan, three years old or newer. We've got people working on it. We pulled the security tape from the County Community Bank on Grow Avenue also. That would have been a logical travel route in that direction, but so far, no car similar to that went by. We're pulling all the security tapes throughout the town. It'll be pretty easy to review since we have the exact timeframe. If we don't find anything, the conclusion would be that the car drove due north leaving town. There are no cameras in that direction from Larson's office. While a cross-reference like that is not impossible, we will probably end up with hundreds of matches just in this county alone, never mind farther away."

"The premise is then that Larson could have been helped meeting his maker?" Grady asked while thinking about what he saw earlier in the day when he entered the Larson's office. "The door was locked from the inside and so were the windows," he reminded Grady.

"A mere technicality for a pro. Did you ever hear of a fast pin?" No one did. "It's a simple little metal clip that can be slipped into the deadbolt of a door lock before exiting a room and closing the door. Anyone trying the door even with heavy force can't open it. It acts like a deadbolt, but it would give way with the right amount of pressure. The door also had a push-button handle lock, but a visitor could depress it when leaving and then just shut the door. When the door was kicked open, everything got busted up, and it looked like an innocent part that fell on the floor. Our guys were down there all afternoon. We found one among the debris."

"This is a pro job?" Mitch added.

"Gentlemen, you've been in some heavy-duty company on this one. We think Larson was killed somehow with an overdose. We're having a detailed autopsy done to look for an injection mark or signs of struggle or restraint of some kind. In fact, if it were two people, they could have just forced the powder in a drink right down his throat. Powder or liquid form is the quickest kill, other than an injection. You absorb it all at once."

"What about the prescription? Was it his?" asked Mitch.

"Oh yeah, pros... remember? They would have probably at one time even been in Larson's company when he used it at his office or home. He kept a bottle in his office, according to his secretary. They could have asked to use the bathroom or even broken in to get their hands on the bottle. Even an old prescription will have a paper trail tracing back to him. Once they had the prescription, they could duplicate it. Tramadol is available online and mailed to the home. It's a common painkiller for extreme cases. Larson was treated two years ago for back pain, and that's when it was prescribed."

"So I guess in order to catch the killer, or killers, we need to act like Larson did a suicide and everything is over, right?" Pete summarized.

"That's it. We are combing over those videotapes and reviewing the autopsy. Now that you are in the loop, be aware of any information that can take this to conclusion. I'll stay in touch with Mitch and let you know of any progress. I don't have to tell you that there is a very small circle of people in the know on our end, and we have to keep it that way."

"We know the feeling," answered Mitch. "We will keep this just among the three of us," he said while staring right at Corporal Grady, the understanding being that Evers would not be told.

The group agreed to get some rest that night and let the forces at work be guided by their findings.

DA Larson Found Dead, Forbes Connection Alleged

By Mary Michelson, Staff writer

Filed: Tuesday, June 24, 2008
Published: Wednesday, June 25, 2008
Susquehanna County News

The Pennsylvania State Police have handed over investigations into the Forbes International Investments, Inc., investment scam to the FBI after arrests made yesterday in the case. State Police Captain Dean Evers headed up a team arresting suspects in the case yesterday in Montrose. The primary person of interest was Susquehanna County District Attorney Lawrence Larson, who was found dead in his office, apparently the victim of a suicide due to an overdose of drugs. An autopsy is being conducted by state police surgeons to confirm the findings. Others taken in for questioning were Susquehanna County Coroner James Davis and Northeast Penn Bank Vice President William Dobson. Both are alleged to have taken part in the Forbes scheme involving the deaths of six people in Wyoming and Susquehanna

Counties in recent months. County Sheriff Ken Petersen assisted in the investigation and arrests.

District Attorney Larson was in his second term, and was said to be preparing for a US Senate run, according to members of his senate election committee. A native and longtime resident of Silver Lake Township, he was very instrumental in bringing federal and state crime fighting grants to Susquehanna County and was active in many civic and non-profit organizations. He leaves a wife and two children.

Forbes president Joseph Pratt was found dead of a heart attack recently in his vehicle parked at his office in Montrose. Forbes had been under investigation by the District Attorney's office and Sheriff Ken Petersen for illegal investment practices in connection with the proceeds clients had received from natural gas well leasing agreements. The Forbes offices in Montrose and Wilkes Barre have been seized by FBI investigators. Clients and anyone with questions or information concerning the case are asked to call the State Attorney General's office in Harrisburg.

32

A month passed, and life went back to normal as much as could be expected in Silver Lake Township. Mitch was preoccupied with physical therapy treatments three times a week, and Pete had made two trips out of town and hosted a few visits at the lake from relatives in the intervening time. The only news they had from Agent Chambers was two weeks ago, and there was nothing substantial then. He was just staying in touch. Without any feedback from Agent Chambers, they each couldn't help but to worry whether they spoke out prematurely about Judge Horvath and their suspicions. They did feel good about addressing Larson, Davis, Dobson, and certainly Pratt. Maybe that was all they should be concerned with after all, they began to think.

"Pete, I just heard from Tom Chambers," Mitch announced by phone.

"It's about time. It's been, what, four weeks since we met with him."

"Well, he's been in touch, but he really hasn't had anything definitive to say, if you remember."

"That's what I mean. Anyway, what's up?"

"He wants to get together. Your place?"

"Sure, any time."

"How about now? He's sitting right in front of me."

"All right, I'll be here."

When Mitch and Chambers arrived, their dispositions gave away their feelings. They walked into Pete's living room and were welcomed with some cheese slices and bread along with an assortment of olives and glasses of merlot, all of which was quite a different assortment, coming from Pete.

"Pete, what's with the spread? Are you going European on us?" Mitch kidded.

"Actually, you two are the most sophisticated guests I've had here all summer. That shows you what a lousy summer I've been having."

"Well, we aim to uphold our status. But what's with the wine? Did you run outta beer?"

"Sometimes I wonder if you deserve anything at all. Try it. It's good for you. Actually, I'm trying to get rid of my food inventory before I leave for the season."

"Pete, really, I appreciate it. Let me tell you guys what's been going on. You two are on our minds all the time, but the wheels of justice grind slowly. And I'm here today to explain the slow progress," Chambers began.

"Thanks. We can only guess how it must be, especially when you're trying to really nail someone," Mitch answered.

"It's true. The bad guys have so many rights these days that you have to get it correct all ways to Sunday and then some. There's nothing worse than falling short on your proof. You become the accused rather than the perp, and I'm not kidding. I've been there once, and it'll never happen to me again, ever," Chambers responded.

"Well, we appreciate the time you're taking to give us an update."

"Mitch, it's the least we can do. You guys have gotten us around to third base on this thing. And I'm trying like hell to bring it home. Let me bring you up to speed.

"First, there really is no news yet. And I know that must be a disappointment after all this time." When Pete and Mitch heard this, they visibly deflated. Their eyes wandered around the room in disgust with the situation.

"But here is the reason," Chambers added. "And when I tell you this, it will be hard to believe, but bear with me. I hope you can appreciate what I go through literally on a day-to-day basis."

Mitch and Pete continued to be attentive, realizing that Chambers was commiserating as much as he was sharing information.

Chambers continued. "Senator Bob Wellman and his committee have been working on an important piece of legislation. It involves the concerns of the natural gas well drilling operations all throughout the state. And it seems that Wellman himself is pretty much the Rosetta Stone on this whole thing. He knows the rural aspects of the Marcellus Shale counties and the absolute need that the residents have in getting involved in gas production. It is in his words, and it's true: the survival of the northeast sector of the state. He also knows the political side, and he is very good at it, not only on the state level, but also on the federal level. But what is really interesting is that he knows the strong interests that the neighboring upstate New York has in competing for the very same limited funding and resources of these gas well exploration companies. What I'm saying in straightforward terms is that Senator Bob Wellman is the single most important key figure in the entire future prosperity of the state of Pennsylvania, believe it or not."

"You have to be kidding me! After all our work and after all we've gone through, the politicians are making this a sacrosanct, hands-off situation!" Mitch scowled.

"Hold on. It gets worse. First, let me assure you, we have enough suspicions as it is about all those bastards on the state level to start digging around to see if they have personal agendas. But it does make sense to let them complete this important work, and we need to cooperate for the time being, at least, until he puts together some very important financial and political arrangements within the state, and also in cooperation with New York state politicians."

"How in the hell does that have anything to do with what we're dealing with? We are overdue in putting this thing to bed. Way overdue!" Mitch reminded.

"I know, I know. The powers that be have commanded, and I repeat, *commanded*, that we hold off with our case until certain assurances are put in place. And those assurances are vital to the future of Pennsylvania and New York if they are conducted correctly with each state's best interests in mind."

"How so? We have criminals on the loose ... killers!" reminded Mitch.

"That's why I'm here. Listen; we all want to resolve this thing: Forbes, Pratt, Larson, killings, the absolute worst things in the world that could come into our lives. But believe it or not, there are some things that are more important, as in the prosperity of the state you are living in and how that affects the lives of millions of people."

"What in the hell are you telling us?" Mitch responded.

"Hold on, Mitch." Pete grabbed him by the arm and pulled it toward him. "I get it already. Just listen, and you will too."

"Thanks, Pete. I know it's unbelievable, but it is what it is. We simply have to wait our turn. I guess that's the easiest way to put it. As serious as you and I think this is, murders and all, there are actually much more important matters to get resolved before we are allowed to do our thing. But I assure you we will get this thing done.

"What the politicians don't want is anything to disturb the progress of getting some cooperative agreements in place between the two states in concert with about twelve of the major gas exploration companies, and a few more if they can get them all up to speed. As far as everyone is concerned, and I mean everyone, the worst thing that can happen is to have an all-out competition for these gas companies to locate in one state versus the other."

"I thought there were antitrust laws against trying to control things like that," Pete interjected.

"There are; for private businesses, that is, but not for governments. And not for governments when they can put some laws in place to control this from becoming an all-out war. It's been bad enough already. The way they explain it, if both states continue separately, everyone will get less than if they cooperate."

"It's kinda like that Betamax and VHS marketing war that Sony had with all the other manufacturers when the video cassette recorders were introduced years ago," Pete interjected. "Everyone wasted a lot of time and energy fighting each other, trying to become the one standard videotape, when they could have decided on an industry standard among themselves. Then they could have used their resources toward improving efficient manufacturing to bring the prices down so that they all could sell more machines and make more profits. The lesson was an expensive one for everybody, and in the end, Sony's Betamax lost out."

"That's exactly what's going on. That's what everyone's trying to prevent. If the gas companies get into a bidding war on just the basic leases, their funds are not going to be able to be used for the actual drilling as much. The drilling is what produces the revenues for the landowners, the gas companies, and of course, the states, when it comes down to it," Chambers continued.

"So what's to keep everyone in line? I mean, how do they control who gets what?" Mitch asked.

"That's what they're working on right now. I guess the leases are going to have to be written so that there is a deadline for when the drilling must take place. This is supposed to keep any one company from tying up too much of the land and from keeping it idle too long. But what is really unprecedented is that the two states are going to set up an agreement to split the business opportunities being presented by the gas companies. They plan to limit the licenses to a fixed number and report the licenses granted and keep tabs on each other so that the agreed upon portions of business opportunities are maintained," Chambers explained.

"This is similar to what OPEC does with the oil production. They don't want any one country to ruin it for all of them," Pete explained.

"It sounds like tricky business to keep all that greed in check," Mitch added.

"Actually, it's almost impossible. Consider the greed element alone: landowners, gas companies, drilling contractors, bankers, politicians—you name it. It's totally out of control, and it's going to take some masterful political maneuvering to pull this off," Chambers cautioned. "It has been taking an excruciatingly long time, but if anyone can accomplish it, Wellman is thought to be the one."

"I really can't see it ever happening," Pete responded. "There is a free-for-all going on now, and it's going to be hard to stop it."

"Well, Wellman is getting a lot of support from all levels, state and federal, and even in New York state. This is huge," Chambers concluded. "Now here is the clincher: the water from the Susquehanna River. That river flows down through New York state, right through the Marcellus Shale country and then all the way down through Pennsylvania Marcellus Shale country to the Chesapeake Bay. Of all the entities involved in this whole thing, the Chesapeake Bay Authority can trump everyone. In other words, what happens upriver ends up downriver, and that is their concern. They wield the overriding authority and have all the say-so. If the two states don't work things out, there could be something like a free-for-all. Each state would end up licensing too many wells and using an unfair amount of the water resources of the river or wastewater disposal resources in an uncoordinated way. Chaos would surely result, at least in the short term. It could be decades before either state realizes the potential that is available to them."

"So you're saying that no one wants to rock the boat by way of a scandal relating in any way to the gas drilling," Pete summarized.

"That's exactly what the issue is. It would definitely be a distraction and could potentially ruin it for everyone," Chambers answered.

Pete just mused and listened to the conversation, but he couldn't help asking, "Tom, there's something more you're not telling us, am I right?"

Chambers just stared at Pete long and hard. He had been wondering if Pete's thought process might come to this conclusion. He paused before speaking. "Pete, you and Mitch now know as much as we do, except for one thing, which we can't comment on right at this time. If you ask me any more, I won't be able to answer any questions. That's all I can tell you."

"Asked and answered. I understand. You've been more than forthcoming," Pete said with a knowing look in his eyes.

"Gentlemen, I've got to save the world, or at least the state. Mitch, can I give you a ride back home?" Chambers asked.

"I'll drive him over later," Pete interjected. "We have some things to take care of, if you don't mind, Mitch."

"Sure, it's okay with me. See you soon, Tom. Thanks for keeping us in the loop."

After Agent Chambers left, Mitch turned to Pete, saying, "Did I miss something?"

"Maybe so; I'm guessing strongly that Chambers gave us a tipoff as to who else might be involved in our little mystery."

"You mean Wellman?"

"Yes."

"How so?"

"While I believe everything he told us about the cooperative agreement between the two states and how important it must be, I think pursuing anything at this time relating to leases and Forbes's investments and Larson's death should be tolerable. In other words, it wouldn't affect the workings of two high-level committees in state governments. However, and this is the clincher, if Wellman is connected to our investigation, that would be disastrous. I think that is what Chambers was alluding to."

"Do you think they have something on Wellman?"

"Possibly, or they might just suspect that he could be involved. He knows so much about these developments that he could have been acting on the inside to provide information that could have been helpful to Pratt and Larson."

"What do we do now?"

"Sit and wait, I guess. It's really in the feds' hands."

"I guess, but I still feel so much a part of it," Mitch bemoaned.

"It looks like they're biting out there. Want to stay for a while?"

"Sure," said Mitch, looking at his watch. "Let's go. These opportunities are far and few between anymore."

"You mean few and … never mind. Let's catch some dinner."

33

One Plus One Equals Three, NY and PA Cooperate

By Mary Michelson, Staff Writer

Filed: Monday, August 11, 2008
Published: Wednesday, August 13, 2008 Susquehanna County News

The Pennsylvania State Senate Agricultural and Rural Affairs Committee announced this week an arrangement of unprecedented proportions and implications. The senate committee has reached an agreement with its New York state counterpart to facilitate the exploration and harvesting of natural gas throughout the Marcellus Shale in both states by cooperating in a series of steps that will prove beneficial for both states.

Previously, each state was struggling with the boom in interest for the mineral rights of landowners by natural gas exploration companies. No less than twenty exploration companies have set up shop in the two-state region, offering five-year lease arrangements with hefty sign-up bonuses now said to be hovering at $2,500 per acre. Landowners then participate in the extraction proceeds at the rate of fifteen percent of the revenues for the five-year period. Needless to say, this has been akin to a gold rush in recent months and government officials in both states have become overwhelmed with unprecedented activities in licensing, inspection and environmental controls. None of this type or volume of infrastructure development was anticipated just two years ago when the potential of the Marcellus Shale was revealed. Geologists say by consensus that this discovery of natural gas is the single largest ever.

The fate of the two states has been modeled by the bi-state committees working with one another for their mutual benefit. It has been explained that if each state acts independently and goes its own way, a serious environmental, financial, and civic opportunity will be missed forever. Each would have to "invent its own wheel" by figuring out problems and procedures without the benefit of the other's experiences. The protection of the environment is at the center of the planning, and in particular, how each state allocates its water resources and wastewater controls. By combining resources and selectively planning the harvest of these gas assets, both states hope to eliminate wasted efforts and finances, and plan to work together to assist in fulfilling each other's needs.

Essential to the process is the allocation of drilling licenses, which will be managed jointly. The intention is to control the resources of the exploration companies while, at the same time, keeping a viable inventory of production real estate in abeyance for near-term drilling without unnecessarily sequestering acreage for long periods of non-productivity. This way, exploration companies can be assured that land inventory will always be available and they will not have to take a strong investment posture in future leases until they need them. The result means that the capital of the drillers can be put right to work on revenue production from any active wells instead of having the capital tied up in land inventory leases. Everyone benefits if the level of trust can be maintained.

All of this has been the brain child of State Senator Robert Wellman, D-20, who has been the organizer and principal negotiator for Pennsylvania. He commented, "While we expect many issues to arise throughout the process in future years, we all realize this natural gas opportunity is a godsend and we are committed to making this cooperation work. Both of our states' futures rest on its success. We have never been given such a gift as this, and if we allow greed and mismanagement to take over it will be the single most shameful event in the history of both states. Everyone feels the weight of the responsibility and has worked extremely hard through special executive sessions all summer long to finally achieve this very worthwhile goal. We are very proud of the bi-state cooperative, and we all intend to make it work, believe me."

Effective September 1st, all state drilling licenses will be issued through the bi-state system known collectively as the Northeastern States Coalition of Mineral Resources. All current applications have been suspended and will be prioritized under the new system with respect to the aging of their applications. A ceremonial meeting of the governors of both states is set for September 1st to sign and issue the first two bi-state licenses, one for New York and one for Pennsylvania. The meeting will be held on Wildwood Road which is just east of both Waverly, New York, and Sayre, Pennsylvania, along the state border where the Susquehanna River crosses from New York into Pennsylvania. The symbolism is profound in that the river is the primary water resource needed by both states to enable much of the drilling process. It is in fact a "quid pro quo" arrangement, whereby New York is allowed to use the water but must pass clean water to Pennsylvania. In order, however, for Pennsylvania to receive enough water for its own uses, New York must allocate its water flow responsibly. Each state has everything to gain by its full cooperation.

34

Summer in Silver Lake is too short, both metaphorically and meteorologically. It is only ninety days between Memorial Day and Labor Day, the only months absolutely guaranteed when the water pipes will not freeze in the cottages and homes around the lake at this elevation. All bets are off in all other months, and there are decades of past records to verify that claim. Snows as late as May and freezing frosts as early as mid-September have occurred over the years. Fall colors can arrive as early as September or as late as November, depending on a myriad of complex interactions from a dry or rainy summer to a warm or frosty September. Usually by early October the summer residents have left, and the beauty of the uninterrupted solitude is unequaled.

 Pete had packed to leave for the trip back home to Michigan, back to nothing, with his wife not a part of his life there anymore. Preparations of draining the water pipes and locking windows and doors for the winter were almost complete, a routine of events carried out by rote after all the years visiting for the summer months.

The car was loaded up, and a brief visit to Helen and Mitch would send him off, regrettably, for another eight months. Michigan itself is no Shangri-La in the winter months, but it was his home, and he enjoyed that part of the year there.

He was leaving with a feeling of angst. His life was one of achievements, never a job left undone, always a project completed beyond expectations. Not this time. His patience and that of his quasi-team members would have to wait for the sluggish speed of governmental developments to unfold. He felt that the meeting with Tom Chambers was the right thing to do, but really the group still had nothing to show for it. He wondered how things would have been if they continued to investigate for themselves without relying on the feds. His patience was more on a business-oriented pace, as in a matter of hours or days, not weeks or months.

Pete walked up the driveway for the last newspaper delivery before leaving for home tomorrow. He enjoyed the weekly paper, especially the section entitled "100 Years Ago," which repeated articles from a century ago week by week. It was widely known and attested to that things never change. Any one of the articles could have occurred yesterday. They were timeless. One thing stood out—the grammatical and highly literate rendering was absolutely a joy to experience. It was something not to be found in today's expedient prose. It was Victorian by any measure, and a throwback to times when only the good is remembered and all of the bad has healed by layers upon layers of time.

100 Years Ago

Water well does double duty as gas well

Published: Wednesday, June 22, 1910 Susquehanna County News

The property of the Rupert Wherthing family in Silver Lake Township has a new addition to its system of business ventures. A new well was drilled recently for the watering of cattle just outside the milking barn with startling results. By statement of Hyde Drilling owner, Alfred Hyde, this is the first natural gas well drilled outside of Salt Springs at the Wheaton property. There is a water flow sufficient to support the herd of forty cattle; however, the presence of gas bubbles in the water indicates a source of natural gas below the farm.

Mr. Wherthing is looking into the possibility of supplying gas on a commercial basis. It should be noted that this has been attempted in the region in years past at the Wheaton farm location, but the uncertain flow of gas in continuous volume and pressure had put the commercial feasibility as too risky a venture for the faint-hearted. Mr. Wherthing has installed a "No Smoking" sign at the well as a safety precaution. The community wishes success for these considerations since it would be of local benefit to all.

> Publisher's note: The above article is shown here a few years early because of the uncanny resemblance to the content of a gas well development article in today's paper. See page 3 for the "Smart Wells" article.

The current news articles still carried the same Victorian flavor, whether by design or long-time influence. The narratives were eagerly anticipated by the community throughout the county, some just for the news content and others absolutely for the literary presentation. The *Susquehanna News* was a gem in a wasteland of rotting daily publications. Fortunately, its future was guaranteed, since it had recently been acquired by the Scranton News Corporation and the new owners left everything intact. It was an anachronism that everyone wanted to preserve. It could be said that it was behind the times, and it would also be praised for being so. Contributing content came from correspondents who were English teachers and writers by trade or training, retired columnists, and highly literate locals who carried great esteem among their peers, neighbors, and community leaders. Again, it was small-town rural ethos at its best. Pete relished its presence when it arrived in the Wednesday mailing each week. Reading the publication provided an hour of antithetical remedy for the concerns of the times. It was nonetheless an update of the state of the county when it arrived every seven days. *The world should be so fortunate as to experience such a gift,* Pete thought.

His preoccupation was interrupted by a call from Mitch. "Peter, you getting ready to hibernate for the winter?"

"Unfortunately, I think my blood is already starting to thicken. It's been cold around here. How have you two been?"

"Pretty good; Helen is getting her fall plantings in. I'm rehabilitating pretty well. I've been back on the job for three weeks now. Everything's looking good."

"Glad to hear it. What's up?"

"Take a look at the paper and tell me what you think about the article on page three. It's the one about the smart wells," Mitch advised.

"Okay. I was just starting to read it. Thanks. I'll give you a call back."

35

"Smart Well" Process Grant Awarded to Sow and Reap

By Mary Michelson, Staff writer

Filed: Friday, September 12 2008
Published: Wednesday, September 17,
2008 Susquehanna County News

The Pennsylvania State Senate Appropriations Committee has announced a $3,300,000 state- and federally-sponsored grant to a small consortium of local property owners organized as Sow and Reap, Inc., Save Our Watershed, and REAlize Profits. The unsolicited grant proposal had been submitted to the Department of Conservation of Natural Resources (DCNR), the Department of Environmental Protection (DEP), and the Environmental Protection Agency (EPA) eighteen months ago and was met with considerable interest. In an unusually short timeframe for any such petition, the concept of reclaiming and recycling our precious water for the hydraulic fracturing process, called fracking, used to blast apart mile-deep layers of shale rock formations during natural gas well drilling was considered ingeniously creative and responsive to the pressure of gas exploration and overnight exploitation of mineral rights agreements already underway. "The approval process was 'fast-tracked,' given the urgent nature and development needs of the Northeastern counties," commented Senator Rick Riley, D- Chairman of the Senate Appropriations Committee. "We hope to have a proven full-size prototype of the concept in operation within 6 to 9 months."

While Pennsylvania is sitting on top of the single largest natural gas reserves ever discovered, the limiting factor has been water. The amounts of water needed per single well is staggering, 3–4 million gallons. Not only is the source of water a limitation, but the post treatment of it to remove salt, metals, and acids before discharging into the environment is a very limited and controversial technical constraint. Existing waste water treatment facilities were essentially established to process local municipal sewage and small amounts of industrial waste water, and are limited in their capacities to handle the new-found volumes of waste water. They must be expanded, and many new ones authorized and built from scratch. Further, the necessity to truck both the water and the waste water to and from the well sites adds an almost inestimable element regarding cost and traffic load on local roadways.

The Sow and Reap grant promises to eliminate the need for fresh water and water treatment transfer for 80 to 90 percent of the water requirements as we now know them. "Smart wells" are the operating terminology of the group and they work like this. Professor John Nordstrom, Houston State University, in collaboration with two local firms, Tunkhannock Engineering and Process Machine Corp., has built lab models of the process equipment. They will now be authorized under the state grant to plan and build a full-scale operation in Silver Lake Township with the center of

HYPOTHESIS

operations based at the property of Nora Connely, a member of the consortium. It must be noted here that while many landowners' properties may have unproven potential, one of the driving aspects of the consortium's proposal was the already proven escape of gas through existing water well on the Connely property. It had been documented as early as 1910 in an article which appeared in the Susquehanna News when the well was drilled by her father's family at the time that large amounts of gas bubbled up through the well water, and some small amounts still do to this day. Many local residents are also familiar with the gas bubbles which were documented in the eighteen century and can even be seen escaping from the open well historic site to this day at Salt Springs State Park a few miles away.

The Connely property is aligned contiguously north to south among the other properties in the consortium along Silver Creek, which originates at Silver Lake and generally runs north to south, parallel to Route 167, as it passes through Silver Lake Township before heading east toward Salt Springs. There are five properties amounting to 1,857 acres; each, as a member of the participating group, will be able to withdraw water from the Sow and Reap setup without having it trucked in, and subsequently pass the water through reclamation equipment and transfer it by way of a water pipeline to the next well on the same property or adjacent property. All of the properties sit above a pre-glacial valley filled with gravel below the surface, allowing high water flow rates to the surface estimated at over 2,000 gallons per minute. Deep water wells will be drilled on two of the properties in the linkup which have quarry pits on them designated as water reservoirs. The reservoirs will be filled from the wells, along with the purely distilled water from the reclamation process, and also diverted Silver Creek water waiting for the next well's fracturing operations. The pipeline system is closed-loop and pressurized. To prevent freezing in the cold winter months, a circulation cycle occurs every 30 minutes if the ground temperature falls below 34 degrees.

The success of the system depends on the viability of two water reclamation processes; namely, thermal evaporation and crystallization. The evaporator can reclaim at least 70 percent of the wastewater, leaving 30 percent to be processed as normal drilling brine, a salt-laden waste product. The crystallizer extracts 90 percent of the balance, and the simple web of pipes directs the purified water to the next well or to the quarry reservoirs for storage. There are no inbound trucking activities and only a small fraction of wastewater needs to be sent to treatment plants other than the simple on-site reclamation equipment. Such a localized self-support system is poised to be recommended as the standard drilling process recommended by DEP, DCNR, and EPA if the system is successful. The design and layout of the system is already completed and installation is scheduled to begin immediately.

"Mitch, I think we might have the missing piece of the puzzle," Pete announced over the return phone call.

"I thought you might say something like that. What do you think?" responded Mitch.

"What kind of car does Nora have?"

"I don't know, but I think it's silver or gray."

"Call Chambers and see if you can get him up here today. Have him get a background check on our friend Nora and see what kind of car is registered to her. See if he has anything on that professor Nordstrom too."

"Will do; I'll get back to you. Geez, I hate this!"

The three of them—Pete, Mitch, and Grady—listened that evening to FBI Agent Tom Chambers as he unveiled the life and times of Nora Connely, the quaint local schoolteacher they all knew and loved. Her career began in the Navy Waves after high school. Her training and assignments were classified, but early on she was stationed at the Marine Corps Training Center at Parris Island, South Carolina. After that, she spent some time in Washington, D.C., as part of a public relations group for the marines. Following her discharge, she got her college degree in secondary education from Penn State University while working part-time in the Wyoming County court system for Magistrate Wilton Horvath. Three years later she started teaching in the Montrose High School and has been with the Montrose Area School District, as it is now known, to this day. She drives a 2005 Chevrolet Monte Carlo, silver in color.

"Are we saying that she's some kind of commando or something?" Mitch responded.

"It's possible. All indications are that her assignments could have been in Special Forces. It's all classified, but that's at least a possibility. As you are aware, we know all about Wellman, and he was in the marines around the same time. When he got out with his law degree, he clerked for Wilton Horvath after Horvath was appointed judge, right after Nora left there to begin teaching as far as we can determine. She did continue to work there during the summers for a while. The connection with Horvath is uncanny, though. We don't think this is at all a coincidence."

Pete and Mitch looked at each other.

"Do you think she went into Larson's office and shoved that medication down his throat or injected him with a needle or something like that?" Mitch asked.

"I do." Pete was silent until now. "If she had any kind of skills training in hand-to-hand combat or assassination techniques, any one of a dozen easy moves on someone with his guard down would be possible. Here is my hypothesis: there is only one person left alive from the original five landowners who comprised Sow and Reap, and that's Nora Connely. She and Senator Wellman's wife and a professor named Nordstrom now control the consortium, according to the land use agreements filed for everyone's estates. My guess is that Wellman had Wilkinson set up the consortium to apply for the grants when that Houston professor came up with the idea. Wellman could easily influence approvals on the state level, and probably federal too. If Wellman was in the marines on special assignments, which are also unknown, I'd bet we could put him and Nora in the same places at the same time."

"I'll check on that right now," Chambers interrupted.

"Wait; there's a lot more." Pete motioned for him to stay. "Nora probably carried influence with her neighbors in organizing the consortium and in the Forbes investment scheme. Remember, she is the only one who hadn't invested yet at the time of Pratt's death. Once Wilkinson got everyone to alter their wills and estate plans, he wasn't needed anymore. His so-called accident more than likely was not, especially with Wellman's wife as beneficiary.

"Further, coroner Davis was enlisted to cooperate on passing the autopsies off as suicides or a heart attack, as in Pratt's case. Larson was involved, probably for his future political benefit, but he was needed to dampen any claims against Forbes in the event that relatives filed suit or complained. The funds were transferred offshore, and the insurance policies were worthless. He didn't look too closely into these deaths, and that's the way the group wanted it. Larson would have been assured great monetary assistance from the proceeds in his upcoming senate run. Once he was in congress, all the bases would be covered, with Wellman on the state level and Larson on the federal level. As a freshman senator, Larson would be sure to get appointed to the lesser committees dealing with farmland and mineral rights, rural developments, and the like. Together they could corner a good percentage of the action on all future natural gas extraction in the county in the coming years."

"Yeah, but that's years away. What did they have to gain today?" interjected Mitch.

"Control," answered Chambers. "You have to start sometime, and if they could put those five properties together as they say, that setup could generate ten times the normal income. And things are happening pretty fast around here with these wells."

"They were until last week," Pete said. "Gasco rescinded many of its open leases to conserve cash due to the credit markets drying up and the gas prices, at least temporarily, having gone down. They plan to finance future leases with profits from the drilling in place already and not rely as much on borrowing. There are very few funds available for borrowing, especially in speculative ventures like gas drilling. The Sow and Reap grants were squeezed in before the end of the budget period while legislators were still in session. Timing was of the essence. I think Wellman's scheme was that people had to sign up and get their lease bonus then invest their money and then be pronounced dead on a tight schedule before the gas companies backed out for this whole thing to work. I would say that Wellman had inside information on the leases being rescinded before most people even in Gasco."

"Then, when Judge Horvath learned that Larson was going down and could conceivably implicate them, there was no need to have Larson around anymore; the lesser of two evils, I guess. Let me make a phone call about Wellman's background check. Can I use your phone?" Chambers asked. Pete motioned him toward the phone, noting that his cell phone must not have a strong signal.

"Now, with everybody dead and the five properties under the control of the consortium, if they can get that 'smart well' concept in place quickly, there is quite a bit of money to be made starting within the next twelve months. If those 1,857 acres were properly developed, even if only 50 percent of the land was suitable, they could support more than one hundred separate wells with that water setup. Each well generates at least two hundred thousand dollars a year in fees for the landowner for an average of five years. You're talking a potential of well over a one hundred-million-dollar project for the consortium once everything is in place, if my math is correct," Mitch summarized.

They waited for Chambers to get off the phone before continuing.

"We'll have something shortly. Wellman was on a watch list for some other reason not related to this case," Chambers confided. "So we already have a pretty good file on him."

"No wonder they call you guys spooks," Mitch offered with a laugh.

"We really deserve the name sometimes. I'm guilty of it myself," Chambers answered. "But you guys have more inside information than all of our agents on this case right now. We'll have to make you honorary spooks or something."

"No thanks. We're hated enough now as it is," replied Mitch jokingly.

"Okay, now I can let you in on some more information. Remember a few weeks ago when I told you we were letting the bi-state committee complete its work for fear of disturbing their progress? That really was the case. But we've been watching Wellman for some time now."

Pete and Mitch nodded knowingly to one another.

"We know he's dirty, but we don't know how. We have some penny ante things on him, but nothing to take him down. This gas scam and connection to the murders are going to make a lot of people on my end very happy. On the other hand, this guy is the golden boy of the region. He has done a lot of good. It's a shame, a gosh-darn shame. We have to get this right. There can be no mistakes. He has to be convicted," Chambers confided. "We have to take our time and make no mistakes."

"We're in your corner. How can we help?" Mitch offered.

"We need to tie Nora into Wellman as a partner in this conspiracy, no doubts allowed. You see what I mean? If we nail her, with her military training and hard-ass approach, it may be difficult to incriminate Wellman. We need to get her out of the house for a few hours while our agents comb through it to try to pick up a current connection to Wellman."

"I can have Helen set up a dinner for Pete tomorrow night. That should give you enough time to do your thing," Mitch offered.

"I was hoping you would offer," Chambers answered. "We'll need a good two hours, more if possible."

"No problem. I'll call Helen now. We'll say it's a farewell for Pete," Mitch volunteered.

"I want to tell you gentlemen how important this is. If we approach it from the Wellman side, it would be awfully difficult to prove any connection. He supposedly lost money like everyone else in the Forbes thing. And his wife just happened to inherit the Wilkinson property. He has no other connections. He's clean. This thing has been set up with so many safeguards that we would never be able to tie him in. We want him bad, let me tell ya."

36

Six o'clock, and the guests had arrived. Mitch and Helen's porch was the perfect venue for observing the changing atmospherics during dusk. The four friends sat and rocked with a glass of wine in hand, nibbling on cheese cubes while looking out over the meadow. Conversation comes and goes in such a sedate setting. One comment barely leads logically to another, but altogether each participant knows well that is acceptable, owing to the relaxing effect of these waning days of summerlike weather.

The leaves were glowing colors of amber and red on the trees already in some spots. The scent of decaying fallen leaves and tall grass wafting through the nostrils gave certain alert as to the coming of fall. Yet evenings could be enjoyed for a short while outdoors before the coolness set in with the darkness.

Talk of Nora's Sow and Reap consortium occupied the conversation. She was somewhat noncommittal, since the deaths in the group of original planners left the venture now only in the hands of an outside adviser from the University of Houston, Kathy

Wellman, who was the niece of Edward Wilkinson, and herself. Nonetheless, she felt confident in handling the project, in particular since she had just retired and could put her full effort into it.

The mechanics of the installation were already assigned to contractors who had been involved for two years in the planning. She explained that the five contiguous properties were unique in their topography. There were stream and lake sources of water on the northern properties and glacial gravel deposits under all of them, which would allow very productive drilled water wells. The quarry on the southern end was to be the main water reservoir, which guaranteed a constant water supply and storage of the reclaimed wastewater, with a capacity of well over one hundred million gallons. The finance side was easy to understand, and she would do that herself using her local accountant.

"It was exciting, rejuvenating," she said. Her wish was only that her husband could be there to share it with her.

Pete and Mitch couldn't help but to regard Nora uncomfortably with the newfound persona of which only they were aware. They saw her differently, as could be expected. Before, her moves were dainty and humble—now they were catlike and canny; before, she was submissively not a conversationalist—now she was hiding something; before, she used her eating utensils with the grace of Emily Post—now she held the knife like an assassin. Everything changed and would change even more.

Helen outdid herself again, with a chicken Wellington dish accompanied with garden-grown carrots drizzled with a dark spicy chicken-based sauce. Everyone could have had seconds if it were not for the promise of a plump Endless Mountain apple pie cooling on the stove. Endless Mountain apples are a combination of tartness and sweetness unlike any found elsewhere. The rocky soil and sparse apple tree plantings yield an unforgettable combination of full taste, moisture, and potpourri of citrus like no other such fruit. Her mastery in creating the perfect lard-dough crust and baking it that extra ten minutes to adjust for the 1,700 feet altitude made all the difference. The crust held together just long enough to get it into your mouth and then almost dissolved along with the soft apple filling. Irish tea was the perfect complement to the tartness of the pie, strong and tasty, but with a mild bite that cleansed the taste buds each time in anticipation of another fresh taste of pie.

The phone rang, and Mitch answered. "Hello...you must have the wrong number...that's okay, no problem." It was the "all clear" call from Chambers. His team was finished at Nora's home, and that was the signal. It was difficult for Pete and Mitch to engage fully in the contrived spirit of the evening, but they did well under the circumstances.

Nora left for home, bidding Pete farewell until next year. Pete thanked Helen for the wonderful dinner, and he joined Mitch in the living room before they both left for Pete's house to meet Chambers and his team. They drove over to Pete's house in separate cars.

"Nothing; I mean, clean as a whistle," Chambers said as Pete and Mitch came through the door. Chambers and two other agents sat slumped into chairs in the living room. "Agents Joe West and Rick Spooner," Chambers added, indicating the two men with him. "We went through everything; no files, phone numbers, pictures, weapons, or anything. These people are good."

They all sat quietly. Pete brought out some beers. "Do you have anyone right now who can get to Frontier Communications in Dallas, just below Tunkhannock?" he asked.

"Yes. Actually, West and Spooner are driving back that way tonight. Why?" answered Chambers.

"My guess is that Judge Horvath did make a phone contact to have Larson taken out, and he did it from a public phone in Tunkhannock. There can't be too many payphones in that town anymore, and certainly not that many being used between twelve thirty and two o'clock that day. Let's see who was called during that period of time and try for a match of some sort."

"We're on it," Spooner responded. "Let me get someone in there to start digging before we arrive." He made a call to another location. "He'll be in there within a half hour." The two agents left with a promise to call back within two hours.

The wait was grueling. It was after eleven o'clock later that night when Pete picked up the ringing phone. "Hold on." He handed it to Chambers. They watched as Chambers wrote down the information and then asked the caller to hold on for a minute.

"There were three public payphone calls in that hour and a half from the eight locations within three miles of the courthouse; not a very prosperous venture in this day and age of cell phones, I guess. Four are at gas station mini-marts, three in restaurants, and one is a stand-alone booth at the airport. Two calls were made to local numbers in town and one to a Waverly, New York, number."

"Waverly? Who is listed for that number?" Mitch asked quickly.

"Hold on; give me the New York name... a Carol Wherthing, at 1400 Chemung Street."

Pete was quick to ask, "See if that number matches to any of the calls made from Nora Connely's house recently."

"It will," Mitch added. "That's Nora's sister. I'm sure of it."

They waited for ten minutes while Chambers held on to the phone. The answer was what they hoped for. "The Waverly number matches a number that is called three or four times a week from the Connely residence. The payphone call was made at 12:47 p.m. and lasted 1.6 minutes. Following that a call from Waverly went out to the Connely number at 12:52, lasting 1.1 minutes. Then at 12:55, another call was made from the Wherthing house in New York to Senator Wellman's private number at his office in the state capital, Harrisburg, which lasted 1.8 minutes. Fifteen minutes after that, the Connely house received a call from a payphone in Harrisburg, presumably from the senator; it lasted 5.3 minutes," Chambers reported. "Thanks, Joe. Stay there. We might need you," Chambers said as he hung up the phone.

"It's still all circumstantial," Chambers cautioned. "But we can pretty much be assured that's how it went down."

"Nora's sister is named Carol. I'm sure that's who the Waverly person is," said Mitch.

"We need a foolproof way to bring this thing all together; any ideas?" Chambers asked.

"Can we trust Captain Evers?" Pete asked, directing his eyes toward corporal Grady.

"I think the answer is no, but under the circumstances, what can he do?" Grady answered.

"You're right. Too many people know about this now, and it has to be Evers connecting with Judge Horvath, or this won't work. We need to have him call Horvath one more time and ask for an arrest warrant for Nora Connely two days from now on Saturday afternoon. That should give the underground communication system enough time to work."

"Great idea! Let's do it!" Chambers said.

Once State Police Captain Evers was brought up to speed by Tom Chambers, he was more than anxious to do his part. Judge Horvath was contacted the next day to issue another warrant, and it was faxed to Pete's house, as were the previous ones.

The subject of everyone's focus was Nora Connely. Predictably, a payphone call was made later that afternoon from the Tunkhannock airport payphone by Judge Horvath, about an hour after he received the warrant request from Evers. This time it was witnessed by FBI agents who recorded everything on video and voice recorders. The call was tracked to the Waverly, New York, number of Carol Wherthing, and a phone tap recording made. From there, a call to Senator Robert Wellman's private number was made, and the same wiretap recorded a brief conversation. After that, Senator Wellman's phones remained silent. Within minutes, Judge Horvath received a return call at the phone booth from a payphone in the Harrisburg state capital area. The caller didn't identify himself, and the conversation was very cryptic and hard to interpret.

"I have a message to call you."

"Yes, I have another warrant request you should be interested in."

"Who?"

"Your number-one partner, NC. Saturday afternoon.

"Thanks."

But the investigators knew exactly what was meant. This for sure had to be Horvath's demise. He hung up and returned to his office.

It was Thursday, and state senate legislative sessions in Harrisburg would be recessed by early afternoon so that everyone could return home for the weekend.

37

Friday evening was a little different in Silver Lake, as is common in most places. Road traffic, although light by any measure, picks up slightly along the two-lane arteries here and there. The few restaurants and bars in the area are visibly more active. Weekend visitors to the beautiful lakes are arriving with family, groceries, and dreams of just a few more summerlike days to enjoy. On Nora Connely's farm property, any day was enjoyable, but today seemed special. Autumn was definitely in the air, and if you have never been in northeast Pennsylvania in September, there are no words to describe the beckoning of the senses and the feeling of well-being even by just passing through. This evening was no different. Life appeared suspended to those who took in the beauty of this consciousness. It lifted the lowest of spirits all month long, at least until the realities of the coming winter set in. It was nature's gift of pleasure before the harsh inconveniences of the cold season.

Nora's visitor was announced in advance, and she was preparing hors d'oeuvres for the meeting. Each minute of anticipation was like an hour. Her affair with Senator Bob Wellman had to be kept under wraps for both their sakes. It had been like this since they met in the marines, when they both trained in boot camp and served in Washington, D.C., on what was called at the time "special projects." Two unassuming but highly talented young people from a part of the Pennsylvania with good work ethic and caring, both were athletic standouts and scholars, the ideal prospects for officer candidate school, a fast-track military education granted to very few for specific purposes. Those days were well behind them at this stage of their lives. They each ended up going separate ways for one reason or another, marrying and having completely different avenues in life; that is, until a few years ago, when they reconnected for business reasons. They still dreamed of happy golden years together, and the plans of the past three years were finally coming together when they could eventually realize their desires.

Suddenly, two hands grabbed her by the waist with a stronghold from behind, surprising her with a mild jolt as she stood at the kitchen counter, and a face nuzzled next to hers over her shoulder. She was only slightly startled at the game of stealth he had played many times before. She had no indication of his arrival, a matter of pride he held from his special forces training days. They kissed, and he put he put his forefinger to his lips, signaling her to stay silent. He pointed to the porch door and quietly led her outside to the old well beside the barn where they could talk freely. She still didn't know about the arrest warrant, and she never would as far as he was concerned.

"Why all the secrecy, Bob?" Nora whispered.

"Just being cautious. This whole thing is coming together now, and I don't want to upset the apple cart," Wellman answered. "I just have a few details to cover in privacy, and then we can talk openly about general matters when we go back inside." They kissed and held each other in a long embrace.

"Do you think we're being surveilled?" she asked, looking lovingly into his eyes at close range.

"Well, there's a lot at stake. The Larson suicide setup is suspect, and my sources tell me that they're coming after you for it. Are you sure you wiped everything down for prints before you left?"

"Come on! I know what I'm doing. I hardly touched anything, and it was over in a minute. I jammed the tube down his throat and hit the ejector before he knew what was happening, and I hung on to him from behind until he went limp. I think he choked to death first. No marks, no prints, his prints on the glass and the prescription bottle, and I was out the door in less than five minutes. Even if someone saw me leaving, it was the perfect suicide setup. It could have happened after I left if the question ever comes up."

"What do you say if you're asked why you were there?"

"I was going to the Forbes office across the hall. It was closed, of course. It still had the crime scene label sealing the door. No one was around to help me. So I left." She had a cool sense about her as she relived the convenient version of her visit. Wellman stood quietly, assessing his options.

"By the way, where is your car?" she asked.

"I'm not here. Remember?" They continued to hug in a tight embrace. His thoughts vacillated between buying into her contrived defense and how effective it would be with all attention on her as the key to the Forbes puzzle, and trusting that she would not give him up under pressure. He decided she had to die, and with one swift, unsuspecting move, he twisted her arm behind her back and pushed her over to the old well and shoved her over the wall. The splash came seconds later, owing to its depth.

"Hands up, Senator! Down on your knees! Get down, I said!" State Police Officer Sheila Gooding screamed, running from the barn toward him. "Hands behind your back! Officer needs help ... Connely farm ... fire location seven, section fifteen ... murder attempt in progress! Now!" she yelled into her portable radio. "Hang on, Nora!" she called amid the splashing below. "Hold your hands behind your back. Put 'em back! Get on the ground!" she shouted. Wellman went prone on the ground, and as she approached to put the handcuffs on, he quickly grabbed at her ankle and pulled it out from under her, scuffling on top of her. He reached for the pistol. A shot went off. The two combatants lay still until one arose and the other lay sprawled in a growing flow of blood. Wellman stood and ran toward the tree line, disappearing into the woods.

Almost fifteen minutes passed without a stir. Sirens sounded in the waning light of day closer and closer. Two state police cars sped up the driveway, sirens screaming and lights flashing until they drove up to an unsettling sight—Officer Gooding lay, apparently lifeless, and a flaccid call of "Help!" came from the well amid all the confusion.

The men jumped out and took cover behind their cars. "Comm, Officer Campbell! Officer down! Send an ambulance right away...fire location seven...section fifteen...Connely farm!" One officer held his pistol, scanning back and forth at shoulder level, while the other gave aid to Gooding, compressing the stomach wound and covering her with a blanket from one of the cars.

No one was aware of Nora's dilemma thirty feet below them. She strained to press against the sides of the old well. Gas bubbles occasioned from the surface of the water, displacing precious oxygen. Her commando toughness was now at a test. She could hardly breathe, only managing faint gasps trying to call for help. No one came. Her arm was broken, and it was impossible to brace her back against the sidewall. Her grip gave out, and she sunk slowly below the surface of the water. An ambulance sounded its arrival above, but it would not help her now.

Two EMTs worked on Officer Gooding by stopping the bleeding with a large bandage wrap and strapping an oxygen mask over her face. They carefully lifted her onto a carrier and into the ambulance.

Mitch arrived amid the exit of the ambulance. "It was Gooding," offered the second officer.

Mitch felt sick.

"She gonna be all right?" he asked.

"It's serious. Lots of blood! It looks like her weapon was used," he said, pointing to the handgun in the pool of blood.

"Damn!" Mitch exclaimed. "Where's Nora Connely?"

"No sign of her," said the other officer as he came from the house.

"Damn!"

"Over here, guys!" called the other officer from the barn. "It must be Gooding's recorder. It's still on."

"Play it!" sounded Mitch.

The three men huddled around the small video recorder's glowing screen in the barn and watched in amazement as the surreal scene of just minutes ago played itself out in the darkness surrounding them. Proof that Wellman was there offered only momentary satisfaction; then the short struggle, ending in Nora's push into the well. "God! She's in there!" They ran to the well and peered down. "Nora! Nora!" Mitch called. There was no response. "Get a rope!" he yelled.

They lashed a rope to the car bumper, and the younger officer jumped to the task, flashlight in hand, lowering himself with Mitch and Campbell holding back and letting out slack. "This thing's deep. I'm down over twenty feet.

"I see her!"

No movement.

"She's dead!"

"That's all the rope!" came a shout from above.

"No matter! We'll have to leave this for the fire rescue guys," he yelled up. "She's gone!"

Amid the sounds of more sirens from the arrival of the Silver Lake Fire Company and rescue team members arriving in their cars

HYPOTHESIS

and trucks, Mitch and Campbell went back to the video camera to watch the morbid spectacle again. They replayed the recording and saw Wellman's act again, this time with acknowledgment to the well. The camera dropped to the ground, and the viewing angle changed to perpendicular. Turning the camera accordingly, they heard Officer Gooding's voice and could see the ensuing struggle with Wellman, then the sound of the gun, and then nothing. It continued to play for sixteen more minutes and then delivered the final scene of the approaching sound of the two state police cars and Officer Gooding's first aid, arrival of the ambulance and Mitch following afterward, some conversation, and then the words, "Over here, guys! It must be Gooding's recorder. It's still on; play it!"

One of the officers answered a comm call on his car radio. "Gentlemen, that was Captain Evers. He's on his way with a forensic team. I told him about Wellman. He wants to see the tape for himself. He'll be here within the hour."

"Are we supposed to wait an hour while we have a killer on the loose?" Mitch scowled.

"No, Chief, he put out an APB for Wellman. It won't surprise me if we have him even before Captain Evers gets here."

The Silver Lake Rescue Team erected a light fixture over the well and lowered a man with a harness to bring Nora Connely to the surface. When she was winched to the top and carried over the wall, her body was laid on a cot. Her arm dangled at an unnatural angle, indicating the severe wrenching and break it received during her quick encounter with Wellman. The well and her body were photographed before she was placed in a body bag. "Leave her there until Captain Evers gets here," Mitch ordered.

Evers's arrival a few minutes later was anticlimactic. Another Andrew Wyeth country scene wrapped in yellow police tape greeted him and two other officers. "Campbell, where's the camera?" he shouted as he unzipped the body bag to look at Nora's face. "So this is the reward you get."

"Let the crime scene team get everything recorded," Evers yelled. "Show me the video. Where is it?"

Officer Campbell and Chief Mitchell stood on either side of Evers as the three watched the gruesome acts on the recorder again. It was hard not to look at the events on the video screen, but Mitch stretched the limits of his peripheral vision to take in Evers's countenance, lit by the playback screen. As Mitch guided Evers's hand to turn the video recorder at the point when Gooding dropped the camera, he was able to see a curious smirk of satisfaction on his face. Mitch figured he was relieved that this did happen, and in a way it was a vindication of his earlier actions acting on his own in getting the arrest warrants for Nora, and especially Larson.

"This thing really did go to a high level, Mitch," Evers thought out loud.

"I still wonder where it ends," Mitch responded.

"Well, even if it goes higher or deeper, I would think all this exposure is going to chase some people out of the picture, if you know what I mean."

"Play the first part back where Wellman walks in from the woods," Mitch told Campbell.

They watched as Wellman came across the field, using every shadow and tree as a cover for his stealthy arrival. "This guy has technique. He had the killing in mind even before he got here. He didn't just stroll over here for a friendly visit," Evers commented.

"He certainly doesn't look like the well-meaning hometown boy I've seen before. This is like a Jekyll and Hyde operation," Mitch added.

Officer Campbell answered the comm call in his cruiser and after a short conversation, came back to Mitch and Evers. "They just took Wellman entering his home in Tunkhannock."

Evers stared at the other two. "That's it, then."

Mitch thought, *Where have I heard that before?*

38

Senator Accused of Murder, Forbes Involvement

By Mary Michelson, Staff writer

Filed: Saturday, September 20, 2008
Published: Wednesday, September 24, 2008 Susquehanna county News

State police officers and FBI agents arrested local officials in their Tunkhannock homes last evening in connection with the murder of Nora Connely, Silver Lake Township, Susquehanna County, and the attempted murder of State Police Officer Sheila Gooding. State Senator Robert Wellman, D-20, was arrested at his home in Tunkhannock. He is accused of the murder of Nora Connely, a friend and long time acquaintance of Wellman and his family, and in the attempted murder of State Police Officer Sheila Gooding. The alleged murder took place at the Connely home in Silver Lake Township at 6:10 pm Friday evening. State Police were on the scene immediately and Officer Sheila Gooding was seriously wounded by a gunshot while attempting to subdue

Wellman before he ran from the home. Officer Gooding is recuperating at Endless Mountain Hospital and is reported to be in stable condition. Further information concerning the event is being withheld while formal investigations are being conducted. Judge Wilton Horvath was also arrested at his home for complicity in the Connely murder and alleged connection to the recent Forbes Investment scandal.

It is known that FBI agents have been investigating all connections to the Forbes International Investment scam and alleged murders and suicide reporting frauds from earlier in the summer. Attorney Lawrence Larson's suicide and the heart attack death of Forbes CEO Joseph Pratt were the subjects of recent questionings of area residents. County Coroner James Davis remains in jail, pending further outcomes in the case. His trial date has not been set yet. He is represented by attorney Charles Rall, Montrose.

The alleged extent of Senator Wellman's and Ms. Connely's involvement is not yet known. Ms. Connely was one of the primary landowners in the recently announced Sow and Reap gas well consortium. She is survived by her sister, Carol Wherthing, Waverly, NY.

Also related to the case is the recent discovery by Sheriff Ken Petersen of a safe deposit box in the name of Joseph Pratt which is alleged by Pratt's Forbes Investments office manager, Martha Hayes, to contain incriminating information involving the named suspects known to date and at least three other participants. Sheriff Petersen has also called for the re-examination and autopsies of three of the victims' husbands bodies, whose deaths had occurred over two years ago and who were pronounced dead from natural causes at that time: namely, Henry Morson - husband of Jane Morson, Brackney; John Carpenter–husband of Charlotte Carpenter, Brackney; and John Connely–husband of Nora Connely, Brackney.

Any further information is being withheld pending a full investigation of these shocking events

HYPOTHESIS

"It seems incredible, Pete, but that's all she wrote. What a gosh-darn summer!"

"Mitch, I don't know if I can take another summer at Silver Lake. I don't think I deserve it. As a matter of fact, I don't deserve it!"

"Come on! Where else can you have a real-life mystery? It's like a dinner theater, only with real criminals and no food."

"Are they taking good care of you, Sheila?" asked Pete.

"Really, they are. It's a very nice hospital," officer Sheila Gooding answered with a chuckle.

"That's like one of those stupid ox things... a nice hospital," Mitch added.

"What's a stupid ox?" asked Pete.

"You know, like *jumbo shrimp*. It doesn't go together," said Mitch.

"What the... oh my God! He means *oxymoron*," Pete figured.

"That's it!" Mitch agreed.

There was a storm of laughter among the group.

Amid all the merriment, Pete asked, "Mitch, I heard the reason that guy in the truck ran into you is that the driver's ed course in Silver Lake was discontinued."

"Oh yeah, why was that?" answered Mitch in a typical straight-man fashion.

"The horse died."

The laughter continued so loud that one of the nurses in the hallway looked in to see what was going on. Everyone was wiping tears from their eyes and holding their sides. It was a funny exchange and probably was the relief needed for this group of unlikely partners.

"Oh my gosh, stop it, you guys. It hurts when I laugh," Gooding pleaded from her hospital bed.

The gathering of Pete, Mitch, Helen, Corporal Grady, Captain Evers, Officer Campbell, Agent Chambers, and Dr. Art Sheehan around Sheila Gooding's bed at the Endless Mountain Medical Center was the ultimate tribute in her mind. They were assured she was recovering strongly, and although their visit must be kept short, Dr. Sheehan couldn't think of any better medication.

The group conveyed their best wishes for recovery to her. "A special extra thanks from me," Mitch added as he stood to leave. "Helen and I really appreciate all you've done. I hope I can repay you sometime."

"You can right now," she quipped. "Get these guys outta here so I can get some rest."

They each forced a smile when they turned to leave one by one. She cried.

The group convened outside in the parking lot before getting into their cars. It now was really over, and they were lacking for something to say that would end it and close the final chapter. Handshakes were exchanged all around, and Pete finally got into his car.

"Enjoy your winter here in action-adventure land. I'll see all of you in the spring," Pete said as he waved and backed out.

"Thanks for all your help," they added in an uncoordinated farewell. "See you next year."

39

Later that fall, three cars sat in the driveway of Nora Connely's home. Carol Wherthing, Nora's sister, drove in from Waverly, New York, to handle some legal issues with Nora's estate—namely, her inheritance of the property—and also to make arrangements for someone to look after the place until she moved there in a few weeks. Kathy Wellman's SUV was parked facing the barn, and when she got out she was greeted with a long, caring embrace by both of the others. Professor John Nordstrom's SUV was next along the barn, and its storage area was stacked with official-looking instrumentation cases, a portable file cabinet, and various garden tools.

The three unlikely associates just stood quietly, gazing at the surroundings they read about in the newspaper while making occasional somber remarks about the recent events on the site, right where they were convened. It was difficult to believe and more so to even discuss, the assault on their lives by people whom they loved and trusted. They were here to mend their lives, but moreover to console and support one another whether they realized it or not.

"Let's move to the porch," suggested Professor Nordstrom. "We have a lot to talk about."

"Thank you both for coming. It means so much to me," said Carol.

"I've been looking forward to it based on what I've heard from John so far," added Kathy Wellman.

"Well, I hope you'll both be pleased with what I've developed," Professor Nordstrom responded. "It's been over a month, but now it's finally just three of us."

"It's almost like we planned; that is, except for Nora's death," Kathy said.

"Well, now that all the bad guys are gone, I think we can make something of this thing," Professor Nordstrom started.

"John, how did you know?" Kathy asked.

"It was when your husband, the senator, assured me things would be in his control at a meeting with him, Larson, and your sister, Nora," he answered, nodding to Carol. "They were cool customers about covering their tracks on everything they did. They said it was to keep the project under wraps until the formal announcement, which made sense to me. They talked about how they would control your uncle, Ed Wilkinson, in coordinating all the legal aspects and then how he would control the individuals' estates, wills, and legal actions about the insurance claims if any came up. And they did come up. It seemed borderline illegal, so I continued to read between the lines on everything that was going on.

"The odd thing is that there was more than enough money for everyone involved. But first one and then another partner died, then another. When this continued happening, I could see how everything was going to end up in the control of the senator and Nora. To me, it was a house of cards that was doomed to fall once they were found out. I actually feared for my own life as well,

HYPOTHESIS

assuming they thought I knew too much. And, Kathy, pardon me, but I have to say here and now that I also feared for your life."

"I figured that out already, but I've kept it to myself. I'm pretty sure I'd be gone by now."

"Well, that's when I looked to the two of you, sort of as a backup plan. I had put too much time, energy, and expertise, if I may say so, in this to see it fail. I wrote the grant requests and nursed them along for almost two years. Whatever anyone wanted to know regarding them, I dropped everything and made it happen. The development of these concepts has been a large part of my life, and the Sow and Reap consortium was the perfect vehicle to implement my work. Finally, I thought I might profit from it. I trusted the senator and your sister, but once I saw that it could fall victim to their criminal undertakings, I didn't want any part of it. Then, when you inherited your uncle's property, Kathy, I thought for sure you wouldn't want to be a part of a criminal activity, but I didn't know how to approach you.

"Weeks went by before the formal announcement of the grants. I was busy lining up contractors and getting all the prep work done, surveying and the like, so that no time was wasted. I didn't think much more about my suspicions until I received a call from an FBI agent. Tom Chambers is the agent who had been working the Forbes investment scam involving some of the partners in the consortium and other people, I presume. Not knowing if I could even trust him, I decided that I had to put my faith in someone. When he came to meet with me, I helped him fill in some of the blanks about those two, things I'm sure he wasn't aware of; sorry to mention them that way, but I hope any feelings for them are now put aside for our sake."

"Go ahead, John. No problems on my end," Kathy assured him. "He's history."

"Nor mine," Carol agreed.

"It seemed that the senator's involvement was very well covered up, and that Chambers had no real idea at the time he called, possibly only a suspicion. I was sure the senator was controlling Pratt and Larson, but it was always done through other people. So it was difficult to make the connection. I told him about them using you, Carol, as a phone message relay to the senator and others when they called. I know you were told it was to keep the project secret so that the consortium could benefit financially without interference or competition. I wanted Chambers to know you were doing it innocently as a favor to your sister and that you were being duped into helping."

"I appreciate that. He mentioned it to me when I was questioned," Carol said.

"Well, right after the call from the FBI, I called both of you. I had no choice. It was going to collapse soon anyway. It was my only chance to remain with a hold on the situation, but only if we three stick together. I couldn't give you the details over the phone, but as you both recall when we first met, you were both incredulous. While we were meeting, the state police were raiding this home. You know the rest of the story."

"I swear if the police weren't invading this home at the time we were meeting, I would never have believed you when you told us what was going on," Carol commented.

"I'm very sorry for all of us, and no matter what, I'm sorry for Nora's death," Kathy added.

"Well, this leaves both of you in control of three of the parcels of land directly, and it leaves the three of us in control of the consortium, which controls all the land parcels for the foreseeable future. We have a very lucrative project to manage, but only if we three maintain our alliance," John advised.

"What bothers me is that I don't feel comfortable in profiting from the misfortunes of others. A lot of people suffered to get us where we are today, and I don't like it," Kathy began.

"You and me both," agreed Carol. "If we are going to feel good about this, we need to first discuss reparations or something like that."

"I have to tell you both," Professor Nordstrom added. "I now know that I'm working with the right people."

"I agree," said Carol. "Does anyone have any ideas?"

"We are here now because of the bad things that happened to some really wonderful people, and I think we should try to do something meaningful to make amends," Kathy replied.

"It's going to be difficult to help the families involved since there really are no relatives left from any of the victims," Professor Nordstrom added.

"We should try to do something for the community, the entire community. They've all suffered through this thing in one way or another," said Carol. "I don't know what we have to do, but we have to do something."

"Here is my pie-in-the-sky thought. Bear with me. Let's see how this sounds," Kathy began. "What a wonderful thing it would be if these lands became the genesis of a community energy center. By the way, it is going to be such a place somewhat due to the Sow and Reap concept anyway."

"Go ahead. You have my interest," the professor added.

"Here are some facts that I learned from my husband during his work as state senator. There is a countywide need for some sort of economic development that can finally, once and for all, achieve a level of socioeconomic independence for its people. This is a very poor county. All around us other counties have some growth and development, but 50 percent of the workforce here has to leave the county to find sustenance elsewhere, usually in those adjacent counties. And the people who find work here within the county are mostly in low-paying jobs. It's certainly a beautiful and wonderful place to live, but the only economic engines are dairy farming and bluestone quarrying, and... really, nothing else."

"It's a sad thing. We are all aware of it. The worst thing of it all is to see our youth leaving the area for careers in other cities and states," Carol agreed.

"We three right here at this table can change all that," emphasized Kathy.

"How so?" Nordstrom asked. "By the way, when is our other visitor arriving?"

"Any minute now."

"It's only a vision, I admit, but we have to start somewhere," Kathy continued. "If these gas drillers and energy exploration companies have their way, they will come in here and drain off all the available natural gas reserves for the foreseeable future, impacting the rest of our lives, for better or worse. In the next thirty or so years of my lifetime, if I'm lucky, that is all any of us have to look forward to. In my opinion, that's not progress."

"I can't agree more," added the professor. "There will definitely be prosperity for some landowners and some minor trickle-down effect they throw off to others in their purchases and investments. But the vast majority of folks will not benefit at all and in fact, will suffer in many ways. For example, you can expect traffic, landscape deterioration, water pollution, and the largest offense of all, the breakdown of the indescribable way of life around here."

"I feel the same, but, Kathy, are you saying we can change that?" Carol questioned.

"Yes, I certainly am. I believe we can make a difference, a big difference."

"Go ahead."

"Well, here comes our last visitor. I'd like to wait. He can explain it better than I can," Kathy noted.

A car appeared moving up the driveway, trailing a cloud of dust in the usual manner of arrival at the Connely farm. When it stopped, the tall, casual figure of Pete Woodard emerged, much to the delight of the group members.

HYPOTHESIS

"Welcome. Welcome from all of us," Kathy announced. "Thank you for coming."

"I'm glad to be here," Pete responded. "How are you all?"

"It's great to see you," Professor Nordstrom added. "I'm doing just fine."

"Hi, Pete; thank you for all you've done for the people around here. It's so nice to see you," Carol greeted in a very sincere tone.

"Well, it's a pleasure to be back, especially in the late fall. I miss the brisk mornings and the occasional light snowfalls this time of year, but this Indian summer week is marvelous."

"Winter's coming. Don't remind us. Let's enjoy this beautiful fall day," said Carol.

Indian summer was nature's last gift before the onslaught of winter, usually a week or more of temperatures above seventy degrees in late autumn; it was a restful period when a person just wants to drop out of life's responsibilities and vegetate. It was truly a pleasure to experience, especially among the beauty of Silver Lake Township.

"I gather you haven't given up on us," Professor Nordstrom joked. "What good things do you have to tell us?"

Kathy began. "Well, I should probably explain. In thinking about what beneficial things we could do for the community, I contacted Jim Mitchell for some suggestions. He was appreciative and, with regard to the circumstances, very gracious. He directed me to Pete because of his business background and his love of the area around us, and after a few discussions, some interesting ideas came of our conversations."

"We are all ears," Carol stated.

"Go ahead, Pete. You can explain better than I," Kathy requested graciously.

"Sure. I'm pleased to offer my opinion, and it's just that, an opinion. No hard feelings if you aren't interested."

"We understand; go ahead," Kathy answered.

"Well, it comes down to this. The gas companies can plunder the region—they use the politically correct word *harvest*—and few will benefit locally. The activities will continue here for many years, and it's probably a sure thing that this fortune will touch the lives of only a minority of the population. Of course, the state will see an increase in tax revenues, but you know how it is with giving the government more money; they will surely find ways to spend it, and not necessarily for the betterment of the residents in this region.

"In talking to Kathy, it became obvious that she was interested in leveraging these riches philanthropically to benefit everyone. It's like the old parable: "Give a man a fish, and you feed him for a day; but teach a man to fish, and you feed him for life.

"One way to do that so that the Sow and Reap site here can keep on giving, or feeding, if you will, would be to have whatever you intend to do here benefit the whole community, let's say Susquehanna County for sure. Am I on the same page with the rest of you so far?"

"You are, Pete; continue," Professor Nordstrom answered.

"Yes, I'm with you," added Carol.

Kathy nodded and listened and watched her two partners begin to embrace the conversation.

"Okay. Well, there sure seems to be an abundance of gas under these properties, enough for continuous flow for the next twenty-five to fifty years and probably many more if scheduled correctly. Development in this rural country atmosphere is almost a dirty word, as you know. It usually means factories, smokestacks, traffic, pollution, strained resources; you know what I'm saying, the dirty baggage that no one wants, which always accompanies supposed progress. However, since the Sow and Reap consortium is going to be an energy exploration center as it is now organized and described in your plans anyway, why not make it a real energy center, which is self-sustaining and generates a continuous stream of future prosperity, prosperity not only for yourselves, but for everyone. I guess this is why I was asked to be included here today."

"Wow, did you ever answer our question!" Carol exclaimed.

"I like it so far, Pete. What ideas do you have in mind?" asked the professor.

Pete nodded to Kathy and gestured with raised eyebrows and his open hand, indicating if she wanted to explain or just let him continue. She nodded in agreement to have him explain and leaned back in her chair with a knowing smile on her face. *This is going well,* she thought.

"Well, when you look at the big picture of what's happening economically, 85 percent or more of the revenues leave the county once that gas enters the pipeline. But what's worse, 100 percent of the problems stay behind—land reclamation, threat of water and land contamination, roadways to be repaired, wastewater disposal, unemployment, and probably a myriad of future issues that won't manifest themselves initially. It's a 'slam, bam, thank you, ma'am', if you pardon my analogy."

"You know, Pete, I once thought it was progressive to be a part of this industry, and now you have me feeling almost ashamed," Nordstrom commented.

"I didn't intend that, but it's not a bad thing that you feel that way either. Here's why. I think you will see how much more could be done with these resources. We could keep all or most of the revenue stream and put it to work right here at home for the benefit of all."

"What's this magic solution, Pete? You have me on the edge of my seat," Carol asked.

"Consider that this group's vision for the 1,857 acre Sow and Reap site is a self-sustainable community based on harvesting its own energy, primarily for its own use. Yes, some of the gas production can be sold into the pipeline to create revenues to build a base of operating assets. You are going to do that anyway. So why not become your own energy company and then have someone do your drilling? You could divide the flow of gas production between raising revenues by selling gas to the pipeline companies and by building an energy-independent community by using the rest of the gas right here in the community. I can envision a community site dedicated to making the entire county self-supporting from this one resource; all 42,000 people can benefit."

"This would truly be Utopian if what you're saying is possible," Carol commented. She was reminded of the possible energy independence dreams of her great-grandfather on this very farm and of the Wheaton family at Salt Springs just a few miles away.

"Oh, it's possible all right," Professor Nordstrom added. "We are sitting on an enviable asset, and the Sow and Reap water recycling method is a very progressive way to extract it; and also, we have the latest technology. But now, when you think of it the way Pete suggests, there is no reason to ship 85 percent of its value out of the county for others to profit from and exploit while we just settle for 15 percent of the return to us and have to absorb all of the infrastructure problems."

"How do you see it working, then?" Carol asked.

"Go ahead, Professor; you seem to have grasped the concept," Pete responded. He was satisfied that the idea had transferred well to the group's thinking. Now they would own it by their continued construction of the concept. Kathy nodded approvingly in Pete's direction. She too felt the idea growing throughout the conversation.

"It's absolutely brilliant what you've come up with, Pete; that is, the realization that we can manage our own resources if we just stop and plan it adequately. That concept alone would be the vision of our energy center, to manage our own resources and to achieve economic independence as a community for the good of all," Nordstrom reiterated excitedly. "I foresee a university-level education center, possibly an auxiliary extension of Penn State University, specializing in energy development and community independence, a new civic model that would be a real-life institution planned and built by the students right here. It would generate its own electrical energy from a natural gas fired electrical generation plant. Even a small fifty-kilowatt peaker unit, which is only the size of a barn, would handle the sixteen thousand homes in the entire county. The entire county! Two or three more could be built and the energy sold to other regions.

"A natural gas distribution center could be constructed right here to do the same for the entire region to heat homes and provide energy for water heating and cooking. We could set up electrical and gas distribution networks from a central manifold, with a few dozen homes as a starter. It's an old idea, but very possible with today's technology."

"What's nice about it, if I understand it correctly, is that it can be developed entirely with the proceeds from just a few wells," commented Carol.

"That's right," answered Pete. "I would guess that five or so wells could start the ball rolling and generate the operating revenues by letting the gas companies set up the infrastructure and pay you the royalties as you were planning to do anyway. Then, using those proceeds to finance your plan, you would have more than enough revenues to build your energy center.

"But don't forget to reward yourselves. You will be doing a very progressive thing for the community, and you will each derive as much income doing it this way as you would if you were to just let the gas companies take the gas and only give you a 15-percent fee. You have absolutely nothing to lose by reversing the process and creating a community association instead of an individual approach."

"I suggest we name it the Alexis de Tocqueville Energy Center," Kathy finally commented.

"The name is familiar, but what's the connection?" asked Carol.

"He was the French social scientist who advocated civil association for the common good and common purpose instead of individual greed and selfishness. He traveled here in the early nineteenth century to study that idea being formed by our government's concept of democracy and concern for liberty and equality," responded Kathy. "I'm familiar with him through my charity work. His is a name that is probably only recognized in philanthropic circles, but now maybe he will get his full recognition."

"What a concept, and what an idea for the name!" Carol responded. "This is exciting! I don't think I have ever felt so good about anything in my life. I would be very proud to be a part of this."

"I agree wholeheartedly," professor Nordstrom added.

"So how do we get started?" Carol asked.

"You already have," answered Pete. "I would suggest talking among yourselves some more. You should think seriously about naming a very responsive board of directors, one that is purposefully built with the different levels of expertise that you will need. You might want to reestablish the Sow and Reap consortium and define the intended purpose more concisely with all these things in mind."

"This is absolutely what life is all about," announced Professor Nordstrom. "I can't wait to get started."

"We are very blessed indeed. Now then, shall we begin discussing our new partnership?" Kathy continued.

"Tea anyone?" Carol asked as she stood and started toward the door.

She stopped and turned. "By the way, does anyone know a good lawyer?"

40

Alexis de Tocqueville Energy Center Announced

By Mary Michelson, Staff writer

Filed: Monday, Dec 15, 2008
Published: Wednesday, Dec.17, 2008,
Susquehanna County News

Silver Lake Township will be the new home for the Alexis de Tocqueville Energy Center, as described in a press announcement this week from the Sow and Reap, Inc., consortium of landowners. The group is the recipient of a recent $3,300,000 state and federal grant to implement its "smart well" concept of natural gas extraction. The consortium has organized its land and financial resources to facilitate a unique hydraulic fracturing concept which will not require the importation of any water for the process, or the transfer of wastewater from the sites for remediation afterwards. The land area consists of five parcels amounting to 1,857 acres, with the center of operations emanating from the Connely farm in south Silver Lake Township adjacent to route 167 and Silver Creek.

The process is a self-contained wastewater purification and recycling system, which will reintroduce the much-needed water to each well from the previous wells for the hydraulic fracturing operations without the need for any outside support. The process is expected to reduce processing costs greatly while assuring no land or water contamination, since there is a miniscule amount of effluent to be disposed of. Each of the wells will operate in sequence with a prescribed schedule of water for fracturing and water transfer treatment. Efficiency is expected to be doubled regarding the utilization of materials and crews. The water used in the fracturing process will be drawn from two quarry pits, which will store the water they receive from a multiple of underground water wells and the wastewater treatment process itself.

Beyond the basic contracted gas extraction process, the consortium has formed a non-profit organization whose credo is to "manage our own resources and achieve economic independence as a community for the good of all." To meet the stated objective, the organization has established an energy development center in the heart of Silver Lake Township named the Alexis de Tocqueville Energy Center. It should be noted that Alexis de Tocqueville was a nineteenth century French social scientist who studied the American system of democracy and was an outspoken advocate of civil associations for the common good and purpose in opposition to a greedy and selfish approach wherein only a few benefit. The educational and energy production center is intended to benefit the entire county and adjoining counties according to a ten-year construction plan established with Penn State University.

The natural gas extraction from the original Sow and Reap consortium will start production by late spring 2009. Proceeds from the first five wells will be allocated to the investors in Sow and Reap and also to the development of the Alexis de Tocqueville Energy Center. Students from Penn State will complete all of the civil engineering and architectural engineering planning as part of a real-life system of infrastructure developments. The scholastic approach is expected to take much longer than a traditional commercial contract development, but the lasting effects are meant to become ingrained within the student population of our community. The curricula will be conducted continuously throughout the year, with no summer breaks, and is intended to be organized identical to a real world business. Students will matriculate in three-year cycles and will be able to continue graduate studies at the site, including an advanced political science curriculum specializing in the teachings and philosophy of Alexis de Tocqueville.

It is expected that there will be six phases of infrastructure development: Planning and layout of the student engineering center; personnel organization and administrative offices; construction of a 50-megawatt natural gas fired electrical power generator; construction of a distribution pipeline manifold head system; construction of a housing community with the initial capacity of supporting 400 homes and student dormitories; and the launch of a county-wide electrical distribution and gas pipeline system. It should be noted that each of the phases is meant to benefit the entire northeast region to become energy independent and self-sufficient economically. The construction activities for all phases will be conducted exclusively by the student and graduate student population of the Susquehanna County Career and Technology Center, Elk Lake. Municipal Engineering Corp of Tunkhannock has partnered with Penn State for on-site coordination of all student activities and endorsement certification of each project.

Ten years from now, everything will be in place and functioning. A self-contained natural gas exploration and extraction company will distribute natural gas throughout the northeast. An electrical generation plant fired with natural gas will service the county and nearby counties as generation capabilities expand. An educational center operating as an extension of Penn State University will be graduating its fifth senior class of engineering and technical specialists addressing the energy and civil engineering sector. A master-planned residential home site and community development will be in place for 400 housing units and three university dormitories.

The much-anticipated plan has developed unquestionably unanimous support among community stakeholders, including Penn State University, Susquehanna Rural Electrical Corporation, the Pennsylvania Chamber of Commerce, and each township in the county.

Martha Hayes, spokesperson for Sow and Reap, confirmed that the first flow of gas production from the initial three wells is scheduled in three months. After that, a new well will be put on-line each month for the next twelve months. The student engineering center and classrooms have been set up in temporary quarters in an old itinerant labor farmhouse and in a barn on the Connely property. Any inquiries can be made by contacting the Alexis de Tocqueville energy Center, Brackney, PA.

BIBLIOGRAPHY

Milgram experiment, Stanley Milgram, 1963: Yale University psychologist who studied the willingness of subjects to obey authority figures to perform acts that conflicted with their consciences.

Fibonacci number,: A number sequence in which the first two numbers are 'o' and '1' followed by the sum of the previous two numbers; i.e., 0,1,1,2,3,5,8,13,21,34,55,89, etc. developed by Leonardo of Pisa, 1202, from the work of an ancient Indian Sanskrit writer, Pingala, who documented his initial studies of these number patterns.

"Susquehanna County Independent," division of The Scranton Times-Tribune and its parent company, Times Shamrock, Scranton, PA, 2007–2008, various news articles about natural gas drilling in the Marcellus Shale formations.

"The Scranton Times-Tribune," division of Times Shamrock, Scranton, PA, 2007–2008, various news articles about natural gas drilling in the Marcellus Shale formations.

"The Binghamton Press-Sun Bulletin," a Gannett News division, Binghamton, NY, 2007–2008, various news articles about natural gas drilling in the Marcellus Shale formations.

"Maygroupinc.com," Ladera Ranch, CA, 2007–2008, various strategic management techniques used to characterize and classify social occurrences and demographics. http://www.maygroupinc.com

"Democracy in America," 1835, Alexis-Charles-Henri-Clerel de Tocqueville, 1805–1859, French social and political thinker and early social scientist known as Alexis de Tocqueville for his studies of American democracy and the limits of true equality; in particular, the association and coming together of people for the common purpose.

"George Schreck," Franklin Forks, PA, 2007, Susquehanna County, PA nature and wildlife photographer, cover photograph. http://www.user.pa.net/~geosan

"Wendy Miller," Mission Viejo, CA, 2009, photographer, author's photograph, back cover. wendy@eclipseshielding.com.

HYPOTHESIS